A CONVENTICLE OF MAGPIES

The Bloodskill Duology, book 1

LMR CLARKE

A Conventicle of Magpies Copyright © 2021 by LMR Clarke. All Rights Reserved.

All rights reserved. No part of this book may be reproduced in any form or by any electronic or mechanical means including information storage and retrieval systems, without permission in writing from the author. The only exception is by a reviewer, who may quote short excerpts in a review.

Cover designed by The Gilded Quill

This book is a work of fiction. Names, characters, places, and incidents either are products of the author's imagination or are used fictitiously. Any resemblance to actual persons, living or dead, events, or locales is entirely coincidental.

Castrum Press
Visit the publisher's website at www.castrumpress.com

Printed in the United Kingdom

First Printing: Jan 2021
Castrum Press

ISBN-13 978-1-9123274-1-6

ACKNOWLEDGEMENTS

My sincerest thanks go to the Arts Council of Northern Ireland and The National Lottery. I was privileged to receive funding for this project through a Support for the Individual Artist grant. In particular, I would like to thank Damian Smyth, Head of Literature and Drama at ACNI, for the talk he gave on funding opportunities and for his quick communication when Covid-19 derailed my plans. His encouragement to apply in the first place, as well as his easy manner when dealing with change, were vital to the completion of this project. Without this support, A Conventicle of Magpies would never have taken flight.

I would also like to thank my husband Barry for being, as always, my greatest cheerleader. Your stern stares when I'm procrastinating and your demands for the next chapter are thoroughly encouraging in the best possible way.

Thanks must also go to Paul Corcoran and Castrum Press for taking a punt on this project. I appreciate the opportunity and the patience you've had with me during an extremely challenging year.

For Mum and Dad.
Without you, I am nothing.

CONTENTS

Acknowledgements	1
One	13
Two	22
Three	31
Four	40
Five	48
Six	56
Seven	63
Eight	72
Nine	80
Ten	87
Eleven	94
Twelve	100
Thirteen	110
Fourteen	115
Fifteen	122
Sixteen	129
Seventeen	138
Eighteen	145
Nineteen	152
Twenty	159
Twenty-One	166
About The Author	175
Books by the Author	177

THE STAMCHESTER REVIEW
Morning Edition
Eith 1ˢᵗ, 4ᵗʰ Year of the Coati

ON THE PROBLEM OF THE SAOSUÍASEI
BY GOVERNOR KEL DREIDCHAIN

Dirty, idle, drunken, lecherous: the Saosuíasei plague we face is grave. It is an ongoing source of contention in our city. What makes it the bitterest of pills is that this is a plague we brought upon ourselves, and we are all too aware of that.

We are all familiar with the actions of our fathers in years past. When we conquered Undténsian land but not Undténsian hearts, and the natives would not obey, the issue of labor became critical. What was the point in expending such energy on taking this land if we could not plumb its vast well of resources? To our forebears, the answer was simple: use the Saosuíasei. We had already taken all they had except their very islands, and we could not take those, for the people still lived upon them.

Our fathers hit upon what until recently we still viewed as an ingenious plan, a way to clear the islands and solve our labor problem with one action: clear the Saosuíaseis' island and bring the people here. We would have their land, and their labor too. Didn't the Sassymen, as we still so affectionately call them, complain that their lives were unlivable? That they desired better conditions, better food, a better life? Our progenitors offered them all of that, but what a mistake it was.

You can take a pig to a library, but that does not mean it can read. In a similar vein, our fathers found that you can give the Sassymen better lives, but that does not mean they will be grateful. Or co-operative. Or productive. Or, indeed, even happy. A generation on, the Saosuíasei have proved themselves every inch the dirty, idle, drunken, lecherous plague we see on the streets of Stamchester and so many other cities today.

That is why, with the blessing of His Excellency Viscount Trass, Lord Lieutenant of Undténsia, I am pleased to announce the first step in ridding Stamchester of the Sassyman stain. That is why, starting tomorrow, workmen accompanied by First Battalion the Black Lions will strip the area of our city, so unfortunately named the Scar, of every last inch of Saosuíasei criminality. After this, the area will be redeveloped into a bastion of beauty and culture.

Just as one cannot teach a pig to read, one cannot teach the Sassymen to be decent and productive citizens. Decisive action is needed to rid ourselves of the scum. We may have brought this upon ourselves, but we can still take action to purge the poison.

Welcome your militia as they pass through our streets. They lead the charge towards a better future for us all.

Eith 3rd, 4th Year of the Coati

His Excellency, Vicscount Trass
Lord Lieutenant of Undténsia

Your Excellency,

I know word of our victory will reach you by telegraph long before you receive this letter, but regardless I feel compelled to write to you. The depth of my joy now that the Scar has finally been cleared cannot be fully translated by a system of electrical pulses. As our world rattles ahead into the greatness of industry under your careful guidance, one sometimes must still put ink to paper to convey the fullness of one's emotion and gratitude.

I write these words with no doubt: without Your Excellency's gift of blood, we would not have crushed the Sassymen so thoroughly. Our militia swooped in with such skill, their resistance was nothing but pathetic floundering in the streets. We made short work of them to a man.

By your kindness and favor, we are now able to move forward with the construction of the underline all the way to the warehouse district. This will be of considerable benefit to the great men of business in our city, who will no longer have to travel the long way by boat via the Eastraine and Allen, or be forced to take an unpleasant coach trip through the Sassymen's hovel. A secondary benefit, of which I know you will also approve, is the opportunity to raze a long-abused section of Stamchester and rebuild it in a style befitting our people's success and superiority.

Those who survived fled across the river to the Shambles, which I am delighted to report is the last stinking enclave that remains in Sassy hands. However, with Dál and Sénnarlann ready to dance upon nothing, I am convinced their spirits are thoroughly broken. Once those leaders of the Shadow of Jaguars are dead, it will take little effort to drive the Sassymen out of Stamchester once and for all. I will delay the execution of Messrs. Dál and Sénnarlann until you can be here to share the joy.

None of this would have been possible without Your Excellency's generosity. All the people of our glorious city are indebted to you. I look forward to the day when the Sassymen are gone for good, and I can invite you to join us in a city cleansed of scum.

Yours in greatest thanks,

Kel Dreidchain,
Governor of Stamchester & Shorbeg Region

Eith 13th, 4th Year of the Coati

Kel Dreidchain
Governor of the City of Stamchester & Shorbeg Region

Dear Governor Dreidchain,

I received your letter with great cheer. Your deduction was correct, for I was aware of the victory of the First Battalion the Black Lions before I received your letter. Regardless, were it not for the telegraph lines strung loop on loop across the country, I would have had no idea until the post train pulled in this very morning. It is just another example of how we bring great improvements to the lands we acquire.

By the time you receive this reply, I fully expect the razing of the district formerly known as the Scar to be complete. It won't be long before the redevelopment can commence, and the extension of the undertrain can begin.

My work detains me on the north coast, but I trust you will continue with our plans as expected. By area, the Shambles is larger, and the population is denser by far. Had the Sassymen more than one brain between them, they would flee not only the city but the continent. Unfortunately, their minds are not nearly as expansive as their families. One assumes the reprobates who fled the Scar have settled in the Shambles as anticipated, and that will only compound the issue.

It will be some time before I can gather a sufficient stock of blood to ensure victory for the Black Lions again. In the meantime, allow the militia to step back and bring the police to the forefront of justice again. I will furnish you with blood enough as soon as I can.

The Sassymen are no doubt frightened, but not yet cowed. I am afraid that my northern business will keep me out of Stamchester for longer than I wish the wretched Dál and Sénnarlann to remain alive. As such, I request that upon receiving this reply, you schedule their executions post haste. By the time this missive is in your hands, the rebels will have lived long enough.

Do, also, move forward with the first step in the attrition of the Shambles. Those with more than half a brain will flee. The rest will remain so terrorized, the thought of regrouping their little Shadow will be the last thing on their minds.

I look forward to my next visit to Stamchester. I am confident I will find it a cleaner and more prosperous place. With the purge of the Sassymen, it cannot be otherwise.

Yours sincerely,

Viscount Edmur Trass,
Lord Lieutenant of Undténsia

ONE

"...and as death approached, Líbhas cast herself over the edge of the precipice rather than fall into the hands of the enemy. The Spirit of Tuachiad, who had loved Líbhas like his own daughter, would not let her die. Before her body hit the churning sea, he lent his Skill and transformed her into the most beautiful magpie the world had seen. The bird swooped upward in a blaze of light and blood, and beat the usurpers back with claw and wing. And evermore the magpie watched over the Saosuíasei, keeping them safe from all harm."

THE TUACHIANNAD, A BOOK OF SAOSUÍASEI FOLKLORE.

To make a decent job of riding by omnibus, one needed at least one false hand. Two was possible for the practiced thief, though it gave the game away in the greatest way possible if one or other hand fell to the straw-covered floor of the carriage. It raised justifiable suspicion that the lady in a corseted dress and fine hat was not as innocent as she seemed. It was safer, then, to stick to three hands: one real and visible, clasped atop a false one, with the third rummaging in the unsuspecting pockets of the man sitting on the thin wooden bench at one's side.

As Rook commenced her third rummage of the day, fishing in the silk-lined pockets of a well-to-do Avanish man's trousers, she kept her eyes forward. Having one's hand clatter to the floor was a dead giveaway that one was a thief. However, paying too much attention to the target with a sidelong glance brought its own problems. The chief one was that Stamchester men had a habit of assuming any subtle look was a flirtatious one, forcing the hardworking girl to change tactics from fishing inside the man's pockets to preventing him slipping his hand under her skirts. That was all well and good if that was your trade, but Rook's line of work was in taking, not receiving.

Oblivious to her hand's conspiracy, the Avanish man stared across the omnibus. If the lining of his pockets and the fine tailoring of his coat and trousers shouted wealth, the proud height of his velvet top hat screamed it. The man kept his eyes forward and stared only at the patter of rain slipping down the exterior glass. To him, neither Rook nor any of the other ten passengers squeezed inside the rattling horse-drawn contraption existed. Rook suppressed a grin. Avanish wealth complemented Avanish arrogance in a way that gave Rook a comfortable existence.

Across from her, one of the other lady passengers reached for the pull cord above her. A bell sounded, indicating to the driver that he should bring his horses to a halt. In the moment of action amid the dullness of the journey, the Avanish man cast a glance at the lady. His distraction was perfect, and Rook slipped his wallet from his pocket without a sound. The lady stood as the omnibus came to a splashing halt, and the Avanish man returned his gaze to staring out the window. Careful to keep her false hand secured, Rook seized the opportunity and disembarked as well.

Her bustle refashioned itself as she stepped from the steep steps and onto the rain-soaked streets. She ignored the driver's mate's offer of a hand down and instead, with one of her real hands, deposited her fare into his outstretched palm. Secreting her false hand into a large pocket in her skirt, she hurried into the churning crowd.

Typical Stamchester rain poured from the grim sky. It cascaded over the rim of her fine hat, and she knew it would destroy the tall arrangement of black and white ribbon piled on one side. That didn't matter. Rook waited until the omnibus had disappeared in the swirl of carts and wagons and other buses before she extricated her umbrella from her voluminous skirts. At the same time, she pulled a ribbon on the right side of her waist. The shape of the top layer changed, pulling upward like a theater curtain to reveal a different-colored underskirt. A similar tug to both sleeves deflated their grand puffs, and with the slinging of a hidden shawl over her shoulders and the flinging of her soggy hat from her head, the change was complete. In a mere half minute, the lady on the omnibus was no more. Rook was now someone else.

Her high-heeled boots rang on the sodden pavement as she walked with purpose, though she had yet to get her bearings. She glanced from under the edge of her umbrella. She'd caught the omnibus at the top end of Banker's Square, and her mark had joined soon after. His wallet hung snug inside her skirt pockets, along with the false hand and the riches of her other two victims. She'd alighted, it seemed, some three miles south and over the boundary into Eastraine's End. The clatter of horses' hooves on cobbles and the shouts of stallholders hawking their wares competed with the endless hammering of the rain. The stink of the Eastraine River hung heavy, trapped under the dank sky.

It was some seven miles back to the Magpie's Nest, but it wouldn't take long to cover the distance without an omnibus. The last four miles were across the Shambles anyway, and the city would not run buses there. Nor would they build either underlines or overlines, or even attend to the most basic repairs of street lights or sanitation. Rook set her teeth and walked with purpose, turning away from the market and down a narrow street that led south to the convergence of the Eastraine and the Allen. That was one of many reasons no guilt gnawed at her over her actions. Avanish men, just like her marks, all declared that Saosuíasei like herself were the scum of the earth, and deserved nothing better than to live in filth like animals.

Never mind, she thought as she navigated around a grungy puddle; the only reason the Saosuíasei were only on this continent because the Avanish had brought them there. Rook shook her head. Such were their lives in the city of Stamchester.

As she stepped onto the northern bankside of the Allen River, a chugging roar sounded above. A train rattled along the overline that ran through Eastraine's End. Steaming belches dissipated into the air as the grand red engine thundered above her. The line rose in a deliberate curve away from the river. Heaven forbid trains be accessible to the south side of the city where the scum lived. Anything south of the Allen was detestable. Now that the Scar had been razed, that was the only place Rook's people had left to call home. She scoffed as the rain poured harder. For now, at least, they had the Shambles, but for how long, no one could be sure.

Rook stopped at the edge of the river, staring at the southern bankside she called home. It was dark, smothered in the smog that rolled in from Blackout Row, yet pinpricks of green gaslight shone like tiny jewels. One side of her mouth pulled up in a smile. It wasn't much, but it was still her home.

Traffic rattled along the road behind her, the sound of horses' hooves and whirling wheels, and even the occasional obnoxious *honk-honk* of a motor car. The noise drew her gaze left, though her mind told her not to look. She did anyway. She always did.

At the convergence of the Eastraine and Allen was a man-made island. Upon that island was a man-made horror. Rising from the gloom of the rain, Purgatory stood as a sentinel in the swirling waters. It spoke of nothing but darkness and pain. Rook pressed her lips together and forced herself to turn away again. There were many prisons in Stamchester, but Purgatory was the most wretched. Its hexagonal walls brought nothing but grief and pain for its inhabitants. The Avanish had put up no smokescreen of moral improvement and rehabilitation of the criminal mind. They reserved Purgatory for the worst of the city, which meant its population was almost entirely Saosuíasei.

Were Rook ever caught in her thievery, she would find herself inside its walls, behind bars and chained like the animal the Avanish thought she was. She glanced once more and allowed herself a single-fingered salute at the ominous fortress before she turned her back on it again. It was a good thing, then, that she was so good at her job. The only way Rook would find herself inside those walls was if she chose to enter them herself.

She picked her way down a set of slippery steps towards a waiting boatman.

"Fare first," he said, reaching his hand out for payment.

With a sweet smile, Rook settled herself in the low bottom of the boat and pulled up one sleeve. At the sight of the beautiful tattoo of a magpie in flight resplendent on her smooth skin, the boatman retracted his hand and took up his oars and dipped them into the sluggish churn of the Allen.

Safe and sound in the Magpie's Nest, Rook divested herself of her corseted dress and heels and returned to the comfort of a shirt and trousers. The young woman fell into an armchair, threw her booted feet onto the battered coffee table, and plucked up a newspaper. Even though she'd been out all day, she hadn't seen the latest in the *Stamchester Review*. As she scanned the page, Rook shook her head, and a lock of black hair fell over her face.

YET ANOTHER BLOODLESS CORPSE

At two o'clock this morning, a police constable came upon the scene of yet another gruesome murder. The body, which has not yet been identified, was found on the southbank end of the Buxridge Bridge. Like the other five bodies found in similar circumstances over the last few months, the corpse appeared to be drained of every last ounce of blood. Suspicion for this killing falls once more on the elusive fiend known only as Billy Drainer, although Inspector Kip Kerstammen declined to comment on this observation.

Rook licked her thumb and flicked to the next page. Inches and inches of news stretched through the broadsheet, as always full of sensationalism and very little fact. Only two parties enjoyed Stamchester's string of murders: so-called Billy Drainer himself, whoever he was, and the newspapers. Both made significant gains from the events. News was always a profitable commodity in Stamchester, but blood was more valuable than gold. Those corpses weren't bloodless for no reason.

A cough came from the doorway. Rook glanced up from the grim columns. A slim figure stood in the doorway, a tiny girl at the end of her teenage years. Pigeon stood in the low doorframe that led to the main Nest bar and jerked her head. The action sent her mass of dark curls tumbling to one side.

"Mama wants you. A job's come in."

Rook stood, cast the newspaper aside, and followed the diminutive messenger. As they left the back room, the stink of stale beer and cheap tobacco hit them. The two women crossed the bustle of the Shambles' busiest public house, the Magpie's Nest. By no coincidence, it also housed the headquarters of one of the city's most notorious gangs, the Conventicle of Magpies.

They dodged a waitress wielding a tray of empty glasses as the noise of the Nest's patrons rose in rowdy waves. Glasses clinked, men caroused, and the occasional stool toppled from beneath a patron so drunk he no longer knew where his own rear end was.

"What sort of job?" Rook called over the fracas.

Pigeon shrugged one bony shoulder. "Something like the usual. Customer looks sad and angry."

Rook's laugh pierced the evening's revelry. "They always look sad and angry, and it's always because someone's robbed them."

Pigeon grunted in agreement. It was true. Most folk engaged the services of the Conventicle of Magpies for one reason alone: to take back something stolen from them. In the poorest parts of the city, like the Shambles, the Conventicle was a better choice than the police, particularly if you were Saosuíasei. Stamchester's uniformed Avanish law enforcement had little time for what they saw as the paltry trifles of scum.

The roar of the evening's revelers transformed into a low background burr as Pigeon led Rook into one of the private rooms. Like the rest of the place, it was lit by dim green gaslight. Men often booked the rooms for secret meetings with illicit business partners or women who weren't their wives, but this room was for official Conventicle business only. Seated in a stuffed armchair with patched upholstery was a woman Rook didn't know. That marked her as the new client. Across from her, behind a desk and ensconced in a high-backed leather seat, was Mama Magpie.

Rook mimed taking off a top hat and bowed with a flourish. Mama Magpie was a woman of indeterminate years, beautiful and strong-bodied, with typical Saosuíasei features much like Rook's own. Her dark hair framed her face, and her skin was the color of copper. Her kohl-lined eyes were sharp. The eponymous leader of the Conventicle, Magpie was one of the most powerful and feared women in Stamchester. With a charge sheet longer than the winding Allen River, she'd seen the inside of most city prisons, but no Avanish bars could hold her. The bounty on her head was the highest in the city, but again, no Avanish hands could catch her.

"You're in luck, Mrs. Gria," Magpie said, a smile tilting her black lips. "Pigeon has fetched us the best in the Nest."

Rook feigned bashfulness at the remark and gave a shallower bow. There was no point in denying it. At only one-and-twenty, Rook was the best finder, acquirer, and thief in Magpie's employ, and everyone knew it. When your business was finding, acquiring, and thieving, being the best brought a certain respect and admiration.

Mrs. Gria clutched her worn felt hat so hard her knuckles paled. She fixed Rook with a suspicious stare. Rook was used to this reaction, for she looked like she should be in school—if her parents had been able to afford school for any of their ten children, which they had not. Rook's young face betrayed her in some ways, but benefitted her in others. Youth meant innocence, and innocence let people allow her access to things their rational brains should never have allowed.

The woman's stare lasted a shade too long. "What's the trouble?" Rook asked, her voice edged with irritation.

Their client snapped back to the issue at hand and, remembering her sorrows, fished a stained handkerchief from her pocket and pressed it to her reddened eyes.

"My husband's left me, and he took everything. Except," Mrs. Gria added with a macabre laugh, "the children. Now I'm left with five mouths to feed and no income. All the piecework in the world won't keep us fed. I've had to take the younger ones out of school to help with making the boxes, and because I can't afford to keep them there. But even the extra help isn't enough."

Magpie laced her fingers together, her prominent knuckles locking together, and looked at the woman with lowered eyes. "We can't bring your husband back, you understand. That's not our business. We can find him for you, but we can't force him to come home."

Rook recoiled as the woman seemed ready to spit on the worn floorboards. "I know where he is," she snapped, "and I don't want him back. I'd sooner have you kill him than I'd allow him to cross my threshold again."

Magpie raised one sharp eyebrow. "That's not our business either."

"I know that," Mrs. Gria snapped again. Then, with a visible effort, she schooled her emotions and fixed her eyes on Rook and Magpie. "Teog took things that never belonged to him, treasures from my mother and the old country that he has no right to. I want them back." Her voice wavered. "It's all silverware I don't want to part with, but I must sell it to survive. But I can't do so if I don't have it." Despite her best effort to keep them at bay, tears spilled down the woman's cheeks. "I need you to get back what's rightfully mine, nothing more."

Rook stopped herself from shaking her head, for fear Mrs. Gria would take the action as an insult. The woman's story was as common in Stamchester as the appearance of bloodless corpses. Many Saosuíasei immigrants, the majority women abandoned by their husbands, came to the Conventicle, for they were more sympathetic than the police. A coil of sympathy tightened in Rook's gut. She understood that well, although her father hadn't abandoned his family by throwing himself into the arms of another woman. Rather, Sionn Artur had left behind his wife and daughters by throwing himself into the Allen River. He'd drowned in its murky depths, the current a noose around his neck.

Rook's sympathy dissolved into the familiar sting of anger. Oldest sister Isiannâ's disappearance had devastated them all, but only her father had taken his grief to such extremes. But now wasn't the time to dwell on it. Rook pressed her sorrow deep into her boots. It was never the time to dwell on it.

Mama Magpie placed a hand atop Mrs. Gria's. "We'll get your treasures back, I assure you."

"And your fee?" the woman replied. Her words were sharp, but she allowed Magpie's comforting to continue.

"Five percent of the total value of what we return to you."

Just like her head shake, Rook suppressed her flinch. Five percent of a paltry collection of old silverware wasn't worth getting out of bed for. Magpie, sensing her irritation, gave her a near imperceptible glare. She might have been the leader of a gang of thieves and villains, but above all else, Magpie was a decent woman. She looked after the people of her community however she could, even if all her actions were less than legal.

Mrs. Gria dabbed at fresh tears but nodded. "It's a deal."

Later, under a silvery half-moon tucked in a clouded sky, Rook set off to retrieve the betrayed woman's belongings. Mrs. Gria was sure that while her husband might have left her, he'd likely followed all his old habits. The most regular of these was propping up the bar in one of several public houses in West Shambles. The Shambles, East and West, were the most impoverished areas of the entire city. Rook would know, considering she and her family had to live there.

Stamchester, even in the Shambles, stank less at night with the horse dung cleared from the roads. But more and more, the city's sprawl of factories belched their acrid smoke long into the night. Along the wharfs and tucked into blocks among the poorest of the population, production continued as long as the foremen decreed, and the workers could go on. Now that blood typing and extraction were possible, that was a long time.

This was the reason for the bloodless state of Stamchester's recent murder victims. Rook pulled the brim of her top hat lower over her face as she strode between the three- and four-story walk-ups that lined the regimented gas-lit streets. Billy Drainer didn't care about their lives, but he'd figured out that what ran through the veins of old and young, rich and poor, Saosuíasei and Avanish alike, was red metallic profit.

Once something became profitable in this fetid city, it became a commodity. Wherever there was a commodity, there was crime. Magpie had warned Rook against going out alone, considering the danger the killer posed, but Rook had never been one for waiting. Drainer wasn't the only menace in the city, and Rook had escaped from many sticky situations in her time thanks to her proficiency in Bloodskills.

Rook tightened her grip on the heavy ball handle of her cane. With her other hand, she checked the time on the tarnished plate silver pocket watch that had once belonged to her father. It was just after two. As she replaced the pocket watch, Rook struck the cannula mechanism strapped to her arm. The accidental action jolted her, though not as much as when the device had first been fitted. It comprised a hollow steel needle already pushed into a waiting vein, with a vial of Rook's own blood strapped to her arm, all held in place by a thick leather bracer. The contraption hid beneath the sleeve of her man's frock coat. At first, her eyebrows had risen near to her hairline in skepticism at the gift of this strange thing. Magpie had told her it would change her life and her use of Bloodskills. She hadn't been wrong, and Rook wasn't sure if she could now survive without it.

She rounded the last corner onto Warmange Street, where Mrs. Gria was sure her husband now lived. Rook ducked into the alleyway that ran along the rear of the row of walk-ups, and counted dark windows until she reached the eleventh across. Bloodskilling had always been her talent. It was something anyone could do, provided they learned, but to Rook it was an art form to perfect.

Since time immemorial, people had been performing Bloodskills, enhancing their own speed and strength and agility by using the crimson power in their veins. Also since time immemorial, there were limits to this power, since you could only burn so much of your own blood before you became ill, or even collapsed and died. Not so, now you could collect and store your own blood for additional use, or find compatible blood from others and inject it into your veins. This was why factories belched smoke into the night. It was why people were turning up dead and bloodless, and why Magpie hadn't wanted Rook to go alone. Blood was valuable. Blood was money.

Blood was worth killing for.

At the eleventh dwelling along the alley, Rook stopped to survey the scene. There were few lights lit in any of the walk-ups, and none in her target. Mrs. Gria had been prescriptive in her instructions. Eleventh house along, second third-floor window. Rook plucked off her hat, and set it and her cane against the building's worn brickwork wall. Little light penetrated from the street, leaving her safe to work in darkness. Lack of light was no problem. With a flick of her hand, Rook engaged the mechanism strapped to her wrist. The vial of her own blood plunged into her veins. The action caused no reaction, but what followed did.

With the merest effort, Rook pulled her power into action. Her body thrummed, her heart pumped harder in her chest, as she willed her sight to improve. In a blink, the darkness was no longer prohibitive. Everything flashed before her in the sharpest detail, as if it was bright as noon. She burned through more blood as she concentrated on her body, pushing strength and speed into her muscles. Every part of her hummed as she scaled the wall, silent and quick as a flickering shadow, and perched on a third-floor sill. Few people could use multiple Bloodskills at once, but for Rook it was as natural as breathing.

Her balance was steady, again thanks to the Bloodskill, as she peered through the dirty glass pane. A pair of what had once been curtains hung in rags inside the frame. The room was empty, and the bed still made. Teog Gria had yet to return. Satisfied it was safe, Rook fished in her frock coat for her crowbar. The thin inflexible strip of metal lingered in a secret pocket of her frock coat, and had been a constant companion through her work in the Conventicle. Rook slipped it into the crack between the sash window and its frame. With a little help from a brief blast of Bloodskill in strength, Rook pushed down, and the crowbar kindly opened the window.

TWO

When she planted her feet on the bare boards of the tiny room, Rook eased off her Skill and sucked in a breath. Talented she may have been, but it didn't mean using Bloodskill wasn't an effort. Her sight dimmed, her heart rate calmed, and the thrum in her veins dissipated. Darkness or not, Teog Gria's new residence was as depressing as anywhere in the Shambles. The sum total of furniture in the room comprised a single bed that sagged in the middle, a battered bedside table with an ancient oil lamp on it, and a tall and narrow closet shoved in one corner beside the door.

Rook pursed her lips and brought her eyebrows low. While the room was grim, it seemed Teog didn't share it with anyone. The cost of privacy was huge in an overcrowded city. That meant he'd taken a sum of cash from his family, or perhaps he felt confident in the fortune he would come into. Not anymore, Rook thought, and began her search of the room.

It didn't take long to discover the loose floorboard underneath the bed. With the help of her crowbar, Rook soon had Mrs. Gria's treasures in her hands. Wrapped in a stained cloth were two candlesticks and an oval platter, all heavy enough to suggest they were solid silver. Rook re-wrapped the treasures and tucked them under her arm. When she stood, something flickered in her periphery. She realized she wasn't alone, and turned.

A tall man she took to be Teog Gria stood in the crooked doorway, scowling in the darkness.

"Bloody thief!"

The man moved like lightning, using his own Bloodskill. His hands gripped her before she could move. He wrenched her arms apart, and the silverware clattered to the floor. Rook's body burned with Skill. She brought her knee up so hard between the man's legs, she might as well have gelded him. Teog keened like a child and stumbled against the wardrobe. It rocked on its spindly legs. Rook seized the moment. With a grin, she wrenched the dilapidated thing down on Gria's head.

Voices clamored in the hallway. Rook winced. The entire house was awake. Someone turned the handle. The door opened an inch. It collided with the collapsed wardrobe and the flailing man underneath.

Rook backed toward the window, snagging the silver up in its makeshift bag. As Gria groaned and swore, someone hurtled into the door, trying their best to clear the obstruction. Rook clambered back onto the sill. With her bounty held firm once more, Rook Skilled her legs for the coming impact. Then she jumped.

Catlike, she landed in the alleyway on steady feet and grabbed her hat and cane. At the commotion, gas lamps flared in every house, but no one could have seen her. With the power of her Bloodskill, Rook sped back into the night.

She didn't ease off until she was halfway back to the Nest. By then her extra blood was all but spent, and using too much more would eat into her body's natural supply. Rook knew her own margin of safety. Anyone could survive losing a little blood, but once beyond that margin, the body's normal functions became more and more difficult. The last thing Rook needed was fatigue. Teog Gria's neighbors, unable to rely on the police, were likely after her. Even if they realized she was part of the Conventicle, some would still have pursued her. Not all Saosuíasei accepted Magpie's form of justice. Though, Rook mused as she strode along Wardlebrook Street, back towards the Nest, things might soon change. With the collapse of the Shadow of Jaguars after the executions of leaders Dál and Sénnarlann, her people were rudderless. Magpie was the closest they had left to a leader.

Rook's skin glowed green in the old gas lamps of the Shambles. She adjusted the bundle under her arm and fished her father's pocket watch out again. Half two. Not bad timing at all. A pang of sorrow passed through her chest as she ran the pad of her thumb over the watch face. The only time her father hadn't worn his watch was the time he'd drowned himself. Symbolic, Rook thought. It was the one time he knew he wasn't coming back.

As always, she shoved the feeling aside. She didn't have time for it. He didn't deserve her pain. Her father had abandoned them, and left Rook as the sole provider for their family. He'd stolen any chance she had to grieve for Isianná, her only older sister, the one she'd loved the most.

Rook tightened her grip on the ball handle of her cane. No. Grief was for the deceased. They'd never found Isianná's body. Until there was a corpse, bloodless or not, Rook refused to believe Ishie was dead. She pulled on her armor of emotionlessness and continued on her way.

She was two blocks from home when a figure stepped into the street before her, a black silhouette in a pool of green light. Rook gripped her cane harder. Despite having no reserves, she was ready to burn.

Rook faced the silhouetted figure for a few moments, neither of them making a move. Rook gathered what detail she could. It was a man, tall and slim and, from his outline, wearing a cloth cap and a short workman's jacket. This could be it, she thought. This could be her encounter with Billy Drainer.

One of his arms jutted out, suggesting he had a hand jammed in a pocket. The more Rook looked, the more she realized his stance was awkward, and a tremble shuddered through his body. Rook shook her head. Her laugh was obnoxious in the darkness.

The sound took her opponent by surprise and he stepped forward. His face was dark with rage. "What are you laughing at? Give me your money or I'll blow your head off!"

Rook tutted and leaned on her cane. "Please, spare me the theatrics. We both know you don't have a revolver in that pocket."

One lesson Rook had learned over her years in the Conventicle was that throwing blunt honesty in someone's face was an excellent way to disarm them. Another lesson learned: no man in a workman's jacket and cloth cap was wealthy enough to own a firearm.

The man whipped his hand from his pocket, though it wasn't empty. Instead of a revolver, he gripped a tarnished blade. It had a slight curve and a wooden handle, and Rook didn't doubt it was sharp.

"All right, I won't blow your head off," the man said. "I'll slit your throat instead!"

He darted forward with Bloodskill speed and Rook matched it, darting back. Out of reach, she allowed her bundle of silverware to clatter to the beaten dirt street. Gripping the ball handle of her cane in one hand and the black stick with the other, she twisted them apart. With a clean *shing*, a bright knife escaped from its hidden sheath and she wielded it before her.

The clank of valuables hitting the ground diverted her opponent's attention. Instead of lunging toward her, he grabbed for the silverware. Unwilling to lose a night's work, Rook grunted and swept her left foot to the side, sending Mrs. Gria's treasures scattering into the darkness.

The man let loose a string of curses and lunged after one of the rolling candlesticks. He still moved with a speed only Skill could grant, and Rook had to suck in a deep breath and push hard to match him. Weariness fell on her like a lead cloak, but she kept going, slashing out at his arm as he laid a hand on the silver stem of the candlestick. The slice of her blade released his grip, and he cursed anew. Rook found herself behind him, leaning over his bent form, and she knew that was a mistake. He sensed her weakness and bucked against her, the hard round of his skull striking her cheekbone and sending her tumbling backwards.

Rook sucked in gasps of breath, fatigue surrounding her like a fog. The man let out a victorious snarl. He bent to retrieve the candlestick. When he rose, he grew stock-still. It took Rook's hazy brain a moment to understand why. Then, when she saw it, she couldn't suppress her laugh.

"That's right, my friend," a fresh voice said. It was sonorous and beautiful and to Rook, welcoming and familiar. "I don't think that silverware belongs to you, does it?" The figure stepped forward. Illuminated by gaslight, broad shoulders picked out in green, stood Kestrel. A fellow member of the Conventicle, she held her favorite firearm aimed at the man's head. "Be a dear and drop that, will you? That's a good boy."

The man was older than either of them, and rankled at the insult. But with a barrel pointed between his eyes, he did as he was told. Swift as her namesake, Kestrel pocketed her revolver and grabbed for him. She twisted his arms behind his back, shoving him against the nearest rough wall. Kestrel was taller than most, broader than most, and possessed a natural strength Rook could only dream of.

The man wriggled against her hold, but couldn't free himself. He twisted his head to peer over one shoulder. "What the hell are you? A man or a woman?"

So used to such comment as her friend was, Rook knew Kestrel wouldn't rise to the bait. "I'm your better, dearest," she said. She belied her kind tone with a rough shove of his face into the brickwork and dropped her voice into a snarl. "Don't give me a reason to show you how strong a woman I am. Now I'm going to let you go, and you're going to piss off. Immediately. Do you understand?"

The man struggled against her grip and grunted his dissent. But it was no use, so he slumped into acquiescence and nodded.

As good as her word, Kestrel released him. The man stumbled away, turning to face them. He didn't pause as he moved backward, but spat at the ground at Kestrel's feet. "Disgusting he-she."

When Kestrel reached for her firearm once more, his eyes widened, and he disappeared as fast as his Skill could carry him. With a shake of her head, Rook struggled to rise. It was only when Kestrel offered her powerful arm that she made it back onto her feet.

"Things didn't go to plan, I assume?" the taller woman asked.

"You could say that," Rook said with a humorless chuckle. "Let's get back to the Nest."

When Rook presented Mama Magpie with her evening's success, the older woman gave her a solid stare across her desk. "You went alone, even though I told you not to."

"I did," Rook said. "But you were right, Mama. I shouldn't have. I was lucky Kestrel came along when she did."

She didn't mean the words, but the lying was better than receiving of one of Magpie's lectures. From the older woman's single raised eyebrow, Rook knew her honesty was in question. But instead of a lecture, Magpie turned her attention to the cloth parcel Rook held out to her.

Kestrel peered over Rook's head for a better look as Magpie revealed the shimmering silverware within, spreading it across the tabletop. There was a foot of difference in their heights, with Rook scraping five and Kestrel coming in just shy of six. Some might feel intimidated by the other woman looming over them. To Rook, it was never anything but welcome. Kestrel had been her best friend since before they'd become Rook and Kestrel. Both were Saosuíasei, from immigrant families, although Kestrel's birth parents had long since abandoned her because of her "unsavory" ways. They'd never loved their daughter the way they had loved their son. But to Rook and her family, Kestrel was Kestrel no matter what clothes she wore, and anyway, what was another mouth to feed in a family so large?

"That lot's worth a Turner or two," Kestrel said.

"Even more," Mama Magpie replied, peering at the maker's mark on the bottom of the candlesticks. "Mrs. Gria can feed her family for months on the profit from these beauties." She glanced at Rook and raised her eyebrow again. "The five percent commission doesn't seem so paltry now, eh?"

Kestrel's estimation of a few Turners, paper bills resplendent with the face of one of the Avanish's most celebrated Prime Ministers, was an understatement. Rook shrugged one shoulder, but allowed herself a capitulating smile. "I suppose."

"It pays to be kind sometimes," Magpie said, covering the silverware again and reaching for her writing box. "Someone in this godforsaken place needs to look out for abandoned women like Mrs. Gria. Now, without the Shadow, it seems we're the only ones left."

She withdrew a sheaf of lined paper and plucked up her tortoiseshell fountain pen. Her penmanship enthralled Rook as always. Her lines were elegant, with indigo ink streaming from inside the barrel of the pen as if by magic. The patterns Magpie's handwriting made on the paper were as beautiful as any piece of art.

"I'll have Pigeon send this note to Mrs. Gria at first light," Magpie said, blowing on the fresh ink before slipping the paper inside a brown envelope. From inside the writing box she withdrew a thin stick of black wax, melted what she needed, and pressed her sterling silver Magpie seal into it once the wax's texture was right. "In the meantime," she continued with a glance at the two women, "I suggest you both get some rest. Give my love to your mother as always, Rook."

A shiver went unbidden through Rook's body at the mention of her mother. "I will."

Kestrel noticed, and gave her the briefest of touches to the shoulder before they retreated from Mama Magpie's inner sanctum. They walked through the emptying Nest, and out into the darkness.

It was near four o'clock when they reached the run-down tenement block they called home. The stairs creaked under their feet as they crept upward to the third floor, obscenely loud in the quiet. One of their downstairs neighbors, Mrs Dimh, made loud comments about the irregular comings and goings of certain members of the Artur family, though there was little malice in her words and more curiosity.

Shabby though the building was, it was all they had. Even better, they could live here rent-free. It was one of Magpie's investments, and if there was one thing Rook had learned in the ten months since her father's suicide, it was that beggars could never be choosers. No matter how good she was at her job, she couldn't earn enough to pay room and board for the entire family, not even with Kestrel's wage to help. Magpie's generosity was just another reason Rook worked to be the best thief she could.

She twisted her key in the rusted lock and pushed open the door with as little noise as she could. For a moment, she listened. The set of small rooms hummed with the sound of sleepy breathing. At least none of the little ones were awake. Then the noise Rook dreaded came, a hacking cough that drove away all semblance of peace. It was her mother. Rook slipped off her heavy boots and placed them at the head of the long line of pairs of shoes, one for each sibling. She tiptoed up the narrow hallway, leaving Kestrel behind to secure the door. Her stocking feet brought her to the parlor room that functioned as a kitchen, dining room, and bedroom for her mother.

"Rébh, is that you?"

The sound of her birth name made her jolt. In the Conventicle, she was Rook. Sometimes she forgot Rébh existed.

"Yes, Ma," Rook said. "It's me."

Another hacking cough erupted from her mother's chest, and Rook hurried to her bedside, ducking under the lines of meticulously-mended clothes drying above their heads. She plucked a cup of murky water from the nightstand and brought it to her mother's mouth. Even as she drank in the flickering light of the lamp, Mónnuad Artur looked more corpse than woman. Rook swallowed against her sorrow. Her mother needed her to be strong.

"I'm glad you're home safe, Rébh," Mónnuad croaked through chapped lips. Rook passed a hand over her mother's forehead. Her skin was paper-thin and stretched tight over her skull. Mónnuad coughed again, and Rook offered more water. "No trouble?" she asked after another sip.

"None." At most, it was a half-lie. The Gria job had gone just fine, and Kestrel's timely appearance had prevented any trouble afterwards. The fact that Rook had overstretched herself by using too much Skill was something her mother would classify as trouble, but she didn't need to know that. "Mama Magpie sends her love," she said.

Mónnuad managed a smile at the mention of the Magpie. "I know I say this every time, but I'll say it again. She's Líbhas returned to us. What would we do without her?"

Rook gave a fond smile. In her younger years, Mónnuad Artur had been the most famous storyteller in Stamchester, and knew the Tuachiannad folklore inside out. As she stood on plinths in parks and on street corners, her tales had enthralled everyone, Avanish and Saosuíasei alike. Even better was that even at the end of a long day standing in the cold, Mónnuad came home and delivered her best performances for her children alone. The Artur brood would cram into one bed and listen, enamored by their mother's skill and the tales of Líbhas and Tuachiad and all the mystical figures from their country's folklore. Isiannà had inherited their mother's storytelling prowess, and would've continued Mónnuad Artur's storytelling legacy.

Rook's smile dimmed. That was all gone now. Her mother could no longer put one foot in front of the other, never mind stand for hours and speak. And Isiannà? Gone.

Despite the three blankets over her, Mónnuad shook with a sudden tremble. Rook tucked the covers tighter around her mother and turned to stoke the dwindling fire.

"Don't worry about me," Mónnuad said.

Rook ignored her, just as she did every time her mother uttered such nonsense. How could she not worry? She prodded the fire with an iron poker until she stirred up warmth. "I want tea anyway."

That was a full lie, but a hot drink would bring some comfort to her mother's aching bones. As she gathered the tea things, Rook found her mind following the same path it always did when she considered her mother's illness. It had been months since Magpie had last sent a doctor to examine her. The dour old Avanish man had spent less than five minutes in their company, declared that Mónnuad had a form of slow consumption, and left with his assurance that he would never be back. There was no point. Nothing could cure her. Doubtless his unsaid reason for not wanting to return was that the Artur family were Saosuíasei scum. Rook could sense it had been on the tip of his tongue to declare her consumption was brought on by a lack of self-control and too many pregnancies. Her mother had borne ten living children, but it wasn't for want of self-control. It was for the love of them all.

Rook turned. Her mother had fallen into a light doze, so she left the water to boil and slipped out in search of Kestrel. As she passed the two doors that led to her younger sisters' rooms, Rook checked if they were fast asleep. Only the littlest, five-year-old Ibheis, needed her patched blanket pulled back in place. She was forever flailing her thin arms and legs in her sleep. It was the only reason she had a thin pallet bed to herself and didn't share like all the others. The tiny girl squirmed and opened her eyes under Rook's touch, and gave her sister a wide grin before she settled into slumber once more. That smile was yet another reason Rook worked so hard. She had vowed to do whatever necessary to keep her sisters safe and well.

She knew another part of her had other motivations. It was a part of her that joined the Conventicle for the very reason that it was dangerous. Danger kept her focused on the present. It stopped her dwelling on the past or the future. When enthralled in her own Bloodskill and performing whatever task Mama Magpie asked of her, she didn't have time to think about her father, her mother, or Isiannà. She was in the present, focused on her body and the thrill of impending success. It was easier that way.

As she retreated from the littlest ones' room, Rook left the door open a crack and listened for any other noise. There was nothing. Where was Kestrel? It didn't take long to lock the front door. Rook's expression darkened. She checked the narrow room they shared, but Kestrel wasn't there, though she'd suspected as much. With a furrowed brow Rook returned to her mother's room, but her friend wasn't there either. If she wasn't in the house, there was only one other place Kestrel might be. Rook sighed. How many times had she warned her?

Rook slipped to the front door and crept to the edge of the shared stairwell. Murmurs floated from below, followed by a single set of footfalls creeping upward again. Kestrel stopped at the lower landing, panic flickering across her face in the dim glow of her candle. Then she shrugged, her expression shifting to one of almost an apology.

"I know what you're going to say," she said as she passed Rook on the upper landing.

"And I know you won't listen to me," Rook said as she secured the door behind them.

Kestrel slipped off her boots and added them to the long line of family footwear that reached up the inner hall. "He's still our Pit."

Rook's expression darkened, and she padded into the parlor again. She added tea leaves to the boiling water. "He stopped being our Pit when he joined the Filth. Once he did, he turned his back on us all."

In the light of her candle, Kestrel's face grew ashen, but she said nothing. She knew Rook was right. Pit was another of Mónnuad Artur's children, though like Kestrel, not one by birth. For the longest time, the half-Avanish and half-Saosuíasei boy who shared Rook's birthday was the only brother Rook had ever known. But then he'd thrown his colors to the Avanish side of his heritage and joined the Avanish police. Now he was the enemy.

"Nothing good will come from seeing him," Rook said as she poured their tea.

Kestrel accepted the chipped cup with an acquiescent nod, but accompanied it with a self-conscious smile. "I know. I wish it was that easy to cut him off."

"It was for me," Rook said with a scowl.

"It's not the same between you and him as it is between the two of us. If I could blot him out of my mind like a stain, I would."

Rook's sullenness softened at the edge of distress in Kestrel's voice. "I know you would."

Kestrel steadied herself with a long gulp of tea. "Do you ever think he'll come back?"

The scowl returned to Rook's face. "No. Things are too hot with the Avanish, and they'll only get hotter. And I'm not sure if the Shambles would have him back. He's taking his life in his hands, coming here to see you."

Kestrel lit with sudden indignation. "Everyone's wrong in this situation, did you know that? We're wrong and they're wrong. Everyone thinks the other is an enemy: Avanish, Saosuíasei, men, women. But we're all the same underneath. You know?"

As she set a comforting hand on her friend's arm, Rook nodded. "I know. I know. But we've spilled too much blood. We're all blinded by red."

Mónnuad stirred under her blankets and cracked open an eye. "Was my Pit here?"

"No, Ma," Rook said before Kestrel could say otherwise. "We were just talking about him."

"I worry about my boy," Mónnuad said, "but I believe no one is ever lost."

Her face slackened as she settled to sleep once more. Rook clutched her cup as she clutched that thought in her head. *We can only hope, Ma. If that's so, maybe one day Ishie will come home.*

THREE

The morning began with its usual flurry. As soon as five-year-old Ibheis woke, the rest of the sisters rose like a row of dominos in reverse. Within minutes, the flock of sisters piled into the parlor room. The girls were brash and cheery, leaping over one another to clutch at their mother's bedspread. Only Maird, next sibling down from Rook, slouched into the room with her arms crossed. Rook glanced at the clock on the mantelpiece just as Ibheis and next-oldest Faibh clambered onto Mónnuad's bed. Six o'clock. She chuckled and palmed her eyes. It was true. There was no rest for the wicked.

The rest of the morning passed as usual. She and Kestrel prepared a modest breakfast of bread soaked in watery milk, made sure each sister received their fair share, and then sent Caío and Maird to fetch water. The former, Maird's junior by two years, walked with her usual jubilant whistle; the latter, with her usual sulk. If it wasn't for their faces, so similar they looked more twins than sisters, Rook doubted anyone could believe they were siblings. It wasn't until after all faces and hands were clean and the work of the day began — piecework for some and housework for others — that Rook allowed herself a few hours of rest.

It didn't feel like a few minutes had passed, never mind hours, when Caío shook her shoulder. "Rébh, Faoiatín. It's time to wake up now."

Rook blinked a few times, unable to clear the sleep from her eyes. Beside her, Kestrel groaned and pulled the blankets over her head. "Rébh and Faoiatín aren't here," she said, her voice muffled under the covers. "You must have the wrong address."

Rook's vision cleared and Caío's grinning face appeared through the murk: as did her hands, and the two steaming cups she held. "Ah well. Neither will want this tea made with fresh tea leaves, then. I'll drink it myself."

Kestrel jolted up in the bed, flinging out one arm. "Now wait a minute! Fresh tea leaves? What heaven is this?"

The girls chuckled, for a moment existing in a moment of nothing but sisterhood. Rook accepted the cup and tipped Caío a wink. She received one in return. Though only fourteen, she'd grown up fast once Isiannà had disappeared. Sullen Maird was unable or unwilling, and someone had to step into the gap.

Rook leaned against the bare plaster wall and closed her eyes, savoring the aroma of the tea. Fresh leaves were a luxury that only came when old ones made nothing but scared water. She had time to linger over the cup. It would be a long moment before they were ready to leave. While Rook was content to throw on whatever clothes were nearby and call it done, things weren't as simple for Kestrel. What God hadn't given her, she created with her own brand of magic. Rook watched, awed as always, as Kestrel painted her face and transformed herself with carefully chosen clothing, Skilling herself into a corset so tight Rook didn't know how she could breathe.

"How do I look?" Kestrel asked as she adjusted the drape of her skirt.

"Beautiful," Rook said as she did every day. It was no lie or half-lie. It was the simple truth.

A thick fog of cloud hung heavy in the dim afternoon. The two women crossed the Shambles on their way back to the Magpie's Nest amid the dullness. Smoke belched from the horizon, rising in never-ending columns from the chimneys in Blackout Row. Huddling families crammed into every doorway, leaning on each other and not even holding out their hands for a spare coin. These were the destitute, the poor wretches from the Scar that had lost everything under the booted feet of the Avanish militia. The heat and heaviness of tea and bread turned to a cold lump in her stomach. Her family might not have been rich, but they had everything compared to those displaced by the razing of the Scar. Now, more than ever, the Saosuíasei needed to rely on one another. The dead bodies of Fiacónn Dál, the Jaguar, and Ro Sénnarlann, his second, flashed to the fore of Rook's mind. She shuddered. The Avanish had let their corpses hang by the neck for days, swinging beneath the Buxridge Bridge. It wasn't until the crows had pecked out their bulging eyes that the Avanish cut them down. The corpses of the Saosuíasei leaders had crumpled into the stench of the Allen, denied the courtesy of a decent burial.

Rook shook the thought away. The Avanish papers called Billy Drainer a monster, but even he didn't deny families the right to bury their loved ones.

As they rounded the last corner on their journey, the two women stopped short on the pavement. Rook blinked several times, then shared a look of perplexity with Kestrel. Something was different. The Nest was a locus in the Shambles, but more people crammed the packed-earth pavements than usual. Rook pushed through the crowd, narrowing her eyes at the dark figures flanking the Nest's entrance. Four men stood in front of the door, dressed in long woolen coats and flat caps. Lines of jagged black circles climbed from their temples down beneath their starched shirt collars.

Rook stopped without warning, and Kestrel collided into her back. "Do you see what I see?"

Kestrel's answer came in a low whisper. "The Shadow of Jaguars."

"I thought with Dál and Sénnarlann dead, the Shadowmen were gone."

The crowd milled around them, the sight of men with jaguar spots a spectacle rather than the usual.

"Clearly not," Kestrel said. "But who's got the mantle of Jaguar now? Sénnarlann was Dál's second. Who was the third? Did they even have one?"

"I don't know," Rook replied, "but something tells me whoever it is is inside the Nest."

They approached with caution. In the slate-gray afternoon, points of bright red appeared as the men sucked on their cigarettes. The deep brims of their caps shadowed their eyes, their free hands tucked into their pockets. Rook kept her back straight and her head high as she strode up to the door. Those hands weren't inside to protect them from the chill. No doubt they clutched weapons, flick knives or even small revolvers.

The men remained in stony silence as Rook and Kestrel stopped before them. Though she had to crane her neck to meet their eyes, Rook did so without blinking. When they did nothing but stare back, she pulled back her sleeve to reveal her tattoo and said, "Move."

It took the men a moment to step aside, but they did as she said. The Conventicle of Magpies and the Shadow of Jaguars both sought to serve the Saosuíasei people, but they did so in diametric ways. The Conventicle never killed. The Shadow often did.

The strange presence muted the Nest's usual buzz. The patrons nursing their drinks seemed to hunch a little tighter and press their heads together closer than usual. Behind the bar, Wren caught their attention and tipped her head towards Magpie's office. Still polishing a glass, she mouthed, "Serious stuff."

"I wonder what they want," Kestrel murmured as they wound their way into the back rooms, passing more Shadowmen in their long coats.

Rook rolled her eyes. "Not kittens and sweeties, anyway."

While Rook set about her usual routine and read the paper—no newly drained and dead bodies overnight—Kestrel hovered at the doorway, peeking through a crack. After half an hour, Kestrel flapped one hand to get Rook's attention.

"They're leaving," she said in a stage whisper.

Rook shook out the paper and gave a non-committal 'um-hum,' but then Kestrel followed her whisper with a gasp and a Saosuíasei swear.

"You'll never believe it! It's Drucách Tial! He must be the new Jaguar!"

That name shot Rook from her chair. She stumbled to the door and ducked down to press her eye to the crack. Unable to stop herself, she let out a low whistle. A tall man walked out of Magpie's office after her, his cap in his hand, flanked by two other Shadowmen. Just as Kestrel said, it was Drucách Tial, a man who as a boy had trailed in and out of her mother's house. While Dru wasn't one of Mónnuad's waifs and strays, he was an acquaintance of Pit. *Was*, Rook thought, scowling. Pit had no friends in the Shambles, now he'd turned his coat.

Dru had a few more ruts in his forehead than the last time Rook had seen him, and many more Jaguar spots swirling down his face and neck. The more spots, the more important the man. From the redness encircling the many recent additions to his skin, Dru had become very important very fast.

"He's so handsome," Kestrel said. She received a jab to the ribs in response. "Ow!"

They watched as Jaguar and his entourage followed Magpie out of sight. Rook's expression darkened as she moved away from the door, pulling Kestrel behind her.

"I don't like it."

Kestrel chuckled. "You don't like anything."

Her attempt at levity fell flat. Rook folded her arms and ground her teeth. "Dru's only our age. How can he be the new Jaguar?"

Kestrel shrugged both shoulders. "What do we know about him? I haven't spoken to him in at least a year."

"A year isn't enough time to learn to lead the Shadow."

"Well, at least someone's stepped up. God knows the Avanish don't care about us, and after they killed Dál and Sénnarlann, things have only got worse. Whether we end up bloodless on the Buxridge Bridge or swinging by the neck underneath it, they'll be happy. We've as much right to live in this city as they do. Under Dru, the Shadow might fight back."

"The Avanish want a fight," Rook said as she fell into a battered chair. "They want a reason to kill us all."

Kestrel nodded and returned to peer through the chink in the door. "Magpie's coming back. God, she has a face like thunder. She's called Pigeon in after her—no, she's asking her something. Now she's gone to her office, Pigeon's speaking to Wren at the bar. Oh, wow!"

"What?" Rook asked, half-amused and half-exasperated.

"Wren's got the Gold Murder down."

Rook let out a low whistle. Still watching, Kestrel continued her report. "Wren's decanted some Gold. Pigeon's got it on a tray. But she's coming this way."

"I thought she might," Rook replied.

Pigeon's solemn face appeared as Kestrel opened the door. "Mama Magpie wants to see both of you."

"What about?" Rook asked.

Pigeon shrugged one shoulder and turned, still clutching the tray laden with a single glass. Without another word, she led them to Magpie.

The Conventicle's leader was ensconced behind her desk once more. The room had no windows, so even in the afternoon gloom it was lit by candles flickering in cracked wall sconces. Magpie reclined in her chair and made a pyramid with her fingers, not looking up as the women entered. When Pigeon placed the tray on the desk, she managed a grin. "Thank you, my chick."

Pigeon offered her a rare smile. There was something akin to a family tie between them, like a maiden aunt doting on a favored niece. "Anything else, Mama?"

"That's all."

As Pigeon retreated, Magpie roused from her fugue. She straightened in her chair and reached for the cut-glass tumbler, gesturing for the others to sit.

Rook nodded to the gold liquid as Magpie brought the glass to her black lips. "Serious drink."

"Serious business," Magpie replied. It was the usual reply to the Saosuíasei saying.

A moment of silence stretched between them, but Rook didn't dare to interject. Magpie was a woman who did things in her own time and never appreciated being rushed. There was a rumor that one of her stretches behind bars had been because someone had tried to hurry her in a grocer's shop. It was said she took out one of the man's eyes in reply.

After some time, Magpie spoke. "It would seem the Shadow of Jaguars is back. And they want our help."

Rook leaned back in her chair, lacing her fingers behind her head. "We're not in their line of work. We might be a lot of things, but we're not killers."

"That's exactly what I told our new Jaguar," Magpie replied. "The fact he came down to petition me himself shows how serious his intent is. Although," she said, taking another sip of Gold Murder, "young Drucách doesn't look old enough to know how to tie his shoelaces, never mind understand how to run the Shadow." She set down her tumbler again. "To be fair, he wasn't asking us to kill anyone. He needs help to steal some papers from an Avanish official. What those papers are he wouldn't tell me, which was another reason I declined. I'm not sending my girls into a dangerous situation, especially when the reason behind the job is shrouded in the unknown."

She spoke the last sentence more to herself. Rook knew from experience that this entire conversation was less about Magpie telling them something and more about reiterating it to herself. She was often strong in her opinions, even during these conversations, but Rook noted a tightness around Magpie's dark mouth that wasn't usually there.

Kestrel, sensing the same thing, leaned forward. "Mama, you don't sound convinced."

Magpie gave a solemn nod and drained the last of her Gold. Her lips left a black crescent moon on the glass. "I'm not."

Kestrel pressed her advantage. "Maybe that's a sign we should make the Shadow of Jaguars our business." Rook jerked her head to the side and scowled. Her friend held up a placating hand. "Listen to what I have to say before you put me down. Most of what we do is because the poor Saosuíasei—that's us, remember—get nothing from the Avanish. Look at what you had to do last night, Rook. Mrs. Gria came to the Conventicle because she knew the police would do nothing to help her. They don't care about us. They call us dirty and say all the problems in the city are our fault. Maybe the Shadow of Jaguars will bring us the equality we deserve."

Rook gave a huffing chuckle. "Your head's stuck in fantasy. It'll never happen."

Kestrel shook her head. "It'll definitely never happen if everyone thinks like you and no one does anything."

"That's enough, ladies." Magpie didn't shout. Her voice carried enough authority to silence them. "Rook, I understand your pragmatism, but I agree with Kestrel. We'll never be equal to the Avanish if no one takes a stand. However, I'm not convinced the Shadow or its new Jaguar is up to the challenge."

Magpie straightened in her chair. She pulled authority around her like a cloak, banishing the uncertain air from the room. She reached for her writing box and pulled out a small notebook bound in black leather. A thin black ribbon marked the last used page, a silver magpie charm hanging on its end, cast from the same design as her signet ring.

"Let's stop considering what isn't our business and turn to what is. I have a few jobs for you this evening."

They split for the evening, with Kestrel accompanying a small group for an acquisition at the docks. Rook declined an escort from anyone, despite Magpie's objections, and traveled northeast towards Little Avanland, where the richest denizens lived. It differed from the rest of the city, a flawless sweep of new development in contrast with the winding maze of narrow streets that made up the rest of the city. Little Avanland was full of wealth and privilege, and seemed a different world to the twisting maw of the Shambles. It was also a place where one was less likely to be horribly murdered and drained of all their blood. Facts didn't lie. Billy Drainer's stalking grounds were steeped in Saosuíasei poverty.

The strains of one of her younger sisters' skipping rhymes echoed in her ears as Rook slipped across the Eastraine River and into Little Avanland.

> *Billy Drainer stalks the night,*
> *Ready to give you a fright.*
> *Seven swift knocks to your head,*
> *Drains your blood and then you're DEAD!*

Rook clung to the darkness. With the systematic angles of the new street plan, there were few hidden nooks and shadows in Little Avanland. She needed to be careful, despite her safety from Drainer. With her worn frock coat and shabby hat and trousers, it was clear she was not a resident. It was clear from her complexion that she was not

Avanish. If seen, she would find herself thrown in a cell for no reason other than being Saosuíasei in an Avanish world.

The best way to cross this part of the city was from above. Rook secured her hat and cane and clicked her cannula into motion. With her veins filled with extra fuel, she pulled on her Skill and vaulted up the rear of a building to land on its tiled roof, fast and fluid as smoke. She stared across the city from one side to the other. To the east of the Eastraine, Little Avanland's square buildings stood in row upon row. They were built in new brick, some finished with gleaming stone, with new electrical wires strung between them. Every underline and overline criss-crossed this part of the city, connecting the rich to the rest.

To the west and south, the difference was easy to see, even under the hood of night. The further one went from Little Avanland, the more the streets twisted like gnarled roots. The trains skirted the poorest areas, neither under nor overlines dirtying themselves with poverty.

Rook crouched as she moved from roof to roof. The Avanish didn't want to dirty themselves with the poor any longer. If they could exterminate every last Saosuíasei, Rook knew they would. Then they'd build more square buildings and right-angled streets, and string more wires on top of their graves.

She shoved the dark thoughts from her mind and instead went about her secret business. She dipped in and out of rich homes like a quill in ink and wrote her own story across the rooftops. Most of her jobs were the acquisition of valuables in lieu of unpaid wages. Most factory owners had the dreadful trait of being selfish bastards. These jobs were more dubious than the recovery of stolen items, because no matter what way you looked at it, Rook was the one doing the stealing. But, she thought as she padded through yet another plush and warm home, it wasn't as if these residents couldn't afford a minor loss. They filled their houses with the finest furniture, papered the walls with the most fashionable prints, and had more silver knickknacks than Saosuíasei families had simple crockery to eat from. Taking from the richest didn't feel much like a crime, especially when they bought their luxuries from denying workers' wages.

After a few hours, Rook had completed her business. Her pockets now filled with ill-gotten gains, she began the journey back to the Shambles. The walk to Little Avanland had taken nearly two hours, though that was because she'd conserved her blood. It was in her interests to make a speedier retreat, and so she evoked her Skill once more. Her limbs sang and burned as impossible speed took her. To any passerby, she was nothing more than a blur.

Within minutes she was across the city, and with her blood reserves flagging, she let go of her Skill and allowed her pace to slow. She continued on towards the Nest, not even winded. As close as she was, however, she slipped another vial of compatible blood into her bracer. Near to safety as she was, one could never be too careful. Her negligence in bringing a backup the night before would've brought disaster if not for Kestrel. Though her friend never admitted to it, Rook knew Kestrel sometimes followed her. Kes was like that. She never left a friend behind.

Rook was within a mile of the Nest when something quivered in her peripheral vision. She stopped and turned, staring down Tenby Row. A figure stumbled in the dingy street. They lurched sideways, flinging an arm toward the closest wall for support. They'd seen the bottom of too many glasses that night, for the figure missed by a good foot and went tumbling to the ground. Rook rolled her eyes. This wouldn't be the only man or woman in a sorry state tonight. She went to move on, but her mother's cursed morality rang in her mind.

It takes nothing to ignore someone in need. But it takes a special something to lend a stranger a hand.

These were times where lending a hand could be the difference between remaining alive or becoming a blood-drained corpse. Rook grumbled. "Thanks, Ma."

She shook her head and jogged along Tenby Row. It was a narrow street, with crumbling buildings rising on each side. Her sigh dispersed into the darkness. The figure hadn't moved since collapsing, but their groan showed they were still alive, if not lucid. Rook kneeled beside the unfortunate. It was a woman, bundled in at least five shawls and under the influence of at least ten drinks. She remained still with her eyes open, though Rook doubted she could make out anything through the alcoholic blur.

"Hey. Are you all right?" Rook received nothing but another moan in reply. "Ask a stupid question," she said as she threaded one arm underneath the fallen woman's back. "All right, up we get. Where were you drinking this fine evening?" The woman burbled a response, locks of matted hair falling over her face. The hot stench rising from her body made Rook recoil, though she didn't let go. "Judging by the state of you, it was a doorway. Can you tell me your name? Do you have a home to go to?"

All sound from the woman's mouth was incomprehensible gibberish, so garbled Rook couldn't tell if she was speaking Saosuíasei or Avanish. Rook blew another long sigh into the night and shook her head. She couldn't leave the poor creature like this. Women were vulnerable enough without a killer on the rampage. Rook would have to bring her back to the Nest. It was common for Conventicle members to fish drunks off the street and deposit them in the bar's side rooms, even more so in the current climate.

Rook shifted onto her haunches and grabbed the woman under the armpits, dragging her upright. "Time to go home."

A step sounded: not in the distance, but right beside them. Feeling rather than thinking, Rook ducked down again, controlling the drunk woman's descent. Her dagger was in her hand again as she was on her feet, skipping a few steps backward to create distance between herself and her assailant.

The moon loomed high and heavy above the city. It gilded the figure standing before her. His breath rose like smoke from his shapeless face. Rook narrowed her eyes, trying to make sense of the vague silhouette. In one hand, he held a gleaming blade.

"Back off," she said. Her words bounced off the brick walls flanking them. "If you leave now, I won't hurt you."

The figure cocked his head to the side. His gloved hand flexed on the handle of his blade. There was something strange about his movements, as if he was someone she knew. But she didn't, of course. She'd never met him. This figure, without doubt, was the infamous Billy Drainer.

He stepped forwards. Rook stood her ground and flicked her wrist, sending her spare blood coursing through her veins. If he went for the fallen woman, Rook would need all the Skill she could muster to scoop her out of his reach in time. But Drainer stepped forwards again, ignoring the easy target and heading for Rook. His pace was eerie in its slowness, and his hand kept flexing on his blade. He kept his head cocked to the side, as if he was an animal seeing a person for the first time. Rook clenched her dagger tighter. As Drainer grew closer, she Skilled her sight just enough to make out the details of his face.

But there weren't any.

Beneath his top hat he wore a sackcloth hood, with only two slits cut for his eyes. Her throat tightened. They were distinct and dark Saosuíasei eyes.

Rook's adrenaline rose, as did her dagger. "Stay away. And leave her, too." She gestured to the woman, who was groaning again. "Leave all of us alone. Why are you doing this to us? Piss off and kill some Avanish, will you?"

Billy Drainer stared at her, making no move to strike. Rook's heart thundered in her chest. Was this it? Would she die helping someone she didn't know? At least her mother would be proud.

Drainer took a step: this time backwards, not forwards. He took another, and another, and then turned on his heel. He walked back up Tenby Row, the moon still coating him with silver.

Sudden anger overwhelmed Rook. "Who are you?"

Her scream came back at her again and again between the narrow walls, but she received no answer from the retreating figure. Without a word, Drainer disappeared. This time he left behind no victims, only many questions.

FOUR

On their journey to the Nest the following morning, neither Rook nor Kestrel could make sense of what had happened. They walked up the broad swath of Solway Road, past the bright canopies shielding the battered shop front. Confusion hung over them like mist, and the sound of the street hawkers' squawking went unheard.

"I don't understand," Rook said over and over. "He didn't even try to kill us."

Kestrel repeated her reply. "At the very least, it would've been easy to drag off that drunken sod."

Rook shook her head, sucking on her lower lip. "I don't understand. Unless it wasn't Billy Drainer."

Kestrel scoffed. "It must've been him. What other lunatic would run around the city wielding a knife and wearing a bag on his head?"

The man's shapeless sacking face hung heavy in Rook's mind, more real than the swirls of Shambles dwellers around her. "I just don't understand."

The anger from the night before turned to sour fear. Why had he spared her? She remembered his dark eyes. It wasn't because she was one of his people. All his other victims were as Saosuíasei as she, and it seemed he, was. Didn't they have enough suffering without inflicting further troubles on themselves? The thought returned once more. *I don't understand.*

They reached the top of Solway Road. The burble of the crowd swelled, but above it all one voice cried clearly. "Billy Drainer strikes again!"

The headline felled them both like a bullet. Rook and Kestrel stopped cold on the sidewalk. They turned in tandem. The newspaper seller, a ragged boy, waved his stolen wares. There were no legitimate sellers of the *Stamchester Review* in the Shambles. South of the Allen, all news was stolen news.

The boy noticed their attention and called out to them, "Three girls dead in latest Drainer killing spree! Stamchester police no further in their investigation!"

Though Pigeon bought a stack of papers on her way to the Nest every morning, Rook flicked a few coins into the boy's hand and snatched one anyway. The ink smudged under her fingers.

Kestrel hunched down for a better look. "Three?" she asked as Rook scanned the front page for details. "He's never killed three in one night before."

Without warning, the roar of Rook's blood in her body overwhelmed her. It could have been her. The headline could have read four girls dead, or even five girls dead. Or, a nasty corner of her mind suggested, it could've read 'Billy Drainer dead.' *But you did nothing. All you did was yell.* She shut the voice down. It was pointless to think like that.

They hurried on to the Nest, weaving through crowds traveling in all directions. Early morning was crossover time for the continual factory shifts. While one set of weary workers trailed back to their dark homes, another set trudged forward to the grimness of Blackout Row. Their feet were slow with the drudgery of their repetitive lives and the blood-sapped fatigue of a night of work.

A dull fog hung around them. When they reached the Nest, this time no ominous figures in long woolen coats flanked the door. Rook relaxed from a tension she hadn't realized she was carrying. However, as soon as she crossed the threshold, she sensed the veil of pain. She and Kestrel shared a narrow-eyed look. Something was wrong. Very wrong.

Despite the early hour, the bar was a hive, but it wasn't full of the usual customers. Every face was that of a Conventicle member. Wren, Crow, Sparrow, Raven, Hawk, Bluebird, Robin, and Jay were all there already, and more women entered behind. Their expressions ran the gamut from horrified, with eyes glittering with tears, to dark and burning with rage. The bottom dropped out of Rook's stomach.

"Who was it?" she asked.

Wren, behind the bar even without patrons to serve, tried to speak. But her grief choked her. Rook gritted her teeth and lurched to Mama Magpie's office. It couldn't be. Not one of them.

As she burst through the office door, Kestrel on her heels, Rook blurted out, "Who?"

Magpie sagged in her chair, sorrow pulling her expansive personality in on itself. She turned to Rook, her face blotchy, her lips strange and red without their black paint. Rook glanced for Pigeon. She wasn't at Magpie's side.

That was her answer.

Rook could barely speak. "Not her."

Beside her, Kestrel swallowed against a sob.

Magpie palmed her face, shaking her head. "Pigeon was making her way home when he found her. She must have just finished her last task. The task I set her. If I hadn't—" Her voice cracked, leaving the rest unsaid.

Bitter sorrow turned to blazing rage inside Rook's chest. "It's not your fault, Mama. It's that monster Drainer's, and the Avanish bastards who leave us to rot."

At her shoulder, Kestrel vibrated with emotion. Whether it was grief or fury, Rook didn't know. The tall woman turned her shining eyes on her.

"Now do you see why I have hope for the Shadow of Jaguars?" Kestrel asked. Her sharp tone pierced Rook, though Rook knew the ire was for Pigeon's murderer. "If the Avanish had a single care for us, they'd send police or even militia in to find this madman. And then no more people would end up dead, like poor Pigeon."

The weight of Kestrel's words slammed down on Rook. She was right. If the Avanish wouldn't give them equality, perhaps it was time to take it for themselves.

Magpie remained still for some moments with her head bowed, as if the silver charm around her neck hung too heavy on its chain. But as Rook found her own chest heaving with sorrow and fury, Magpie's breathing calmed. She closed her dark eyes for a moment, then reached under her desk to extract a woven bag. Its contents clinked, and Magpie pulled out the unguents and paints she used to beautify her face. With the greatest of care, Magpie held up a hand mirror and applied powder and rouge over her grief-stricken expression, and completed her appearance with her usual glistening black lip stain. Then she stood, adjusted her corset, and smoothed down her black velvet dress.

"I'm going to speak to the whole Conventicle within the hour," she said, her voice back to its familiar cool and collected tone. "Everyone will be here by then. Pigeon's death must be marked."

There was something ominous in the way the statement left her lips. Rook shared a sidewards glance with Kestrel before they both nodded. "Yes, Mama."

They took her silence as a dismissal and made their way back to the bar. The dull rumble of conversation stilled as Rook and Kestrel entered. Sparrow jumped up and skipped towards them.

"What did she say?" she asked, her eyes blinking too fast as always. "Did she say what happened? Did she say what he left state poor Pigeon in?" Her words came as fast as her blinks.

The rest of the Conventicle leaned inward, all ears pricked in interest and all faces pulled with despair.

Rook shook her head. "Mama Magpie will speak to us all within the hour, once everyone's here. She'll tell us more then."

Sparrow's body wilted, though her eyes kept blinking and twitching. "All right, all right," she said, more to herself than anyone else, "within the hour."

By the time Magpie emerged from her office, all members of the Conventicle had perched on seats and barstools, filling every inch of space in the bar. Old gas lamps and sooty candles cast a patchwork of green and yellow light across their drawn faces. Grebe, Pelican, Heron, and Swan clustered together as always. Crake stood apart from everyone, but her near-translucent skin and pink eyes still drew attention. Distress pinched even her disinterested face. Redshank and Greenshank, twins identical down to the clothes they wore, leaned against one another for comfort. They were only a handful of months older than Pigeon, and the shock fell hard upon their youth.

Magpie walked to the bar with clear-cut purpose and a straight back. Wren reached for a bottle of Gold Murder, but Magpie waved her off. Instead, the leader of the Conventicle turned to face the gathered women, righteous anger gleaming in her eyes.

"As you know, Pigeon is dead." The silence that followed the statement was palpable. "Last night, she became one of Billy Drainer's victims. He dumped her body half-in and half-out of an alleyway not five streets from her home." Despite the trauma of her words, Magpie's voice remained steady. "He beat her to death, no stab wounds to waste any of her precious blood." She spat the last phrase. "Then he drained her body and threw into the dirt. He treated her worse than an animal slaughtered in an abattoir." A wave of indignation passed through the crowd. Magpie lifted her voice above it. "And what will the Avanish government do for us? What justice will poor Pigeon ever receive?" She paused, then brought the next word down like a gavel. "None." The Conventicle's indignation became a tumult of fury. "Enough is enough!" Magpie spat, her volume quieting her audience. "I am no longer prepared to sit by and allow the Avanish to treat us like beasts. Perhaps it shouldn't have taken the loss of one of our own for me to see things this way." Her eyes flicked towards Rook, but they settled on Kestrel. "Regardless, that is how I feel now."

Magpie drew in a deep, steadying breath, and Rook knew what turn her speech was about to take.

"The new Jaguar came to see me yesterday. Drucách Tial asked for our help in several matters. I told him I wasn't interested, that I didn't want to involve the Conventicle in the business of the Shadowmen. Well, Billy Drainer has brought that business to our door and taken one of our own. Therefore," she continued in a voice of iron, "I intend to contact the Jaguar and tell him I am willing to co-operate with his plans."

A strange ripple passed through the crowd. Rook looked at no one except Magpie.

"I wish to let you all know now that I require none of you to follow my lead in this one matter," she said. "You came to me for work and protection. I will not change the nature of your work, nor put you into the path of unnecessary harm without your consent. If you choose not to associate with the Shadow of Jaguars, that is your choice. However, if you wish to join me, if you want to be part of a scant vengeance for my beloved Pigeon"—her voice wavered—"I will welcome your support."

There was a beat of silence. Then Kestrel spoke. "I'll join you, Mama. Not just for Pigeon, but for us all."

Murmuring followed her pledge. Then came more declarations.

"I'll join you," came Sparrow's half-frantic reply. "It's the least I can do."

"Us too," Redshank and Greenshank replied together.

Soon, the whole Conventicle called out their support. Even Crake raised a pale hand in a silent pledge. Magpie's eyes swung to Rook, dark and unreadable. When the others saw on whom their leader's gaze had settled, the room fell silent once more.

Rook drew in a slow breath and let it out with deliberate control. She repeated the action again and again. Pigeon had been her friend. She had been a sweet girl, undeserving of a brutal and undignified death, and Kestrel had been right all along. Nothing would change for their people under Avanish rule. It was what the Avanish did: control and conquer. The city of Stamchester hadn't started life as an Avanish place. Stamchester wasn't even the city's original name. The Avanish had taken it from the Undténsians and made it their own through the insidious press of a dominating force. They'd also been happy to displace Saosuíasei from their homes, forcing them across the sea to take advantage of them for cheap labor. But that was all their people would ever be. Disposable. Unimportant. Just as Mama Magpie said, nothing better than animals to use and dispose of as they saw fit.

Rook thought of her mother, her sisters, the future nieces and nephews she might one day have. What sort of life did she want for them? Was equality a mere fantasy? Or was it worth fighting for?

When Rook spoke, she echoed Kestrel's words. "I'll join you, Mama."

Magpie's black lips split into a wide grin, even as tears slipped from her eyes. "Thank you, Rook." She caught each Conventicle member's gaze one by one. "Thank you all."

The Jaguar returned the following day, once more flanked by his burly entourage. This time Rook found herself inside Mama Magpie's office. She stood to the side of the desk while Magpie and the Jaguar faced each other across it. Rook took the time to inspect her old acquaintance. Just as he'd been a handsome boy, Drucách Tial was a handsome man—as far as men went, anyway. Rook wasn't interested in men, or any of the respective parts Kestrel enjoyed fawning over. Dru had smooth dark skin, unmarked by anything other than his jaguar spots. His eyes were glossy and brown, and his dark hair gathered in a curling flick over his forehead. He set his flat cap on Magpie's desk in a sign of respect.

"I'm sorry for your loss," he said.

"Thank you," Magpie replied.

Her face remained impassive. Rook was glad. It was one thing to help the men of the Shadow of Jaguars. It was another to fawn and flutter under their influence. The Conventicle had never bowed to the influence of anyone.

The Jaguar flicked his gaze to Rook. He offered her a smile. "Long time no see, eh, Rébh?"

Rook raised an eyebrow, unsure how to respond. Dru remembered her, but they weren't friends. They weren't even equals, not now little Drucách had risen to the lofty title of the Jaguar. "In the Conventicle, I go by Rook," she said at length.

Magpie nodded. "I've invited Rook to listen because she's one of my most trusted girls, and we'll need her for what you propose."

Rook straightened under the praise. She turned to the Jaguar, regarding him with half-closed eyes to suggest indifference. She resisted the temptation to raise a hand and look at her nails instead of his face. That would have been a few steps too far.

The Jaguar nodded, flicking his eyes from Rook to Magpie. "If the Shadow of Jaguars is ever to strike a significant blow against the Avanish, we need to know details of the Avanish plan of attack. We can't have a repeat of what happened with the Scar." He leaned forward, and Rook could see no remnants of the little boy he'd once been. "Our beloved governor, Kel Dreidchain, is planning to discuss his plans with his close circle. We need someone to get inside and get us that information."

"So," Rook said, keeping her expression deadpan, "you need me to eavesdrop for you."

The Jaguar replied with a wry smile. "Yes, we need you to eavesdrop. But we don't know when the meeting will take place. You'll need to find that out first."

Magpie twined her long fingers together on the tabletop. "You'll have to do some reconnaissance."

"Watching from the outside won't do much good," Rook said.

"Not from the outside," Magpie replied. "From the inside."

Everything clicked into place. Rook closed her eyes for a moment in a silent curse. "You're making me go as a maid, aren't you?"

The thought of it disgusted her. She'd have to wear tight stays and a corset to scrub floors. She'd spend days on her hands and knees while the bloated Avanish governor and his family ogled her bent body. She'd done this once before, though not in a home as opulent as Dreidchain's. It was disgusting. Humiliating. Even worse, depending on how long the job took, it was time separated from her family. Most of those who served the Avanish lived in. It was the way the ruling class liked it: no time wasted by traveling from home. It was, Rook thought with a scoff, better value for their money.

"We'll arrange for a vacancy to become available for you," the Jaguar said. At Rook's incredulous raise of her eyebrows, he lifted a hand. "Don't worry. We're paying a servant a significant sum to persuade her to step aside. It's nothing more nefarious than that."

Rook opened her mouth to object, but Magpie spoke before she could. "You're the only one I trust with this. You're the only one I can guarantee will get herself out of danger, should danger arise. I know servant's work horrifies you, but it can't be worse than the horrors done to my poor Pigeon."

How could Rook object to that? She asserted her agreement with a tight-lipped nod, and the Jaguar reached for his cap. "Thank you for your help, Ms. Magpie," he said as he rose. "Together, I hope the Shadow and the Conventicle can make lives better for all of us."

The rest of the day passed in preparation. For Rook's part, she sat and brooded over a solitary drink for some hours. Others flitted in and out, and around noon Kestrel dragged Rook from her chair and onto the street.

"You've been inside too long," she said as they made their way out of the Shambles and towards the Kenmon shopping district.

The morning's fresh bread mingled with the tantalizing aroma of halfturns, stuffed pastry parcels named for their twisting shape. Kestrel purchased two, and though her poor mood objected, Rook's stomach overruled it and she accepted the meal. They crossed to a low wall and perched as they ate, the city bustling around them. The streets teemed with people going about their daily business. Kenmon was a bustling mix not only of Saosuíasei and Avanish, but of Undténsians and people from other nations, too. They wove among one another, the colorful eddies of the rich mingling with the undyed darkness of the poor. The contrast was stark.

Stamchester's motto, "Formed from many, now as one," was an unending source of irony for people like Rook and Kestrel. There was no 'one' in Stamchester. Anyone who wasn't part of your 'us' was a 'them.' And in a city with a metropolitan 'them,' most of whom would slit your throat as quick as look at you, it meant you had to rely on your 'us' alone. For Rook, that was the family she had found in the Conventicle.

She ate the last of her halfturn and cast the twisted crust onto the pavement. Even before it hit the ground, several pigeons strutted over on gnarled feet, ready to fight one another for the morsel. They squawked and bobbed their feathered heads. The birds from which Pigeon had received her namesake were nothing like the girl. They were noisy where she had been quiet. They were cumbersome on their feet, where Pigeon had been swift upon hers. Magpie had named the girl after the racing kind, beautiful and well-kept and coveted. There was no doubt Mama Magpie had adored her.

Kestrel's crust joined the remnants of Rook's. "It's going to be dangerous," she said.

Rook let out a soft laugh and watched as more birds fluttered over to fight over the morsel. "Everything we do is dangerous. Magpie knows I can handle myself." She touched the bracer and needle that lingered under her coat sleeve. "If anything goes wrong, I'll be out before anyone can sound the alarm."

"I've volunteered to be your runner," Kestrel said. "Whatever you need, I'll get."

"Make sure you keep a store of my blood on you at all times. That's all I'm likely to need." Rook shifted her balance onto one leg. "What I need is for you to look after the girls and Ma for however long I'm gone."

"You know I will," Kestrel said, her words earnest. "It'll only be for a few days. God knows if anyone can creep around a house and snoop and not get caught, it's you. I swear, I don't know how you don't get caught, even when you're in plain sight. I know you'll get what the Shadow needs."

Despite her galvanized attitude towards the Jaguar and his men, something strange still rippled over Rook's skin. "I'd like to know what they intend to do with the information."

"Start a revolution," Kestrel said.

Rook shook her head. "More like start a war."

Her last word fell upon the pigeons at their feet, still fighting over the scraps. Two birds had clamped their beaks on either end of what little remained, and tugged back and forth with increasing violence.

"If it's war, it's a war the Avanish have brought on themselves," Kestrel said. "They have only themselves to blame."

One pigeon triumphed, wrenching the crust from its opponent and hobbling away. Not accepting defeat, the other bird trailed after it. Rook watched as the fight began again, and after a few moments, the prize disintegrated between them.

FIVE

The transition from the Shambles to Little Avanland was like stepping into another world. Wide boulevards lay perpendicular to pin-straight streets. Modernity dominated the cityscape, boxing the inhabitants into blocks and rows. In the darkness of early morning, beautiful gas lamps shone with clean light. The Avanish reserved the muggy green of coal gas for the poor. Tall buildings rose in opulence, the endless tangle of wires strung between them. Some carried electricity, some telegraph messages, and some even carried voices. It was a thing called telephone, though Rook's mind spun as she tried to puzzle out how it worked. How could sound travel through the wire? She shook her head and dug her free hand into her coat pocket. It didn't matter much. The Avanish wouldn't give them a train line, never mind new-fangled things like telephones.

"Hand out of your pocket."

Rook stopped and turned. She stared up at her Shadowman escort, keeping one hand where it was and the other clenched around the handle of her battered case. Her sudden stop caused consternation, and self-entitled Avanish financiers huffed and stepped around them, muttering about an inbred lack of manners in some people.

The Shadowman, Cian, shrugged his shoulders. "It's not a very ladylike thing to do," he said. "You'll get turned away before you cross the threshold if you carry yourself like that. You know what they're like."

Rook stayed silent, but tightened her grip on her case. Cian was right, but that didn't mean she wanted to agree. He was typical of the new Jaguar's men, young and tall, with wiry muscles and a half-grin you were never sure was flirtatious or mocking. Though he had the telltale tattoos of the Shadow, Cian was Skilled enough to camouflage them. Though she begrudged the feeling, Rook couldn't help but respect that Skill. Morphing your appearance required a constant low flow of blood burning, and a lot of concentration. For all her talent, it was something she'd never been able to do.

On the walk from where the Jaguar's taxi carriage dropped them off, Cian stayed a little too close for Rook's liking. His intent may have been to provide protection, but that didn't matter. If he'd tried to touch her, she would've ripped the offending arm from its socket. He'd kept his hands to himself, however, and thus no violence occurred. It was for the best, of course. A woman who might tear a man to pieces wasn't the most desirable candidate for service.

Rook continued to stare Cian down, her concentration broken only by the rattle and roar of an overline train passing through. It was on the tip of her tongue to tell him it should be a woman's prerogative to decide what was ladylike. But, she thought as the train's gray smoke melded with the dark morning sky, it was pointless.

"Let's get this over with," she said instead, and took off along the road again.

The governor's mansion sat in beautiful grounds, surrounded by lawns and rows of flowerbeds. The white stone building swept out in two wings, with a grand clock tower rising from the middle. Several carriages and motor cars stood on the tree-flanked drive. Just like all Avanish, Governor Dreidchain tailored everything to scream out his wealth and power.

Rook and Cian passed by the tall front gate. Hung between black wrought-iron railings decorated with panels of gold filigree and flanked by vermillion-clad city militia, it was the entrance for the important. Instead, they skirted the periphery of the grounds and arrived at the servants' entrance at the rear. The gravel crunched under their boots as they made their way up the path. As they reached the nondescript though well-maintained door, it opened. An equally nondescript but well-maintained houseboy appeared in the frame, pulling up short in surprise.

"Who are you?" he asked, narrowing his eyes.

Both Rook and Cian noted the immediate flick of his gaze to Cian's temples. He searched for jaguar spots, but found none. Cian's Skill never wavered, holding his secret within his skin.

"I'm from Brookers Employment Agency," he said. "I'm here by appointment with a girl for consideration."

All suspicion disappeared from the boy's expression. "Oh. Follow me, then."

The back-of-house corridors were dark and narrow, in stark contrast with the opulence of the grand front facade. The houseboy gestured for them to follow him into a spartan side parlor. As he announced their presence, a prim woman with olive skin and an angular face stood from her patched chair.

"Are you from Brookers?" she asked. Her accent marked her as not Saosuíasei, but not Avanish either. She was Undténsian.

Cian nodded. "I am, Miss." He clamped his hands on Rook's shoulders. "This is the girl you requested, Miss. Goes by the name Rébh. She's a hard worker, and very keen to please."

Had she been able to get away with it, Rook would've delighted in shoving her battered case backwards into Cian's crotch. As it was, she stayed silent and kept her head bowed, playing the detested role of a meek little girl.

"My name is Miss Vost," the prim woman said, "but you will address me as Ma'am."

Dutiful, Rook bent into a shameful curtsey. "Yes, Ma'am."

Vost harrumphed in response and regarded the potential new maid with narrowed blue eyes. She wore a smart black uniform with a white collar and flat leather shoes that bore not a speck of street dirt. Over the top of her uniform she wore a crisp apron, its strings looped several times around her tiny frame and tied in a symmetrical bow. It was clear the apron was for display only, for Vost's hands were untarnished by the roughness of coal soap. Rook flexed her fingers. She'd spent half the night scrubbing her hands raw by washing her sisters' bed linen. She hadn't developed a sudden urge to be domestic. It was because they would never take her as a serious candidate for servant labor if she looked like she hadn't washed a sheet in her life. Rook had scrubbed much laundry in her time, but since joining the Conventicle, most housework had fallen from her to the younger girls.

As expected, the first thing Vost did after her initial visual appraisal was to point at Rook's hands. "Let me see."

Rook lifted her hands to show off her raw skin, turning them over when commanded. Vost harrumphed a second time and grabbed Rook's elbow to propel her around and inspect her from the back. It took all Rook's self-control not to clamp her fingers around the woman's wrists and fling her against the faded paper of the parlor wall.

"And you say she has some experience?" Vost asked.

Cian turned her to face the woman once again. "She does, Ma'am. She's worked in a few different households and comes with good references." He fished in his pockets for a thin packet of forged papers.

Vost took the references and clicked her tongue against her teeth. "Of late, many of our Saosuíasei girls haven't worked out. Some are too stupid to follow instructions."

Rook hoped her jaw clench wasn't too obvious. A meek servant wouldn't be so affronted. Vost might not have been Avanish, but it was apparent she shared their prejudice. Perhaps that was how she, a non-Avanish woman, had risen to a high rank in the governor's household.

"This girl is smart," Cian said. There was an edge of flint to his words in the wake of Vost's ignorance.

"Not too smart, and hopefully not smart-mouthed," the woman said. "All right, I'll give her a trial week. However, if she doesn't work out, I won't make any payment to either you or her."

"Understood."

Vost called for an attendant, and the same houseboy returned so fast it was clear he'd been listening. *Idiot*, Rook thought. He'd make a poor spy.

"Quin, show Miss Rébh to her new quarters."

The houseboy, Quin, nodded and jerked his thumb towards the door. He didn't take her bag, and Rook was glad for that. She didn't need anyone to carry anything for her.

"Good luck, Miss Rébh," Cian said as she left.

Rook half-turned and dipped in the slightest of curtseys. She could give him that. He wasn't the worst.

With her place in the household secured, Rook settled into her temporary role. They gave her a bed in the attic. *Bed* was too generous a term, as it was little more than a wooden board with a scrap of cloth for a blanket. Cold air wheezed and rattled through the mansion's eaves, joined by the snores of the other servant girls. Rook's was one of ten beds in the grim dormitory. She was by far the oldest among them, with the rest ranging in age from eleven to eighteen. At least, that was her guess at their ages. So far none had ventured to speak to her. Miss Vost had sent her to the laundry to join four other girls and Rook spent her first day elbow-deep in coal soap. Her laundry skills still untested, she'd scrubbed other servants' bed linen. The clothes of the governor and his family were too expensive to trust to an unknown girl.

The laundry didn't stop all day: unsurprising, considering how large the household staff was and how many clothes the governor's family seemed to go through. Rook knew Dreidchain had three children, only two of whom lived at home. Yet it seemed like there were enough garments to clothe Rook's entire brood of sisters five times over.

She labored on, the repetitiveness of scrubbing clothing against the washboard lulling her. Her heart pumped only from the vigor of the work. Her mind was calm. At this moment, all she needed to do was remain inconspicuous. She'd be just another Saosuíasei servant, unseen and unheard. It was the perfect cover for her task.

The grand outside clock struck nine in the evening. The other laundry girls sat back on their haunches, stretching their backs. At Rook's quizzical look, one of them spoke to her. It was the first time any of them had. "Nine o'clock is the end of the day," the girl said. She seemed young, and unlike the others, she wasn't Avanish, but was Undténsian. "Finish what you're scrubbing and then we can have dinner."

Rook took her meal in silence. No one attempted to speak to her again, but that didn't matter. She didn't want to engage in conversation. She was more interested in listening. The most junior members of the household staff, such as her fellow laundresses, the houseboys like Quin, and the younger chambermaids, sat at a long table in a narrow dining room. It was a windowless inner room, lit by a few gas lamps and a line of stubby candles trailing the length of the table. No one said anything of much importance. Most of the conversation was idle gossip, but it was good to know there were plenty of loose lips among the staff.

On her first night, Rook remained in her bed like a good little servant girl. On the second night, however, she began her prowl. The day's work had fatigued her more than the last, but she'd made it through using no Skill. That left her with plenty of reserves for her nighttime excursion. The enormous clock was silent after midnight, but Rook still had her father's pocket watch. She'd stashed it under the secret bottom of her case, which she'd shoved beneath the creaking frame of her bed. Servants' wages were woeful, and Rook couldn't blame any of them for stealing what they could if the opportunity arose. Apart from that, there were certain other items in the case she didn't want discovered. No genuine servant girl needed a stash of blades and lock picks.

Once the watch's hands showed two in the morning, Rook grabbed the tools of her trade, stepped into her boots, and wrapped a threadbare shawl around herself as if she were going to the outdoor privy. But as soon as she closed the attic room door behind her, she set to work.

Her Bloodskill flowed through her like an ethereal warmth. This time she sought not the explosive power needed for a high jump or a fistfight, but allowed the blood to burn like a candle, slow and controlled. The day's fatigue disappeared, replaced by a steady stream of energy. If she was careful, she could make her Skill last for hours. Renewed, she set to work.

Confined to the laundry as she had been, Rook hadn't been able to explore the mansion during the day as she had hoped. Had they had employed her as a junior chambermaid, she would've had reason and opportunity to find the lay of the place before her search. It was riskier this way, but she had no choice, though no fears either. This wasn't her first such secret excursion.

She tiptoed through the dark corridors, limiting her use of Bloodskill for sight. Too much would burn her out too soon, and Kestrel wasn't scheduled to appear until the following night. While Rook would pass on what information she had gleaned so far, Kestrel would supply her with a vial of compatible blood. It was only good for a few hours once taken from the large icebox in the Nest, but a little extra blood never went to waste. Bad blood, however, was dangerous. If injected, it could cause severe sickness, and even death.

Governor Dreidchain's mansion was unnerving in its silence. For such a large house with an enormous staff, it was strange that no one stirred. Convenient, but strange. Rook crept through the long corridors, her primary ambition to learn the floor plan of the building. Before she could engage in any serious eavesdropping, she needed to know where to listen.

Rook explored on silent feet, lock picks in hand, a knife strapped to her thigh and hidden under her nightgown. She explored wing by wing and floor by floor, and the hours passed in darkness. There were occasional footfalls that drove her into hiding behind tall potted plants or within the deep folds of velvet curtains, but nothing of significance happened.

Until something did.

As she approached what she took to be the gentleman's wing of the mansion, voices rose at the end of a long hallway. Rook paused, her body tense and still as she used her Skill to sharpen her hearing. There were at least three different voices: one Avanish, one Undténsian, and a third with a familiar lilt. Rook's stomach lurched in sudden revulsion. It was distinctly Saosuíasei. Her mind could find no other reason. Could someone from her own community collude against them?

After hours of slow burn, fatigue encroached and her Skill waned. Rook eased up on sharpening her hearing and instead crept closer to the source of the voices. Three doors down from where she stopped, a light glowed from beneath a door. Not cheap green gaslight, but bright and buttery yellow. Nothing but the best for the governor, Rook reminded herself. She slipped another door closer, her natural hearing picking up the conversation well enough.

"...must do something about this Drainer character," the Undténsian said. "If we're not careful, he'll incite the rebels further."

The Avanish voice, pompous and self-assured, scoffed. It was Dreidchain. "If so, they're even more idiotic than I thought. Whoever this so-called Billy Drainer character is, he's one of their own. Your men are certain of that, Captain, are they not?"

"We are, sir," the Undténsian replied. *Captain*, Rook thought. That was curious. Avanish didn't place Undténsians as low as Saosuíasei, but she'd still seen few of them in their police. "From the few victims who've escaped," the captain continued, "the man speaks with a Saosuíasei accent. Though since he covers his face, no one has confirmed his looks and coloring."

Rook thought back on her own encounter with Drainer. There was no doubting his accent was Saosuíasei.

"The more of them he kills, the better," Dreidchain said. "No offense intended to you, young man, but at least you're only half-Saosuíasei."

Dreidchain's initial words made rage flare in Rook's chest, but the follow-up chilled her again. A half-Saosuíasei policeman. There couldn't be too many of them. Could it be? When the Saosuíasei spoke, the sound cut Rook to the bone.

"No offense taken, sir."

That voice was one she had heard all her life, the voice of a young boy and then a young man who had grown up in her mother's home, taken under her wing when abandoned by his own. It was Pit. Rook's hurt fermented into disgust. Pit wasn't just part of the Avanish police. He was attached to one of their captains. And not just any captain, but one reporting to the governor. The man she had once considered a brother hadn't only turned his back on his community. Now he was part of something worse. The police engaged in active inaction against the man terrorizing her home. If the captain sought permission to do something, it meant Dreidchain had given him an order to do nothing. Rook's disgust twisted into revulsion. Her hand flexed over her knife, not sure which of the three she'd enjoy petrifying the most.

"I don't want to waste any resources on this Drainer issue other than keeping him out of Little Avanland," Governor Dreidchain continued. "If he wants to kill Saosuíasei, he's welcome to. I want our priority to remain protecting the city from the Saosuíasei. It would seem killing their leaders wasn't enough to cow them. I don't want you coming here with any further pleas about saving the Saosuíasei from one of their own. They're tainted and not worth the trouble. Have I made myself clear?"

"Yes, Governor Dreidchain," the captain said.

"We're to have a committee meeting in two nights' time. All required parties will be in attendance. I want you to double the security from last time. There were concerns that you didn't bring enough men. And make sure they're all the sort that know when to keep their mouths shut. If there's a leak, I'm holding you responsible, and you alone."

"Of course, sir. We'll show ourselves out."

From within, someone pushed a chair back. Rook retreated up the corridor and flattened herself against the wall, cloaked in shadow. Two men emerged, both tall, but one with the familiar lanky build of Rook's childhood friend. Even in the darkness, the silver buttons on their chests and shoulders glinted. The rest of them disappeared, their dark uniforms melding with the shadows. They trooped away from Rook's hiding place, and risky as it was, she crept after them.

"I hope that regardless of the candid opinions expressed by the governor," the captain said, "I can still trust you to keep silent, Constable Akker."

Rook drew up short for a moment before continuing after them. That wasn't Pit's surname.

"You can, Captain Veng. I've left my old life in the gutter behind."

"I'm glad to hear it."

Rook had to seize every modicum of self-control she had to stop herself racing forward and smacking Pit across his arrogant, ungrateful, turncoat face. Gutter? Mónnuad Artur had raised him in no gutter. She'd cared for him in a loving, if simple, home and treated him as one of her own children.

The two policemen said little more as they passed from the gentleman's wing into the back corridors, leaving through the servants' entrance. Even with fatigue plaguing her, anger coursed through Rook's veins, burning as hot as any Bloodskill could. She wrested enough control of her emotions to make the journey back to the attic without incident, but by the time she'd stowed her knife and lock picks in her case again, she couldn't stop herself from slamming the lid. The girl in the bed beside hers jolted upright, her breath coming in fearful gasps.

"What was that?" she asked, but Rook remained silent and still. The girl settled back into slumber and Rook shoved her case under the bed again. She pulled the musty blanket over herself, shivering more from emotion than the cold that pervaded the room.

Pit had called their family home a gutter. Now he used an Avanish name instead of his own. He was glad to identify as one of their enemies and leave the rest of himself behind. A flash of dread passed through her. Rook squeezed her eyes shut. She would have to tell Kestrel. It would devastate her.

The tiny thread of friendship Rook might have kept for Pit snapped. How could he do this, not only to his people, but to someone as kind and good as Kestrel? How could the person she'd considered a brother be so cruel?

Rook gritted her teeth and twisted her hands into the grubby sheet. The voice she'd heard belonged to a man she didn't know and didn't want to know. To her, the boy she once knew was dead.

SIX

As she scrubbed through the next day, all Rook could think about was Pit. His words. His betrayal. How much this would hurt Kestrel. Vost appeared in the laundry at some point, though when, Rook couldn't say. She'd been taking her frustrations out on a nightdress with a very stubborn bloodstain, imagining it was Pit's disgusting face as she raked it over the board.

"You're a lot stronger than you first looked."

To her shame, Rook let out a squawk at Vost's voice. Lukewarm water, tinged orange, ran down her arms as she lifted the stained cloth above the wooden tub.

A few of the other girls tittered at her, but Vost looked impressed. "Keep up the good work, Rébh. Perhaps you'll work out better than the others did." She snapped her head to the others, an edge of venom in her voice. "Get on with your work! You could learn a thing or two about industry from this one."

The laundry girls bent their heads and their backs to the washtubs again. As soon as Vost disappeared, Rook received a round of spiteful looks.

"You don't want to make us your enemies," one of them said. It was Fialta, a Saosuíasei girl with a pretty face but a foul expression.

Rook shrugged one shoulder in response. She didn't care if they hated every bone in her body. She wouldn't be around long enough for it to matter. The other girls sent her another round of vile stares, but then Rook noticed the exception. One of them, a girl with the most enormous brown eyes Rook had ever seen, gave her a sympathetic smile. While she hadn't paid the girl any attention until before, Rook did now. Her skin was smooth, and like Vost's, her complexion had the distinctive olive tone of Undténsians. The girl flicked her gaze towards the others before rolling her eyes, and Rook allowed herself a wry grin.

The day went on as the others had, although at dinner Rook found herself on the receiving end of a friendly, if brief, conversation from her new acquaintance.

"My name is Özdo," she said in an accent similar to Vost's. "What's yours?"

Rook almost laughed at the innocence of the question. If only this Özdo knew why she was here. It wasn't to make friends. Regardless, she answered. "Rébh."

Özdo fished a chunk of gristle from her stew. "Don't worry about the other girls," she said as she chewed. "They're just bitter. Nearly all the new girls start in the laundry. You only stay there if you're no good for anything else."

Rook raised an eyebrow. "Is that the case with you?"

The girl grinned. She looked around Maird's age, and there was something both playful and wicked about her expression that made Rook smile. "I let them think that's the case, but I like the laundry. I don't want to fetch and carry for the two daughters, or spend my days running around after the governor's wife. The laundry is peaceful. No one bothers me. And I get paid just the same."

"It's tough work, though." Rook scraped her bowl for the last morsel. The food was bland, but with her blood reserves low, she needed all the energy she could get from the tasteless rations. "Wouldn't you prefer something easier, if less peaceful?"

Özdo shook her head. A strand of dark hair fell from underneath her bleached white cap. It coiled in a perfect ringlet. "I'm no stranger to tough work. I enjoy it. And I suppose when I'm in the laundry, I can pretend it's just a job. I don't like feeling like a servant, and I know I'd feel that way if I was at the ladies' beck and call."

She pressed her lips together in a tight line, as if realizing she'd said too much. To reassure her, Rook gave a solemn nod. "I feel the same way. I might stick around in the laundry too."

With her worry dissipating, Özdo managed a low chuckle. "I'd like that. You've already spoken to me more than any of the rest ever have."

"Oh?"

"They don't like me because I'm not one of them," Özdo said as she finished her food. "They're all Saosuíasei. I'm not."

"You're Undténsian, right?" Rook asked, reaching for Özdo's plate. She stacked it atop hers.

Özdo's eyes widened, as if no one had ever before shown her simple common courtesy such as lifting a plate. "I am."

Rook gathered their utensils. "I've never had much to do with Undténsians. You don't see many of them in the Shambles."

"We stay in Ezkantíl," Özdo said. "At least in that part of the city, we can pretend this is still our country."

"So why are you here?"

Rook's directness took the other woman by surprise, but Özdo answered regardless. "Miss Vost is my aunt. When my parents realized she was earning money and being treated with the tiniest bit of respect, they sent me here to work for her. They wanted me to be successful in something instead of dirt poor, which is what they've always been. They saw this as an opportunity I couldn't miss." She huffed and shook her head. "I wish I'd stayed far away from this house, or even better, this whole city."

"Understandable," Rook said. "Unless you're Avanish, rich, or even better, both, Stamchester can be an appalling place." She stood, their plates in hand. "It's been nice to speak to you, Özdo. A friendly face makes things that bit easier."

The Undténsian woman nodded. "It does, though you don't seem like the sort who needs much support. Vost wasn't wrong when she said you're stronger than you looked at first. Most girls who come here don't raise their heads for weeks. They don't even respond to simple conversation. But you," Özdo said, nodding at the stacked plates in Rook's hands, "aren't like that. Where did you get your confidence?"

Rook tapped her fingernails on the crockery and smiled. "I got it from my mama."

On the third evening, Rook grabbed her knife, shawl, and boots and disappeared from the attic room once again. She slipped into the crisp sting of the foggy night. Her breath clouded as she made her way to the rear gate where she was to meet Kestrel. The moon was a waxing crescent, hanging in the sky like a blue sickle. While Rook looked forward to seeing her friend and replenishing her blood stocks, she didn't look forward to the conversation she was about to have. Kestrel needed to know about Pit.

"What is it?" Kestrel asked as she handed over Rook's needle bracer, already stocked with fresh blood. "There's something wrong."

Rook strapped the device to her arm, only then realizing how much she'd missed its weight and presence. "I saw Pit last night."

Kestrel's cheeks blanched under her rouge. She stepped back. "Where?"

There was no point dancing around it. With a sigh that sent another cloud of breath into the air, Rook shook her head and prepared to inject the blood. "He was inside the mansion with some police captain and Dreidchain."

"Why? How?" Kestrel shook her head in astonishment. "He only joined a few months ago. He's just a recruit. It doesn't make sense."

Another sigh escaped Rook's lips as she engaged her bracer and fresh blood flowed into her veins. "I don't understand why he was there, but he was," she said as strength flowed into her. "But what I know is that we're never getting him back. Ever."

Kestrel's astonishment turned to fresh hurt and confusion. "What do you mean?"

"The things he said, Kes. They were awful. Hateful. He said he didn't see himself as Saosuíasei any longer, said he was raised in a gutter." Kestrel's eyebrows rose to her hairline, then plunged in a scowl. "I know," Rook continued. "He called our home a gutter. Pit's pledged his allegiance to the Avanish now. You need to stop seeing him. Next time he comes sniffing around you, tell him to piss off. Forever."

So many emotions passed across her friend's face, cycling over and over. Anger gave way to crushing hurt, replaced by abject disbelief and back to anger again.

Kestrel's eyes shone glassy in the cold moonlight. "I saw him just a few nights ago. He was normal. He didn't give me any reason to think he'd abandoned his Saosuíasei half. I mean, if he had, he wouldn't come anywhere near me, would he?"

A dark thought crossed Rook's mind. "He would if he was trying to get inside information on what's happening in the community. He could be trying to spy for his new friends."

Fresh hurt slashed across Kestrel's face. "No."

"It's possible," Rook said, but she softened her tone as the first tears slipped down her friend's cheeks. They tracked through her makeup. "We don't know his motives and we won't find out, because he'll never tell us, not if what he said to the captain is true."

Kestrel's face flashed with hope. "Maybe it's not true. He might be trying to play them."

Though she didn't want to, Rook replied with a reluctant, "Perhaps." But she didn't believe it for a moment. Instead of furthering the conversation, she passed on all the information she'd gleaned about Dreidchain's view of the Billy Drainer problem.

"That's disgusting," Kestrel said. "If he could exterminate us all, he would."

"He would, and he's hoping Drainer will take care of as many of us for him as he can." Rook shook her head. "At least we know Drainer isn't working for the city. I half thought I'd find out Drainer was working under Dreidchain's instructions."

After giving Kestrel the details about the committee meeting Dreidchain had spoken of that was to take place the following night, the two women shared a brief embrace.

"Take care," Kestrel said.

"I always do," Rook said. "Look after yourself and the family. And will you do me a favor?"

"Anything."

A sly grin spread across Rook's face. "When Pit comes calling again, give him an extra boot in the balls from me, eh?"

Unable to stop herself, Kestrel let out a deep laugh. She slapped a hand over her mouth, but her shoulders bobbed with mirth.

They embraced again; then Kestrel disappeared into the foggy darkness. Turning on her heel, Rook started back towards the servants' entrance.

The morning hung on Rook like a sodden woolen coat. The days of backbreaking work in the laundry and the nights sneaking around in the dark were catching up with her. Even with the fresh injection courtesy of Kestrel, fatigue hovered around her like a gray mist at the edge of her vision. It must have shown on her face, for Fialta shot a sniping comment toward her as soon as she saw her.

"If you worked at our pace instead of galloping off at your own, you'd feel less dead."

Rook ignored her. She wasn't worth engaging. Had she been working here as an honest servant, she would have. People like Fialta needed a powerful lesson on boundaries; otherwise they became unfailing in their persecution. Rook would've made plans to deliver the lesson in a dark place and smack the teeth out of her smart mouth. Thankfully for Fialta, Rook wasn't an honest servant. That, she thought with a grin, was one of the many reasons the work in the Conventicle suited her more.

"What are you smirking at?"

Fialta's voice brought every set of scrubbing hands to a standstill. Soap bubbles popped in the silence. Rook sighed, shaking her head. Perhaps she'd have to teach that lesson after all.

"I'm smiling at your wisdom," she said. "You're right. I should slow down."

As she returned to her scrubbing, the others did too. Her words were so deadpan, it wasn't clear if they were genuine or not. The other girls took them as the former, perhaps as part of an unconscious collective decision to keep the peace. Özdo, whose hands were still beneath the murky water of her tub, gave Rook a strange look.

Fialta, though, was unplacated. Like an imbecilic mutt trying to steal a bone from its master's plate, she pressed again. "You're a liar. You were laughing at me."

Rook heaved another sigh and sat back on her haunches. Özdo withdrew her hands from the water and tensed as if bracing for a conflict. However, rather than creased with fear, her face was tight with determination. It was the same look Rook often saw on Kestrel's face when she was ready to jump to her aid.

"You don't want to push me," Rook said. She kept her tone even and every word deliberate. "I promise it won't end well."

Just like that mutt, Fialta was too stupid to take the cue. Instead, she took it as bait. "Listen, new girl." She spat the term as if it were the most dreadful insult. "You've been here all of three days. Don't speak to me with such disrespect."

Unable to stop herself, Rook burst into a peal of laughter. The other girls ceased their scrubbing again. The atmosphere in the humid room sharpened with anticipation.

Rook set aside the sopping sheet she'd been scrubbing and dried her hands with excruciating care. She rose to her feet in one fluid motion and smoothed down the front of her apron. A flicker of uncertainty passed across Fialta's face as she followed suit.

"You talk as if you run this place," Rook said. She lifted a hand to inspect her nails, the action nonchalant. She didn't care what her nails looked like, but she wanted Fialta to know her attitude didn't intimidate even her little finger. "But you don't run this place, do you?" She locked her gaze with Fialta's, staring her down with a grin. "You're just the same as everyone else, a servant working at the whim of your employer. You're not entitled to my respect—not because you're a servant, but because your attitude is appalling."

Özdo uttered a low 'ooh' of delight and disbelief. Two of the other laundry girls let out nervous giggles.

Fialta's face flushed with rage. She spluttered, but Rook cut her off before she could speak, not with her own words but with her hand. Rook crossed the room so fast no one could react, a burst of Skill humming through her. She shoved Fialta against the wall and clamped a hand around her throat, squeezing tight enough to make her point clear without leaving a mark.

"I'd advise you not to speak to me again, not with 'such disrespect.' I promised you, pushing me wouldn't end well. This is your last warning."

Fialta squirmed under Rook's steady grip, her fingers scrabbling against the whitewashed wall Rook pressed her against. Her eyes were wide and unblinking, the mark of a bully who'd picked the wrong target. Like every bully Rook ever knew, Fialta was terrified now the tables had turned.

"Do you understand me?" Rook asked. She released her grip enough for Fialta to speak unhindered. Once she'd delivered her capitulation, Rook withdrew her hand. "Good."

The other girls were silent as Fialta rubbed her throat and seethed. It said much about Fialta's reputation that none of them jumped to her aid. Unsurprising, Rook thought. People like Fialta often thought they were liked when, in fact, they were feared. She'd seen it happen with short-lived members of the Conventicle. When they pushed too hard in the wrong direction, no one came to their aid.

When Rook returned to her scrubbing, she glanced at Özdo. The girl grinned, though she said nothing until dinner that evening.

"That was amazing. No one's ever stood up to Fialta's stinking behavior before."

Rook tore a chunk off her bread roll and dipped it in her thin broth. "Maybe her attitude with freshen up now."

Özdo laughed, the sound rich and tinkling. "I doubt it. But," she said, her tone sobering, "it wouldn't surprise me if she goes running to Vost."

It was strange to hear her address her aunt by her surname alone, but Rook supposed they weren't close. They'd shared nothing other than the clipped conversation Vost had with any other servant.

"Not that she'll do anything about it," Özdo said. "Vost would tell her she should have kept her mouth shut and her attention on her work. But you don't want a reputation as a troublemaker. Plenty of girls have come and gone because Vost decided they were too much hassle for not enough work."

Rook fished the solitary slice of unknown vegetable from her bowl and sniffed it before she ate it. "I'm not concerned. Jobs come and jobs go."

Shaking her head, Özdo grinned. "If I didn't have this job, I wouldn't have anything. And doing this job is barely enough." She tilted her head as if marveling at Rook's nonchalance. "You're not like anyone I've met before. You don't act like a laundry girl."

"I'm not," Rook said, "and neither are you. You're a girl who works in a laundry. Your job is your job, but it isn't what makes you. Not unless you let it. Fialta, she's let it define her." Rook cast a glance down the table. Sure enough, Fialta was brooding over her broth, the steam curling around her face. "She wants to be the boss, but why would you want to be the boss of a laundry? What does she get out of lording it over coarse soap and scummy water? She'll get so caught up in that tiny world, she'll forget about the outside. She won't try to be anything else. She'll get stuck."

As she spoke, she knew the words weren't her own. They were parallel to the conversation Rook had overheard years before when Magpie had convinced her parents to let her join the Conventicle.

Rébh could go into service like Isianná and earn a pittance, but she'll never better herself. All she could aspire to would be a higher rank in someone else's domain. If she joins my little birds, she'll earn, but she'll be her own woman. My girls aren't my servants. They're free.

The next day, Rébh had become Rook, and she'd never looked back. Mama Magpie was true to her word. She'd never felt like a servant, and the better she became at her profession, the more respect she'd gained. That was something Rook wouldn't have had in service. It wasn't something Isianná had found, either.

The thought of her sister brought a dark cloud over Rook's vision. Özdo noticed the change and cocked her head to the side. "Rébh?"

Rook waved off her concern. "Nothing." She forced herself to brighten and gestured to the slice of something unknown floating in Özdo's bowl. "So what do you think that is?"

The girl chuckled. "Sometimes it's best not to know the truth."

Those, Rook knew, were wise words.

SEVEN

That evening Rook prepared herself for her reconnaissance. The few nights of prowling had given her enough information to know where Dreidchain's meeting would take place. The only room large enough to accommodate all "required parties," whoever they were, was the dining room, unless the governor had some secret room Rook hadn't come upon. She doubted it. It was hard to keep anything secret when she was around. For another, if Dreidchain spoke about his hatred for the Saosuíasei people in front of someone who shared their blood, he wouldn't be one to hold meetings in hidden rooms or underground chambers. Thus, Rook found herself ensconced in the warren of back corridors surrounding the kitchen.

Sure enough, that night the dining room filled with men of importance. The policemen did their checks, poking in every shadowy nook where a miscreant might hide themselves. But since Rook was no mere miscreant, she evaded them with ease. Pit wasn't among their number, though that was more of a benefit to him than to her. One policeman was much like another, and he wouldn't have been a greater threat. But the thought of him sent flares of rage through Rook's body again, and she mightn't have been able to stop herself extricating him into a dark corner to beat him half to death. She wouldn't kill him. That wasn't what the Conventicle did, and it wasn't in Rook's nature. However, knocking seven bells from someone was.

Once the police were certain that there was no danger, they entered the dining room. The man hadn't closed the door, leaving a thin sliver of view for Rook to watch the proceedings. The policemen lingered on the periphery of the huge lacquered dining table, standing guard behind the eminent men of Stamchester. Rook, now free to move, lingered in the shadows behind the servants' entrance. In the daytime this was the door through which servers brought course after course of fine food from the kitchens. Now the entire kitchen complex was empty and plunged into darkness. Servants had prepared the room long before anyone arrived, with bottles of fine wine and shimmering crystal glasses shining like elaborate decorations. There wasn't one member of the household staff present, not even Dreidchain's stiff-backed butler.

As the men reached for the glasses, deigning to pour their own libations, Rook memorized their descriptions. She might not have recognized their faces, but the Shadow of Jaguars could match the descriptions she gave to known or suspected enemies of the Saosuíasei. Then they would know who was plotting against them. Legitimate targets, they called such men—and they were all men, for no women appeared.

Pit returned with Captain Veng, standing at ease behind him with the other policemen. A thought jabbed Rook like a rusty blade. The moment she reported on her former friend's presence, he would become a legitimate target too. Despite all Pit had said, she didn't wish death upon him, but that was what the Shadow of Jaguars might bring. Another thought jabbed her, this one laced with venom.

Maybe Pit deserved it. He was a traitor.

Once the doors closed, signaling all were present, Rook set aside her anger and used her Skill to sharpen her hearing. Not only could she listen in on every nuance of conversation inside, but she could detect footsteps coming from the depths of the kitchens. If they caught her now, whatever intelligence she was about to gather would disappear, and they'd ship her off to Purgatory. Her throat tightened, and she clenched her fists. She couldn't afford to do time: not just because of her reputation as the Conventicle's best, but because her family wouldn't survive without her. The little ones would have no one to look out for them. It would put too much pressure on Caió and Maird. But worst of all, her mother would disintegrate. The loss of one daughter was dreadful, but Mónnuad had coped. But to lose two? Rook knew Mónnuad was too frail to survive that.

At the head of the table, with a fine crystal glass in his hand, Dreidchain stood to address the audience. Rook forced her fists to release and threw her attention to the governor's words.

"Before we begin," Dreidchain said, intoning with a voice more suited to a prime minister than a mere city governor, "I'd like to thank all of you for coming to this final meeting before we commit to our course of action and begin. Our plans, while noble in the outcome they seek, are unprecedented. Some might say our actions are questionable in their morals. But your presence in this room gives me hope not only that we will succeed, but that we are justified in the course we have chosen."

The hairs on Rook's arms rose. Whatever this was, it was huge.

Dreidchain turned his attention to one man in particular, an officious-looking sort with a thin face and gold-rimmed spectacles perched on the end of his nose. He didn't look like he could threaten a mouse, let alone the entire Saosuíasei people. Yet the words Dreidchain spoke next turned every inch of Rook's skin cold.

"Grayson, have you selected the site for the bombs?"

Rook's grip on her Bloodskill loosened and her head spun, but she fought through the freeze of shock to regain control. Bombs. The Avanish were going to bomb them.

"Yes, Governor," the man named Grayson said in a light voice that, again, sounded like he couldn't threaten anyone. His words belied that. "We've chosen two sites on Providence Road."

Rook blinked, unsure if she'd heard the right name. Providence Road? That wasn't a Saosuíasei area. It was in the Northbank Business District. Where was the sense in that?

"We'll detonate the bombs in the early hours of the morning tomorrow." Grayson adjusted his glasses, pushing them up to the bridge of his narrow nose. They slid down again. "To do so will make it seem like the explosives went off early, and will ensure no one gets hurt while we make our point." He chuckled and grinned at his compatriots. "Not to mention the alleged mistake will make this new Shadow of Jaguars look even more bungling and cack-handed than they already do."

A chorus of laughter drifted around the room. Even in her fury, Rook's eyes flicked to Pit, gaging his reaction to the insult against his people, but there was none. That brought a fresh flood of fiery anger upon Rook, which fought with the coldness of her shock. How could he stand there and not only listen to such plots against his kindred, but protect the men who plotted too? She resisted the urge to spit in disgust. He had turned against them all.

"We'll have the articles ready for insertion in the paper," an unfamiliar voice said. "News of the Saosuíasei attack on us will be all over the city by nine in the morning."

Whoever he was, he was another man distinct only in how ordinary he seemed. Rook looked from one Avanish face to another. None of them had the marks of criminality the papers suggested all reprobates bore, the dreadful scars or eyepatches or missing limbs. They were just ordinary men sitting around a table, sipping wine and looking pleased with themselves. They might have been discussing business prospects or the achievements of their children. But they weren't.

"Excellent," Dreidchain said. "Once it becomes known that the Saosuíasei planted bombs with enough force to kill hundreds of Avanish in one fell swoop, the last of the doubters will fall in line. Even the Lord Lieutenant will condone our retaliation, and our city will flourish with the scum gone."

Cold disgust curdled in Rook's stomach. The self-styled great men of the city weren't planning on bombing the Saosuíasei. They were setting her people up, giving themselves justification to kill them all. Rook fought down the urge to vomit. There was no doubt the Avanish would use the opportunity to perform a thorough extermination. It was villainous. Reprehensible.

"What are you doing here?"

The words snapped Rook from her thoughts, her horror turning to a moment of sharp fear. She'd allowed her Skill to drop again, and had heard no one approach. It was too dark to see who it was, so Rook sharpened her sight and raised her fists, ready to strike.

Crouching in the shadows beside her was someone Rook at first wanted to punch, then hug in relief. It was Özdo.

"What are *you* doing here?" Rook whispered back.

Özdo's face flushed, and she averted her eyes. "I'm not a thief," she said as she hugged something to her chest. "I just take what they don't give me, and they don't give me much of anything. You know that, they pay us a pittance, so don't judge me."

Rook's eyes bulged as she tried to make sense of the other woman's words. Then she noticed the little package pressed against Özdo's front and the breadcrumbs stuck to her lower lip. She'd been taking food.

The irony of Özdo trying to defend her actions to Rook almost sent a burst of laughter from the latter's lips. She seized control of herself again and pressed a finger to her mouth, signaling for silence. Özdo clutched her food parcel tight. She said nothing, but the vibrations running through her spoke her meaning. What was Rook doing? What was going on? There was no time to explain, not even with a concocted excuse. The conversation in the dining room was too important, and she might already have missed something vital.

"So, we all know what we must do," Dreidchain's voice drifted in from the dining room. "Gentlemen, I invite you to join me in a toast." He reached for his wine glass, and the others followed suit. "To the cure to the Saosuíasei plague!"

The men responded with aplomb, but Rook's attention diverted from their macabre salute. A tingle of fearful anticipation passed through her. She had a problem. Instead of watching the proceedings, Pit was now staring at the servants' entrance. Rook's breath seized in her chest. Though his focus could only be on the door, for it was impossible to see through the crack, it looked like his eyes locked with hers. Those strange eyes, one green and one brown, as if his dual and opposite identities had manifested in his flesh.

Rook released her Bloodskill for hearing and transferred it into stillness. Pit wasn't as Skilled as she was, but he wasn't Unskilled either. If he'd enhanced his own hearing, he would've detected their whispers. He leaned towards the policeman beside him and said something Rook couldn't make out. The other man glanced at the door and narrowed his eyes. Rook remained still, hoping Özdo would do the same. If they moved, the game was up.

The door twisted off its hinges as the second policeman wrenched it open. He'd acted with the speed and strength of Skill. Rook blanched, revealed to the room before she could react. Though many sets of eyes stared at her, she returned the glance of only one. Pit's jaw dropped to his chest. He shook his head and, though she couldn't hear him, Rook knew what single word he mouthed.

"No."

The room erupted into chaos, the gentlemen of the city throwing their chairs back in indignation and fear. Their secret meeting wasn't as secret as they'd thought. The guard of policemen lunged towards the servants' entrance, some faster than others, and Rook turned. She seized Özdo's wrist and wrenched her into the darkness of a narrow corridor. A cacophonous roar followed them, and they ducked into a side passage. The servants' corridors were too winding for the policemen to use Skilled speed without careening into the walls, but that didn't mean they were safe. Rook couldn't use it either, and she didn't know if Özdo was Skilled at all. Not only that, but her own reserves were low. If she burned too much she would collapse, and that would be the end of everything. They would catch her, throw her in prison, make her mission a failure and cast her family into abject destitution.

Özdo pulled her wrist free. Her little food package was long discarded, and she turned her face to Rook. However, instead of the disgust and fear she expected, Özdo gestured for her to follow. "This way!"

Rook's gut reaction was to ignore the other woman and flee her own way, but she pushed her arrogance aside. Özdo had been here longer than she had, and it was clear this wasn't the first time she'd sneaked around the kitchens after dark. With a curt nod, Rook followed close on Özdo's heels.

Rook didn't know the kitchen complex well, since her sneaking had focused on the main house. In the darkness, the place was impossible in its unfamiliarity. Rook reached for the walls, as if touching them would help her find her way. She didn't dare use more Skill to enhance her sight, but Özdo had no issue navigating. Whether that was through knowledge or sight Skill, Rook didn't know, but soon they were in the kitchen proper. It wasn't too far from there to the exterior door. Once they escaped into the dark embrace of the garden, the shadows would protect them, and they could disappear into the night.

They. That thought stopped Rook short. "Özdo!" The sharpness of her voice in the darkness made the other woman flinch into stillness. "I can make my way out from here," Rook said. "You need to get back to your bed before anyone notices you're gone."

This time it was Özdo's voice that was sharp. She jerked a finger at the kitchen door. "Those men saw me as clearly as they saw you, Rébh. I can't just go back to bed and hope for the best. They know I was there. I'm the only Undténsian here, apart from Vost. It doesn't matter how much I'd lie to them. They'd never believe me."

Rook cursed her stupidity. Özdo was right. Regardless of why she was creeping around the kitchens in the dead of night, considering what she'd overhead, she was in as much danger as Rook. There was no time to plan, no time to explain. They needed to get out before anyone found them.

"Rook!"

She closed her eyes, mouthing a silent curse. That voice. It was as familiar as it had been the night before. Rook turned on her heel, finding herself face to face with the man she'd once considered a brother. Now Pit was nothing but an opponent in a dark uniform.

"I don't want to hurt you, Pit," she said, the words sharp on her tongue, "but I will."

Özdo let out a sound that was half scoffing and half choked. Pit stared at them, but there was no anger in his mismatched eyes. There was only a strange look of fear and regret.

"You won't need to hurt me," he said. He glanced over his shoulder, back towards the sound of encroaching policemen. When he looked back at them, his odd expression disappeared, replaced by one of determination. "Go. Get out. Now."

Rook drew her eyebrows low. "What?"

"I said go!" Pit said through gritted teeth. Then he turned his back on them, hurtling toward the kitchen door. "They're not in here!"

He didn't turn back, and the rest of his words disappeared as he joined the herd of other men. They careened away from the kitchen, clattering through the rest of the dark hallways. Rook stood with her arms limp and her feet rooted by shock. Had that just happened? Had Pit, who only the day before had denounced the entire Saosuíasei people, just let her go? Why? It didn't make a thimble's worth of sense.

She jerked from her confusion when Özdo clamped a hand around her wrist, reversing the gesture from earlier. "You heard him, Rébh. I don't plan on waiting around until they come back. Let's go!"

Rook blinked away her inaction. "Of course. I'm sorry. Let's get out of here."

Together, leaving the hurricane of police pursuit behind, they fled, weaving through the gardens and vault over the high railings before one police boot hit the grass. As soon as they burst into the winding streets of Little Avanland, a high-pitched whistle rose in the air. Brief terror clenched in Rook's gut. There were more policemen outside. Of course there were. Exhausted beyond anything she'd felt in many years, her usual fearlessness had ebbed away. It wasn't that she never felt fear, but she could control it. However, in this moment she was tired and confused, and more afraid than she cared to admit. It wasn't because Dreidchain and his eminent men had seen her. It was because of Pit. What was his game?

When the initial whistle wasn't followed by the frantic pattern of peeps policemen used to signal for backup, Rook glanced around for its origin. Özdo followed suit. The streets were empty, gray under a thin film of mist. There was no police carriage. There were no more men. In fact, for a long moment Rook saw nothing.

Then a voice cracked the still darkness. "Over here!" A taxi carriage drawn by two gigantic horses stood at the corner of the block, shrouded in fog. From its driver's seat, a figure stood, gave a frantic wave and called again. "Yes, here!"

Despite everything, Rook grinned. The tall silhouette was as familiar as her own reflection. Kestrel. Of course. Beckoning Özdo to follow her, the two women raced through the darkness, fog parting around them, their breath billowing from their open mouths.

Kestrel leaped from the carriage and wrenched the door open for them, shaking her head underneath her driver's cap. "I hope you appreciate this!" she said as she bundled them into the carriage and slammed the door behind them. She didn't question Özdo's presence, but instead jabbed a finger at her head. "This thing is the most unfashionable headwear I've ever allowed to grace my head! You owe me big time, even more than how much you owe me for sitting outside in the freezing fog in case everything went belly up—which it seems it did!"

Rook exploded with a cackle as Kestrel tipped the brim of the cap, then threw herself into the driver's seat once again. With a crack of the reins, she jerked the horses into motion, sending them galloping through the darkness, leaving Little Avanland and Governor Dreidchain far behind.

For now.

THE STAMCHESTER REVIEW
Evening Edition
Eith 1ˢᵗ, 4ᵗʰ Year of the Coati

SHADOW OF FOOLS: BOMB PLOT FOILED

In the early hours of this morning, two bombs exploded on Providence Road in the Northbank Business District of the city. The plot to kill hundreds of innocent Avanish people was foiled by the incompetence of the bombers themselves. Even with its ringleaders dead, the Sassyman organization the Shadow of Jaguars has made an attempt to return to operations in the city, but has shown itself to be a collection of bungling dolts. The bombs detonated at five o'clock in the morning, long before any Northbank businesses began operations.

Inspector Kip Kerstammen told the Review, "This goes to show that while the Saosuíasei are ineffective, their threat is still present. As a result, we are in consultation with Governor Dreidchain about plans to step up protection for our city."

Speaking at the site of the explosions, Governor Dreidchain gave assurances on these plans: "We will not bow down to any threat. I have no doubt this is revenge for our reclamation of the area the Saosuíasei once occupied. Previously nicknamed the Scar, the area will be redeveloped into a site fit for Avanish habitation, and of course the Sassymen cannot abide this. Their love of filth is legendary. This attack on our city cannot stand, and cannot be repeated. I intend to discuss with Viscount Trass, Lord

Lieutenant of Undténsia, the potential of bringing in military support for our noble police service. I promise I will protect you. We will not be intimidated by the Saosuíasei. We will not bow down to their baseness. We will flourish in spite of them."

EIGHT

The day after the bombs exploded in Providence Road, Dreidchain kept his promise, and the military trooped in. They brought with them a fresh dusting of snow and the promise of a bitter winter. Rook stepped out of the Nest and into a wall of freezing wind. She held her flat cloth cap in place as she stalked up the street, away from the place that had once been her second home but now seemed more like a boys' club. Mama Magpie's establishment had become an official meeting place for the Shadow of Jaguars, and she had long since abandoned any pretense of keeping distance from them.

Most of her regular bar patrons were gone, no longer traveling along streets now considered too dangerous to frequent. Few but the most hardened of alcoholics considered a drink worth the risk of being gunned down by the Avanish military. The other side of Conventicle business had dried up too, for few came to Magpie with their troubles now that their main problem was the distinct threat of being shot in the head by an Avanish soldier. She was paid a retainer fee by Jaguar for allowing the use of her premises and her girls, but that money wasn't enough. Thus, Magpie opened her bar and her bottles to the rebels. Why not? Shadow of Jaguars money was just as green as any other cash.

Unfortunately, the presence of so many loud and often drunken young men meant the Nest was not the sanctuary Rook had once found it. More often than not she took to her feet and fled, escaping into the outside world. Sometimes even the threat of being shot was more palatable than spending another moment in that rowdy fraternity.

Walking with no destination in mind, Rook turned onto Tenth Avenue. Something thin and white crackled and collided with her legs. She scowled as she snatched up the crumpled front page of a newspaper that had spread across her trousers. The loose cover was torn and damp, as if it mourned the loss of the rest of itself. The lone page flapped in the wind that forced its way through the Stamchester streets and rattled every window in its frame. Rook snarled as she read the headline:

ANOTHER KNOT OF REBELS EXTERMINATED BY AVANISH ELITE

No newspaper sellers dared to darken the streets of the Shambles any longer, but she could hear their cries in her mind as she scanned the columns of type under the thick headline.

> Saosuíasei Shadow of Jaguars failing under the pressure of Avanish military! Governor Dreidchain confident that threat will be destroyed by end of the month!

In disgust, Rook crumpled the newspaper and threw it away. The icy wind carried it away, the paper ball skipping along slushy streets. Rook tucked her chin into the high collar of her man's woolen coat, acquired from a careless rebel who'd left it unattended. Rook had first taken the coat to see how many Turners lined its pockets. Its owner spent an unending amount of money at the Nest's bar, and the bright vermillion lining spoke even louder of his fortune. Then, after running the soft weave of expensive fabric between her fingers, she'd kept it. Rook figured she'd appreciate it more and be less likely to vomit down its front from excess alcohol. Plus she'd needed a new coat, and now she had all but joined the Shadow of Jaguars, she decided she might as well look like one of them.

She was about to continue her aimless stalking when a set of heels clattered up behind her. Rook turned, grinning. Only Kestrel would venture out into the ice in heels. Her footfalls slowed and when she reached Rook's side, they fell into step beside one another.

"Couldn't take all that man any longer?" Kestrel asked, arching one artfully painted eyebrow.

"Couldn't take all that man *stink* any longer," Rook corrected. "The sooner my nose dies from the stench and falls off, the better."

Their chuckles disappeared into the high wind. Rook's cheeks burned with its coldness. The brief levity was a welcome break in their now heavy existence. They were safe enough to walk the streets around the Nest, as it was far enough away from any Rebel blockades and conflict flashpoints, but to venture beyond was to take your life in your hands. Not that they hadn't done it, but when they had, it had been carefully planned, with their blood reserves topped up and spare vials in their bags. You couldn't have enough Skill these days, especially when a speedy departure often meant the difference between life and death.

Kestrel smirked and tweaked Rook's nose, the thin leather of her gloves creaking. "Aww, don't let it fall off. You'd look too odd. I don't think I could be friends with someone who was noseless."

Rook batted Kestrel's hand away. "You're too concerned with looks."

"And you're not concerned enough." Kestrel plucked at Rook's coat. "This thing is far too big for you. And don't even get me started on that cap."

They continued around the block, turning away from the wind. Without its bluster in her ears, the street now seemed eerie in the quiet. Rook dug her hands deep into her pockets and glanced up at the buildings. What had once been a thriving area within the Shambles, a place that hummed with community, was now more like a graveyard. Every window was shuttered, and even the washing lines strung between buildings were empty, as if the residents were too afraid even to hang out their drying. Not that it was drying weather, Rook mused, but regardless of snow or Shadow of Jaguars, the mundane chores of life still went on.

Where the street joined Eleventh Avenue, a cluster of armed Rebels crouched around a fire they'd lit in an improvised brazier. While they warmed their stiff fingers, they'd tucked their pistols into their pockets and waistbands.

"Afternoon, ladies," one of them said as they passed. "I wouldn't go much further if I were you."

Another of the men nodded along Eleventh. "The Avanish are planning a push into the Shambles from that direction. Unless you want a few extra holes in your bodies, I'd head back from where you came."

A third man chuckled in what Rook assumed to be a crude interpretation of his compatriot's words. Unlike the other two, he wore a thin jacket and not one of the thick wool coats they sported. There was good reason for that, and Rook knew why. She grinned at him and flashed the bright silk scarlet of her coat's lining.

"Hey! That's mine!"

He went to jerk a hand towards her. Rook was ready to snatch his wrist in her fingers and twist until he begged for mercy, but she didn't have to. One of the man's fellow rebels pulled him backward and gave him a swift slap to the back of the head.

"You'd take a coat from the back of a lady in the middle of this weather?"

"But it's *my* coat!" He received another smack for that. "Ow!"

The third man chuckled and shooed them onward. "Not any longer. And anyway, it looks better on her. So give over."

"But—"

Their voices disappeared as Rook and Kestrel turned back on themselves and into the wind again. While she wasn't usually one to do what she was told, Rook had no desire to find herself riddled with bullets.

They returned to the Nest for a little while, but with an excess of men and without any business to attend to, the two women left again to make the short journey home. Magpie hadn't tried to keep them.

"There's nothing for you to do except polish glasses," she had said. Her kohl-lined eyes were lidded with sadness. Then they returned to Magpie's signature sharpness. "I want you both back later, though. Jaguar's coming in this evening to discuss something he wants our help with."

As soon as Rook slid the key in the lock of their apartment door, there was a slam from inside. She and Kestrel shared a wide-eyed look before Rook threw open the door, ready for whatever fresh conflict lay inside. As they entered, a figure tried to spirit past them, but Kestrel grabbed it by the coat collar.

"Let me go!"

"Don't let her go!" another voice called from inside. It was Mónnuad.

Clarity arrived, and Rook pressed her lips together. She grabbed the collar too and together, she and Kestrel dragged Maird, kicking and screaming, up the hallway. The rest of the sisters watched with wide eyes as they tossed Maird onto the rickety chair beside their mother's bed. The dark-haired girl fumed with anger and tried to leap to her feet again, but Rook glared so hard she sat down again. All of the sisters knew that sharp home truths followed that glare. Now sullen, Maird flopped back onto the chair and allowed her curtain of hair to fall across her face.

Rook folded her arms. "What have you done?" she asked. When Maird remained tightlipped, Rook tapped one foot against the bare floorboards. "I'm waiting."

Her sister's reply came as an explosion. "It's not fair! *You* got to join the Conventicle. Even Kestrel got to join, and she's not even a real—" Maird caught herself before she said something that would elicit more than a few home truths. She held up her palms in apology. "Sorry. But I'm just saying that both of you got to join. Why can't I?"

Rook shared a weary glance with her equally weary mother. She raised her eyes to the water-stained ceiling and mouthed a silent curse. Not this old argument again.

"Maird, we've talked about this a hundred thousand times. You're too young to join, and," Rook added with a sweeping gesture, as if to take in the whole of the city, "now isn't exactly the best time, considering everything that's going on out there."

"Maybe now *is* the best time," Maird snapped back, "considering everything that's going on."

Her temper flaring, Rook took a step forward. She lifted a finger and jabbed it at her sister's chest. "You don't understand the real dangers out there—"

"*You* don't understand—"

"Children!" Mónnuad's voice rang louder than it had in years, bringing her warring offspring under immediate control. The effort exhausted her, and she fell back against her pillows, drawing in labored breaths. "Stop," she managed. "Stop your fighting."

A wave of shame crested, and Rook's face grew hot. She stepped back again, giving them both space for their ire to cool.

After a moment, Maird spoke again. This time her voice wavered with tears. "You don't think I'm good enough."

"Maird, no," Rook said. "That's not true."

"We're all simply concerned for you, my sweet," their mother said. She reached out a trembling hand to grasp her third-born daughter's fingers. "We know you're good enough."

Rook nodded her agreement and offered her sister a smile. The word 'good' was a strange description for a job that was by its nature 'bad,' considering that before the Shadow of Jaguars the main part of their work had been stealing. Virtuous stealing, but it was still stealing.

"Once the Conventicle gets back to our usual business, I'll talk to Magpie," Rook said, "as long as Mama says it's okay."

Mónnuad hesitated to respond, but gave a small nod.

"All right," Maird murmured. She pulled her hair back from her face. "But you have to promise."

Though she rolled her eyes, it was in mock irritation. Rook said, "I promise," and for now, at least, the issue was settled.

They spent the rest of the afternoon getting the apartment into order, since things had gone awry in the week Rook had been gone. It was also apparent that the youngest girls hadn't been bathed in that time, so Rook found herself elbow deep in soap once again.

The time came to return to the Nest. Before they left, Rook and Kestrel made sure the youngest girls were snug in their beds and, more importantly, that Maird was left to understand in no uncertain terms what would happen if she disappeared from the apartment.

"With us gone, you're in charge here," Rook said. "Mother and the girls rely on you to keep them safe. If you want to be part of the Conventicle, you have to be responsible. This is a good way for you to show us you can do that."

While she did it with a sullen twist to her mouth, Maird nodded her understanding. With that, Rook and Kestrel took to the street once again.

It was coming upon midnight and the streets glittered with ice, picked out in green by the gas lamps and silver when the moon managed to break free of the clouds. The air bit at Rook's face and she buried her chin deep in her coat collar again. The streets were empty during the day, and by night they were much the same. They passed by the brazier where the three Rebel men had stood, now manned by a larger cadre of others. The Avanish had a habit of striking in darkness in the hopes of catching the

Shadow of Jaguars off-guard. All it did was push more men into the dark freeze of the night.

Kestrel shivered as they turned onto the next street. "What do you think Jaguar wants this time?"

Rook shrugged one shoulder, the movement jerky with cold. "Who knows? Whatever it is, I know Mama will ask me to do it."

"Ah, the woes of being the Conventicle's best," Kestrel said with a mocking lilt.

Rook jabbed an elbow into the other woman's ribs and grinned. "Shut up. If I have to do whatever it is, you're coming with me."

"Ah," Kestrel said again, "the woes of being the best friend of the Conventicle's best."

Their laughter bounced off the high brick buildings before Rook forced herself to quiet again. She gripped the handle of her cane. If they telegraphed their location to any Avanish lying in wait for an unsuspecting victim, they had no one to blame but themselves.

Sensing the same thing, Kestrel's gloved hand touched the pistol concealed beneath her coat. "Things have changed around here, and not for the better."

"Lots of things have changed," Rook added. She flicked her gaze sideward. "Have you seen Pit yet?"

Her friend's back straightened with a flash of indignation. "No."

Rook snorted. "He probably doesn't want to show his face when he thinks I might be around, although maybe he just doesn't want to show it at all. He'll know I've told you I saw him."

Kestrel harrumphed. Her furious eyes shone like diamonds in the gaslight. "I hope he never shows his face again. For his sake he'd best not appear in my presence ever again, even by accident. I'll knock out every one of his teeth, stick them back in, and knock them out again. Bastard."

"I'll keep some glue handy for that very occasion," Rook chuckled. "That's something I'd love to see."

They turned off the street and down a thin alleyway. It wasn't the best route, Rook knew. No easy way to escape, too likely they could be penned in from either side. But it was a shortcut that would bring them out close to the Nest's door. Between their weaponry and the full vials of blood strapped to their arms, she figured they could handle themselves. They always had.

The earthen pathway between the rear of two buildings was solid and slippery, and the narrow passage seemed to fill with the clouds of their breath. They were near the far end when the first strains of someone's panic reached them.

"Please, don't. Please!"

Whoever it was, their words were swiftly muffled, likely by an Avanish hand. The women shared a look before taking off, bolting one after another through the thin slit between buildings. Rook went first, skidding out onto the street with Kestrel close behind, her pistol already drawn. With a twist of her wrist, Rook drew her knife from her cane. The *shing* sliced the cold air, and she was ready to fight this fresh Avanish threat.

She blinked as her mind processed the sight before her. It was a woman whose mouth was covered by a hand, preventing her screams, but the hand wasn't Avanish. The clothes weren't Avanish. And the face, it wasn't anything. Underneath his battered top hat, it was covered by a shapeless sacking mask with slits for eyes.

"You," Rook breathed. The word rose like smoke.

Billy Drainer tightened his grip on his terrified victim's face, pressing his grimy hands into her skin. The dark eyes under his mask narrowed for a moment, then widened in realization. "You."

There was a deafening click as Kestrel cocked her pistol. "Let her go, you animal."

Rook huffed a laugh, still brandishing her blade. "Don't insult animals that way."

His breath steaming from under his mask, Drainer took a step back, though he didn't release his victim. "I've still got the wound from last time, little girl."

"Let's see it," Rook said, tilting her chin high. "I always like to admire my own handiwork."

That was true, but it wasn't the real reason she wanted to see his face. His voice, those words, the way he said 'girl.' It was so familiar. Whoever this villain was, Rook knew him.

"Nice try," Drainer replied. "I'm not that stupid."

"You're stupid enough," Rook replied. "Why are you doing this to us?" Governor Dreidchain's delighted interpretation of Drainer's actions came back to her. Let them kill each other. "Don't you have any sympathy for your own people? Because you're Saosuíasei, right? With those eyes, you can't be anything else, and you speak the language like a native." Drainer made no response, so she went on. "You're playing right into the Avanish's hands. They're loving this, and you're doing their work for them."

"No," Drainer said. His every word was laced with poison. "I'm doing my work for them."

When the woman in his grip gave a sudden terrified jerk, he tightened his fingers until her skin blanched. Her tears drew clean lines across his hand.

"Let her go," Kestrel said, her voice low, "or I will blow your head clean off your shoulders."

The woman tried to scream, but the sound was nothing more than a muffled bleat of terror. Drainer took another step backward. Rook glanced behind him, but there was no one else around. Where were the Rebels when you needed them?

"I know you will. Your aim has always been good, Faoiatín."

Kestrel's arm wavered, and the muzzle of her pistol dipped. "What?"

Before either of them could react, Drainer released his victim's face. He shoved her with Skill-enhanced force, and she hurtled towards them so fast Rook cast her knife aside without thinking, instinctively reaching to save her. She steadied the weeping woman and glanced around, her heart thundering. Where was Drainer? As Skilled as he seemed to be, he could be halfway across the city by now.

Laughter rained down on them like shrapnel. Rook and Kestrel's heads jerked upward in tandem. Drainer was perched on the edge of a building, hanging with a Skill-enhanced grip of just one hand.

"You've saved this one," he said with a macabre chuckle, "but I'll just go and get another one. I have an order to fill, you see, and my employer doesn't like to be disappointed." He flipped up onto the flat roof of the three-story building and doffed his hat at them in mocking cordiality. "Good evening, ladies."

Then he was gone.

NINE

They brought the woman who could've been Drainer's latest victim to the Nest. Redshank and Greenshank took her into a side room for comfort and a stiff drink, shooting Rook twin looks of concern, though it wasn't about the woman.

"Jaguar's in with Magpie," Redshank said. "I think he's planning something big."

Magpie summoned them to her office as soon as they arrived. The Jaguar reclined in the patched and stuffed chair, the picture of relaxation as he rubbed the pad of his thumb across the tips of his fingers.

"Mama," Rook said with a nod. She gave the man the briefest of looks. "Jaguar."

He parted his lips in a wry smile. "Come on now, Rébh. You can call me Dru. We've known each other long enough."

For her employer's sake, Rook beat down the urge to slap him and instead said, "Like I told you before, I go by Rook."

The Jaguar smiled. "As you wish."

Rook turned away without response. She gave all her attention to Magpie, whose face was solemn and her eyes as hard and dark as coal. "I see you arrived with some commotion," Magpie said.

"We did. We saved someone from an attack."

"A happy accident," the Jaguar said, his smile still present. "The Avanish?"

"No," Rook replied. "Billy Drainer."

The Jaguar's grin disappeared. "I'd hoped that bastard might take himself off, considering the Avanish threat."

Kestrel crossed her arms. "The Avanish don't seem to be a threat to him, at least not according to what he said."

Magpie leaned across her desk. "You spoke to him?"

"He recognized me from last time," Rook said. "He said he was doing his work for the Avanish, whatever that means."

The Jaguar's entire body tensed, as if the news had coiled him tight as a spring. "I thought you said Dreidchain didn't know who he was, or why Drainer is killing Saosuíasei."

"Dreidchain isn't the only Avanish man of importance in this city," Magpie said, her words quiet with contemplation. "He might be the governor, but he has superiors in the government. It's a terrifying thought, but perhaps Drainer is in league with someone higher up. Perhaps even the Lord Lieutenant."

Rook suppressed the chill that rattled up her spine.

"That's not the only thing he said," Kestrel continued. A new waver entered her voice. "He knew my name. Not my Conventicle name, but my actual name. He called me Faoiatín. I think he knows us."

Magpie sat back, letting out a slow breath. Jaguar's expression was still with thought.

"There was something about his voice too," Rook said, "something strange. I've heard it before, but I don't know where. It sounds like he's trying to disguise his words somehow, but there's something so familiar about him, I'm sure I've met him before."

Magpie drummed her long nails on the table, the black-on-silver rings she always wore glinting in the lamplight. "None of this is good news, but it's not our primary concern right now." She shifted in her chair, the mantle of Conventicle leader draped around her shoulders once more. "The Jaguar has a job for you."

"I thought as much," Rook replied. "What information do you need this time?"

The Shadow's leader laced his fingers together and tilted his head, looking up at her beneath his dark brows. "It's not information I need," he said. "It's infiltration. But I want something brought in. A little gift for the Avanish, you might say."

"A gift?" Kestrel asked. However, Rook had already followed his meaning. She shook her head and turned to Magpie. "No. I won't do it."

"Do what?" Kestrel asked.

Rook shook her head again and took a step backward. "He wants me to plant a bomb." Kestrel made a strange strangled noise. Rook locked eyes with Magpie. "That's what it is, right?"

The older woman pursed her black lips and nodded. "Yes."

At the confirmation, Rook and Kestrel shared a look. While it was momentary, they communicated more than any words could. Rook's thoughts swirled. If she didn't do what the Shadow of Jaguars wanted her to do, would that be a betrayal of the Saosuíasei? Would it be an insult to Pigeon's memory not to strike against the men who'd permitted her death? Rook kept her face immovable, unwilling to belie her feelings.

The Jaguar's laugh was sharp. "You're suddenly high and mighty, Rook. You were happy to spy on Dreidchain and his bedfellows and pass that information on to us. We found our targets and where to plant the explosives because of what you told us. But now you're too moral to help us further?"

Rook's head spun at the accusation. Everything in her wanted to scream at him, 'This isn't what we do. It isn't the Conventicle's way, and it isn't my way.' But Magpie sat before her with a face still etched with the grief of losing Pigeon—Pigeon, killed by Drainer, a murderer running rampant on the streets of Stamchester unchecked and unchallenged because Governor Dreidchain and his cronies didn't care. Perhaps if they'd given half a damn, they might have caught Drainer before he crossed Pigeon's path. It was, by proxy, Dreidchain's fault her young friend had died. His fault and the fault of all the 'eminent' men in league with him.

So why wouldn't she plant the bomb?

Rook balled her hands into fists. Because it was different, no matter what the Jaguar tried to say. To find information was one thing. To set a trap was another.

She pressed her lips into a hard line. "I'm not too moral to help. I haven't changed and decided I don't want to be a part of this." She glanced at Magpie. "I haven't forgotten what we all lost when Pigeon died, or how the city government is doing nothing about it." She let out a choked laugh. "I'm not too moral to spy or to steal. But"—she took a controlled breath before she continued—"I won't kill. If you want me to steal or sabotage something, or plant a bomb to destroy property, I'm game for that. But I won't do it if the intention is to kill." Her mother's face flashed in her vision, the look of abject horror she would wear if she discovered her daughter was a murderer. "I just won't do it. I'm sorry."

She delivered the apology to Magpie. She couldn't care less about the Jaguar's feelings, but Rook cared about disappointing the woman who'd looked after her all these years. However, when she met Magpie's eyes, there was only soft understanding within them.

"That's all right, Rook," she said. Her black lips twitched in a smile with pride.

The Jaguar wasn't at all moved by her words, and only homed in on what was useful to him. "All right, no deliberate killing. But I'll take you up on that offer to sabotage and destroy. There are plenty of other ways you can help us." He let out a derisive snort. "Killing is men's work, it would seem."

Kestrel snapped at him. "It's nothing to do with men or women. It's about what's right and wrong. What the Avanish have done and still do to us is wrong. Letting a murderer run around the city killing as many Saosuíasei as he likes is wrong. But their killing doesn't make other killings right. We've got to be better than them."

An unexpected and grateful wave washed over Rook. She'd expected her friend to deride her stance.

The Jaguar, unmoved by Kestrel's words either, snorted again. "Such lofty morals in the Conventicle." He rose from his seat and reached for his cap and coat. "But here's something to consider, my dears." He allowed the last word to hang in the air like smoke. "Even if you don't pull the trigger or plant the bomb, if you've given us the information on where to point our weapons, you're still accountable. Does that make you better than me?" He locked eyes with Rook. The peak of his cap shadowed his face. "At least I'm honest with myself. At least I take responsibility for the weight of my actions." He turned to Magpie. "I'll be back tomorrow with details on a few other jobs. Perhaps her ladyship here will deign to help a lowlife like myself with one of them."

With one last glance at Rook, he tipped his cap and left. The atmosphere hung heavy with his parting words.

With little Conventicle work to do and no desire to listen to the drunken antics of the Shadowmen, Rook and Kestrel left the Nest again. They walked back much the way they had come. It was partly because it was the quickest route. It was partly because Rook would have relished another encounter with Drainer. If only she could get his mask off, if only she could see the face of the man who wasn't just playing into Avanish hands but was working for them, and who seemed to know them.

The night was still with frost. A black cat padded before them, disappearing into the narrow nook between two buildings. They neared the corner of Lomond Street and Broadridge Lane, and someone stepped out of the shadows. Rook's hand was on her bracer, ready to plunge into action. Drainer was about to feel the sharp point of her wrath. But the figure was smaller, thinner, and wore not a top hat but the flat cap of a Saosuíasei Shadowman. He held his palms up to them. They shone pale in the moonlight.

"It's me."

Fury and hope and fear twisted in Rook's chest like a strange braid. "Pit."

There he was in the flesh, the man she'd once called her brother. Beside Rook, Kestrel was still. Her face was deliberately blank. Pit approached them, his hands still raised. His eyes glimmered in the moonlight, one green and one brown. When he tried to speak, Rook lifted a finger in warning.

"Don't," she said through gritted teeth. "Don't you dare."

Pit glanced from her to Kestrel and back again, his hands still up. "I need to talk to you. Both of you."

"I don't care. You don't deserve our attention."

Frustration crossed Pit's face. "Rook, it's not as simple as you think."

"It seemed simple in Governor Dreidchain's mansion when you stood in that room and listened while those men plotted against us. And it sounded simple when you said you'd renounced your Saosuíasei heritage and called my mother's home a gutter." His arms fell, and he stared at her, dumbfounded. Rook snorted. "Yes, I was there when you said that too."

Voices sounded in the distance. Pit jerked around, seeking the source. When he turned back, desperation warped his expression. "We need to talk."

"We need to *leave*," Rook said, but when she went to grab Kestrel's elbow and pull her onward, the other woman resisted. "Kes?"

"Let him speak." Kestrel's voice was low and soft, and Rook knew she couldn't reason with her. Besotted as she was with Pit, even though he was a traitor, Kestrel would always give him another chance. Pit made a move forward as if to embrace her, his mouth opening in a thank you, but Kestrel stepped back. "I said to let you speak, not touch. What do you have to say?"

Stung, Pit shook himself. "Is there anywhere we can go?"

Rook feigned nonchalance and crossed her arms. "I only know of a dump nearby."

Even in the darkness, his flush was clear. Kestrel waved off her rudeness. "Just say what you have to say, Pit. Then we can all get on with our lives."

The implication hung between them like a raised blade. Kestrel didn't mean a goodbye for now. She meant a goodbye forever.

Pit swallowed, his throat bobbing under the collar of his coat. "I'm sorry."

There was a beat of silence as they waited for the rest, but nothing more came. Rook's laugh was obnoxious in the night's silence. "That's it?"

Their former friend squeezed his eyes shut as if forcing back tears. "I don't know what else to say."

Rook was about to jump in, her tongue burning with scathing anticipation, but Kestrel spoke first. Her words, instead of hot with anger, were cold and low.

"How about, 'I'm sorry I turned my back on you all?' Or maybe, 'I'm sorry I've behaved like a first-class bastard.' Or even"—her voice cracked—"'I'm sorry for breaking your heart.'"

The tears that threatened now tracked down Pit's face. "I'm sorry."

That did it. That tore it. Pit didn't cry. It wasn't in his nature. Rook clenched her fists, recalling tragedy and disaster upon tragedy and disaster where Pit had shed not one solitary tear. Rook could take no more of it.

She reached for him, and he flinched away. But she didn't strike out. Instead, she laid a hand on his shoulder and squeezed.

Beside her, Kestrel snapped toward her, face scrunched with confusion. "You believe him?" She formed the question from equal parts disbelief and hope.

Rook nodded, unable to stop her cursed forgiveness from seeping out. "I do."

Despite everything, this was the right thing to do. There was a note of genuine sorrow in his words that he couldn't fake. Pit had never been an accomplished actor. If he had tears to shed, they were genuine.

"Come on," she said. "A gutter it might be, but we'd better finish this conversation at home. It's too important to have out on the street. Plus, if we stay out here, we might get shot." Rook flashed a lopsided smile. "That won't do any of us any good."

Pit sniffed out a laugh around his tears and nodded. "All right."

As expected, the girls were all in bed by the time they arrived, for it was well after two o'clock, though Rook knew being in bed was one thing and sleeping was another. She was certain at least one pair of ears would perk up. Not that it mattered. There were no secrets in the Artur family.

As the door closed behind them, Rook motioned for Pit to wait in the hall. He stood at the end of the long line of boots. Rook peeked into the living room to see her mother staring at her, dark eyes shining in the buttery light of the oil lamp.

"Ma, I have someone with me. May I bring them in?"

Mónnuad, despite her terminal exhaustion, lifted herself onto her elbows. "Do I need to make myself presentable?" She didn't ask why her daughter was bringing someone into the house at the late hour. It was a given that the rhythm of Rook's life ticked to a different clock.

Rook shook her head. "No, Ma. It's someone you know."

She raised an eyebrow as she nodded and sank back onto her pillows. "Yes, go ahead. I'm sure whoever it is will understand."

"I do."

Pit stepped into the room, wringing his cap in his hands, his head bowed. Rook watched as her mother's face lit with joy. She didn't know what Pit had said about their home. Rook hadn't had the heart to tell her.

"Pit!" Mónnuad said, holding trembling arms out to him. "I haven't seen you in so long."

Pit hesitated, glancing at Rook, seeking permission to accept the embrace. Rook gave a curt tilt of her head in response. Pit crossed the room in less than a second and wrapped his arms around Mónnuad's thin form. She pressed her face into the side of his short-clipped hair and held him as tight as any of her daughters. "I've missed you, son."

There was a strange sound, like the yelp of a dog clipped by a cartwheel. Mónnuad drew back, holding Pit at arm's length. There was a beat of silence before he blurted out, "I'm sorry," before pressing his face into her neck. Stunned, Mónnuad looked to Rook for an explanation. Within minutes, she knew it all.

Ensconced between Kestrel and Rook on the sofa, Pit wiped his face on the cuff of his shirt sleeve and shook his head. "This isn't what I wanted, Ma."

Mónnuad spoke with a level but loving tone. "What did you want, Pit? What did you think you could get from the Avanish that you couldn't get from us?"

He flinched. "I don't know, and that was the problem. I set out with the stupid notion there was something missing in my life, but the more time I spent with the Avanish, the more I realized I wasn't one of them. That I don't *want* to be one of them. It isn't all of them, but so many are so hateful. They think we're..."

He broke off, so Rook offered one of Dreidchain's words. "Tainted?"

Pit flushed anew. "Dreidchain and the others direct the hatred. They spread lies, perpetuate the idea that we're scum. I don't think most of the Avanish would care about us one way or the other if it wasn't for what the powerful say and do."

"It's been this way for decades," Mónnuad said. She closed her eyes and placed her hands over them. "Even in the old country, the Avanish tried to justify what they did to us by telling each other we deserved it. We were too stupid to farm our own land, too base and devious to run our own government. But their words weren't the fundamental problem then, and they aren't now. It's the firepower behind them that's always been the issue. They came into our country with guns and blades and drove us from our homes. Now, in this city, they're going to do it with bombs."

"I wish there was something we could do about it," Pit said.

"There is something," Kestrel said. She was sitting close to Pit, but not quite touching him. Forgiveness only went so far, so fast. "We're fighting back. Mama Magpie has us working with the Shadow of Jaguars."

Pit turned to Rook with a light of understanding in his eyes. "That's why you were in Dreidchain's mansion. You were spying for them."

There was an edge of incredulousness in his tone that made Rook want to slap him. But she, like Kestrel, kept her hands to herself. An idea formed in her head, something amorphous that came together along with the smile on her face.

"What?" Kestrel and Pit asked in unison. They shared a half-embarrassed smile at the similitude.

"I have an idea about how you can redeem yourself," Rook said. "You're in deep with the Filth now. You must be, since you're attached to that captain."

Pit's face darkened. "I think Captain Veng was the only one who would have me. He's Undténsian, not Avanish, so he's not like the others. He isn't against the Saosuíasei, and some things he's said make me think he wants to help us. Veng doesn't talk the way everyone else does."

"Then keep working with him." Pit's face scrunched with confusion, so Rook continued. "You're on the inside. You have access that no one else could. I infiltrated Dreidchain's mansion so easily because to him and the rest of them, one Saosuíasei servant is the same as another. It would be impossible for someone to infiltrate the police from the outside."

"But from the inside," Kestrel said, realization dawning, "you're already trusted. You can feed back everything you hear."

Pit paled. His tongue flicked over his lips. At his hesitation, Rook scowled. "You owe us. All of us. You turned your coat, and you can't take that back. But you can do something with what you've done. You can help us now. And," she said, thinking back to her words with the Jaguar, "you might help save Avanish lives too."

"How?"

"If the Jaguar agrees to my suggestion," Rook said, "not only that, but we might all be able to sleep easier at night."

TEN

"Are you sure this is a good idea?" Pit shifted, trying to get comfortable on the stuffed and patched armchair. Rook leaned against the wall of Magpie's office and rolled her eyes.

He's asked that question at least ten times. "I'm sure," she said.

Kestrel, who leaned on the back of his chair, nodded and ruffled his thick black hair. "It'll be fine, Pit. We know Dru and he knows you. He'll understand."

Rook cast them a curious look. "Well, I hope he will. I mean, otherwise he'll shoot you on the spot."

Pit's face blanched. Kestrel glared. "She's joking. Aren't you, Rook?"

She'd had her fun, so she nodded. "Yes, I'm joking. Dru won't shoot you." She waited for a beat. "But he might beat you black and blue instead."

"Rook!"

Kestrel's screech mingled with the scrape of the door opening. Magpie entered, her silver namesake glinting in the hollow between her collarbones. The Jaguar followed, his spots standing dark on his temples. Pit rose, and their eyes met for the first time in many months. The recognition on the Jaguar's face was like whiplash, and he thrust his hand into his coat pocket. Rook's heart was in her throat as she made to dive forward with her dagger drawn, but Magpie was there before her, with her hand clamped around the Jaguar's wrist. His fingers stayed tight around the gun.

"Not under my roof," Magpie said.

The Jaguar tried to pull his wrist free, but Mama Magpie held on. "But traitors are all right under it?" the Jaguar asked.

Kestrel plucked the gun from his hand. "Pit's not a traitor."

His weapon confiscated, Magpie released him. The Jaguar curled his lip. "He looked the part of a traitor in that Avanish uniform."

Magpie walked to her seat and lowered herself on the other side of the desk. She clasped her hands and nodded at the chair Pit had vacated. "Take a seat and Rook will tell you her idea."

The Jaguar's dark eyes slid to her, and he stared for a long moment before he did as Magpie asked. He turned his gaze from Rook to Pit, though he spoke to her. "Go on then."

With her heart returning to a sensible rhythm, Rook slid her dagger back into her cane and gestured to Pit. "This is an exchange."

The Jaguar kept his cold eyes on Pit. "Go on."

"Yesterday, you and I had words about how culpable we all are for what we do." Rook glanced at Pit, then back at Jaguar. "I agree with you." At that, the Jaguar broke his stare and turned to her. "Just because I don't plant the bomb or pull the trigger doesn't mean I'm innocent, especially if you're working from my intelligence."

He tilted his head to one side. "So where does my dear old friend Pit the policeman come into this?"

Rook took a careful breath as she prepared what she had to say. "Pit wants to help us. Life on the Avanish side of the city didn't treat him better, but he's now in a position of trust among them."

"He turned his coat and he regrets it, you mean." The Jaguar narrowed his eyes. "Tell me, Pit. Why did you do it? What made you turn your back on all of us?"

Pit shifted, folding his hands behind his back in a way Rook had never seen him do before. He must have learned it in his training. "Do you want the truth?"

The Jaguar nodded. "You'd best believe I do."

After a deep breath, Pit shook his head. "I did it because I was stupid."

There was a beat of silence, followed by another one. Then the Jaguar barked a hard laugh. "That is the truth," he said. "You're stupid, all right. So we have a half-Saosuíasei policeman in the room." He turned his attention back to Rook. "How does this fit in with an exchange?"

"I'm attached to Captain Veng," Pit said, "who reports to Governor Dreidchain. I know things and hear things a regular man on the beat wouldn't."

"All right," the Jaguar said. He crossed his arms. "So the exchange is that I let you live if you give me information."

Magpie leaned forward, her necklace gleaming in the candlelight. "Not quite, Drucách. If that was the bargain, we would never have brought Pit here."

"The deal I propose is this," Rook said. "In exchange for what information Pit can give you, you allow him to feed us information that will help keep innocent Avanish lives safe. And before you say anything," she continued before the Jaguar could interject, "there are innocent Avanish in this city. Not everyone is like Dreidchain and his cronies. Many people aren't involved at all."

Jaguar closed his mouth with an audible clack of his teeth. He sat back, considering. "You could do that without a deal with me. And there'd be nothing to stop you turning your coat again."

Rook shook her head. "We want to play as honest a game as possible. You pinned me to the wall when you said what you did last night. You're right, I'm not any better than you, but we can all become better together. I want to do what I can to minimize the danger to innocent people. In exchange for what Pit tells you, you allow Pit to pass information back to tell those not involved in this conflict where to avoid."

The Jaguar remained silent. Magpie spoke into the void. "The Avanish government needs tearing down, there's no doubt about that. We're not asking to stop the Shadow of Jaguars. We're asking to stop unnecessary deaths. For every killing like my poor Pigeon, there's a death on the other side just the same. Whether it's by the Avanish militia, or the Shadow of Jaguars, or Billy Drainer, it doesn't matter. Pigeon did nothing to deserve what happened to her. We want to be better than the Avanish," Magpie finished in a voice now thick with grief, "not the same as them."

The Jaguar kept his arms folded, looking only at Pit. He considered for a long moment before he spoke. "Please understand, my dear old friend, that if you double-cross me, I won't kill you. First." A heavy ominousness hung from the last word. "I know you. I know where you used to live. I know everyone you know. I'll take out everyone you love"—he nodded at Rook and Kestrel—"and only once that's done will I put you out of your misery."

"Understood," was Pit's only reply.

With a shade of his wry expression returning, the Jaguar leaned back in his chair and laced his fingers behind his head. "That wasn't what I expected when I came here today. Shall we talk about my business now? I have a few jobs for your ladies, and I can't hang around here all day."

That evening, Pit parted ways with them again.

"I won't be back here," he said as they lingered on the street outside the Nest. "I won't be back at your apartment either. I shouldn't have been going there anyway, but now I'll stay away for sure. I don't want anyone to link your mother's home to me."

"It's a home now, is it?" Rook asked, but her voice bore no anger. "Thought it was a gutter."

Pit gave her a sidelong smile. "You're never going to let that go, are you?"

"Nope. Never."

Their shared chuckle dissipated into the cold. "I understand," Pit said. "If I were you, I wouldn't either."

They fell into a silence that edged on awkward. It took Rook a moment to understand why. When she realized, she took a step back. "I'll let you two say goodbye."

Kestrel mouthed 'thank you' and Rook walked to the corner of the block, swinging her cane and whistling no particular tune. She didn't turn around. While she might have invaded people's houses when they deserved it, she wouldn't invade someone's privacy when they didn't. Doubtless Kestrel and Pit were now engaged in tongue wrestling, their hands roaming over one another. Rook maintained, for now and forever, that such things were a waste of time.

As she waited for the extensive goodbye behind her to finish, her mind went to Özdo. She was inside the Nest, as Magpie had offered her temporary shelter. What she was planning to do afterward was anyone's guess. Where could she go? Rook had considered suggesting she join the Conventicle, since she had the skills to steal. But, just as with Maird, she wasn't sure if it was wise. Theirs was no safe profession. Then, she thought with a snort that echoed into the darkness, nothing was safe now the city had fallen into war.

A cough drew her attention, and she turned back again. Only Kestrel remained, illuminated in a pool of pale lamplight. Rook walked the short distance up the street again.

"You'll be floating on thin air all night now," she said, passing her arm through the crook of her friend's arm. "Maybe I'll sleep on the couch in Ma's room. I don't want you getting confused in your sleep."

Kestrel's laugh was light, filled with a happiness Rook hadn't heard in some time. "You wish."

As they entered, the strains of the bar's music and conversation rolled towards them like a welcome party. It was a strange comfort to hear the normality. The Nest's new Shadowmen patrons destroyed that sensation in seconds as they sent up a bawdy 'Yeoooo!' as Rook and Kestrel crossed the bar.

At the sound, young Özdo turned from her perch on a barstool. She grinned and waved them over. "This is some place," she said.

"It's our home from home," Kestrel said. She slipped her arm from Rook's. "I'll leave you two to have a drink. I'll be in the back if you need me."

Rook's immediate response was to form the words 'don't go.' She wasn't the most social of people, often relying on Kestrel's friendliness to mask her own silence. But Özdo patted the vacant stool beside her and smiled. Rook gave an internal shrug. What harm could it do?

"Well, that looked serious," Özdo said as Rook leaned her cane against that bar and perched on the barstool. "Who was the fella? I didn't see his face."

Rook gestured to Wren, who mouthed, 'The usual?' and set about pouring the drink. Rook thanked her for it, but raised a finger to stop her retreat. She downed the bitter quicksilver in one smooth gulp, then gave Wren a grateful smile as she poured another.

"He's working for the Shadow of Jaguars," Rook said, then added after another sip, "for now, at least."

Özdo lifted one thin brow. "Now? What did he do before?"

"You've met him." Rook rolled the glass between her palms, the transparent liquid picking up traces of green gaslight.

It took less than a second for Özdo's quick mind to put the pieces together. Her jaw dropped. "No. That policeman?"

Rook's 'hush' was too slow. At the sound of that dreaded word, the bar fell silent, and all eyes glared at them. "What are you all looking at?" Rook snapped, and gradually the birds of the Conventicle and the Shadowmen alike slid their gazes away.

Under the weight of Rook's scowl, Özdo lifted a hand in apology. "Sorry, sorry. I didn't mean to say it so loud." She dropped her voice to a stage whisper. "That policeman? He's got some set of balls on him to come here of all places." She spoke as if the Nest had been her haunt for years, not just a few days. "What was he doing?"

Rook tilted her head back to drain her second glass of quicksilver. This time she didn't gesture for more, but instead tipped the glass upside down on the bar. "Remember I told you he was an old acquaintance?" Özdo nodded. "Well, he's more like a brother, though we're not blood related. His name is Pit. My mother helped bring him up after he lost his parents. He's half-Saosuíasei, half-Avanish, and had some idiotic notion to find his Avanish heritage and joined the Filth. All he found was that the Avanish didn't want him any more than a full-blooded Saosuíasei, that the police don't care about us, and the governor is an irredeemable bastard." Rook drummed her fingernails on the bottom of the upended glass. "In short, he made a disastrous choice. Now he's going to redeem himself. It was that, or I kick his arse all the way to the homeland and back."

Özdo's laugh drew another round of stares, but Rook waved them off with one well-chosen finger. The younger woman was a breath of fresh air in the stinking smog of city politics. "That's a threat I'm sure he took seriously," she said. She took a gulp of her own drink, a deep purple wine. "I'd take it seriously, all right, after what I've seen you do."

Rook gestured to the glass. "Are you even old enough to drink that?"

With another tinkling laugh, Özdo raised her glass in a toast. She kept an unblinking stare at Rook as she downed the rest of her wine, finishing with a dramatic 'ahh' of satisfaction. "What age do you think I am?"

Cocking her head to the side, Rook tapped her chin. "About fifteen?"

For the third time, Özdo's laugh drew the gaze of everyone. From their corner table, Redshank, Greenshank and Jay tittered and pointed. Rook glared.

"Thank you for the compliment," Özdo said, "but I'm older than that."

"Sixteen?" Rook asked. When Özdo shook her head and pointed upward, she tried again. "Seventeen? Eighteen?"

Her glass now empty, Özdo slid it away from herself with a sigh. "Nope. Try twenty-five."

"Twenty-five?" Rook repeated, her eyes wide with surprise. "You don't look it."

"I feel it," Özdo said. Her voice lost its joviality and was now flat and gray. "Twenty-five with nothing to show for it, not even a bad reference from an awful job. My parents sent me to my cousin because they thought I couldn't destroy that too. Well, surprise," she finished with irony, "Özdo Vost ruins her life again."

Though she wanted to, Rook didn't ask for elaboration. Even brimming with hot curiosity as she was, she wasn't the sort who divulged much information about her own life, and didn't ask others about theirs. Instead, she gestured for Wren, who came to them with a bottle of quicksilver in one hand and a bottle of wine in the other.

"Shall I leave the bottles?" she asked in an empathetic tone. Wren was like that, a woman of few words but open ears.

"No thanks," Özdo said, "not the wine, anyway. One more glass will do me."

Rook tapped the upended glass. "And I'm already done for the night."

Wren poured the purple wine. Özdo closed her eyes to savor another sip. Rook drummed her fingers on the glass again. "What are your plans for your next steps?" she asked. "I'm assuming you don't want to go back to your parents."

"You're correct." Özdo leaned low on the bar. For a moment it looked like she would touch her forehead to the flat surface, but she stilled her slump. "I don't know what to do. Can't go home, no reference for another job. I guess there's always the Bloodhouse."

"No," Rook said. "Absolutely not." When Özdo blinked in surprise at her conviction, Rook shook her head. "Those places are death chambers. They make it sound like you can go in, have blood drawn, then leave again, but it's not like that." Her face darkened at the memory of so many tragic stories. "Most people don't realize the Bloodhouses charge you for drawing your blood. You end up owing more than your blood is worth, so you have to give more. Then they indenture you for the debt, and you have to keep giving your blood, and you have to work for them too. It's a trap."

"That can't be legal," Özdo said, sitting up straight again.

"It is," Rook said with a shrug, "because the Avanish are the ones who run it and who make the laws. They're not the ones who go there. Most Bloodhouse victims are Saosuíasei."

"Or Undténsian," Özdo said.

"Exactly."

The weight of the conversation made Özdo sag once more. Rook's chest tightened in sympathy. Then she ventured an idea she didn't know was wanted or not. "You could join the Conventicle."

This time Özdo's laugh was soft and sorrowful. "I might be good at sneaking around stealing food, but that's the height of it. I'm not cut out for what you do."

"You don't have to be. Wren's a member of the Conventicle just the same as me, but she doesn't go out and do what I do. She stays inside the Nest, tends the bar, does odd jobs. There are plenty of ways you can be one of us." Rook thought of Maird and all the reasons she'd given her sister to dissuade her from this very choice of path. "I won't lie. It can still be dangerous. We're all wanted by the Filth the same, whether you're like me or like Wren. The only one the Avanish want more than the rest is Mama Magpie, but they'll never touch her."

Özdo wound her fingers around her glass, leaving dull smudges on the smooth surface. "Do you think she would consider me?"

"I'll speak on your behalf, give you a better reference than Miss Vost ever could." They shared a chuckle before Rook gave Özdo what she hoped was a comforting smile. "Everyone in the Conventicle looks after one another. As long as you toe the line and do what you're expected to, you'll be welcome here."

"You make a compelling point," Özdo said. She drained the last of her wine. "So will I get a bird name like the rest of you?"

Rook chuckled. "You get to pick your own, so long as no one else has it."

Özdo spread her fingers in a grand gesture. "I want something epic, something that'll make people respect me."

Rook shook her head. "Sometimes the humblest birds are the ones we love the most." Pigeon's quiet smile shone in her memory. "You don't need an epic name to get respect."

Özdo was about to say something else, her lips poised to deliver another wry and humorous comment, when an almighty hammering started at the Nest's door, followed by an explosion of splintering wood. Rook's stomach dropped.

"This is a raid! Weapons down and hands in the air!"

Of course, her hands didn't go into the air. They went straight for her cane.

ELEVEN

With one hand on her cane and the other lifted in a protective cross in front of Özdo, Rook took a moment to gauge the chaos. The door splintered under the impact of a solid black boot and dangled limp on one hinge. Men rushed in like a tidal surge, men Rook at first thought were police. But at a second glance, she realized they weren't. Instead of the black uniforms with silver buttons of the Stamchester police, these men wore the saturated viridian velvet of the Avanish militia. Instead of batons and whistles, they carried guns. Some even had strange textured spheres on their belts. Rook's body flashed cold. Those were explosives.

As the soldiers fanned out, all Shadowmen and Conventicle women jumped to their feet. Like Rook, everyone kept their backs to the walls, each training their weapon at the chest of an enemy. The Avanish lieutenant stood in their midst, wielding a pistol. The gold embroidery at his collar and cuffs spoke of his rank, but that was all that did. He looked too young, even greener than the fabric of his uniform.

"By order of Governor Kel Dreidchain, you're all under arrest," he said, waving his weapon as he spoke.

The bar now descended into cold silence. Rook kept her hand clenched on her cane and calculated. There were more Saosuíasei rebels than military men.

"I don't think so," said a voice.

Footsteps rang into the silence, and the soldiers hesitated, looking to their lieutenant. The young man had none of the decisiveness a military leader, and his forehead creased in confusion. As he lowered his weapon by a fraction of an inch, Rook could see the cogs in his brain turning. She shook her head, bringing her brows low. Something wasn't right. The Avanish conquered with military might, but the soldiers on display here were far from mighty.

Magpie stepped into the room, her painted face poised and beautiful. She wore a long black coat, unnecessary for indoor wear, though Rook knew why she wore it. It wrapped her in power.

"You've made quick work of my door, friend." Magpie's black lips twisted at the last word. "I'm afraid I must ask you to clean up your mess before you go."

Her words were as sharp as the blade nestling in Rook's cane. Rook flexed her hand on its ball handle. Beside her, Özdo drew a little closer.

The lieutenant, jarred by Magpie's words, tilted his chin, and a self-important snarl came over his face. He trained his pistol on her and spoke again. "By order of Governor—"

Magpie waved a hand to cut him off. "Yes, you've said that already." Some Conventicle members chuckled at her nonchalant tone. She planted her hands on her hips. Her coat parted, showing the faintest hint of the dual revolvers slung on her belt. "If we're going to repeat ourselves, I'll say it again." All levity disappeared from her words. "Clean up your mess and leave."

Rook watched the anger flicker across the military man's face. If he was a real lieutenant, he was a substandard one. The more she took in the details of their uniforms and the way they held themselves, the more suspicion rose within her. The insignia each wore on his breast was strange, though Rook couldn't put her finger on why. It was familiar, yet different in some near-imperceptible way. Their viridian coats were of varying shades, and some were shabbier than any proud soldier would ever allow. It was as if they'd cobbled together their uniforms from the cast-offs of actual soldiers. Something wasn't right.

The lieutenant, whose jacket looked the newest of all of them, strengthened his arm and cocked his weapon. "We're not going anywhere. You don't tell us what to do. Now come quietly or—"

There was to be no quiet acquiescence in the Nest that night. A single shot went off—from which side, Rook didn't know. And the whole place erupted.

The bar became an instant battleground. Rook grabbed Özdo by the scruff of her neck and dragged her over the top of the bar. The bar's grand mirror exploded above them, glass raining down in glittering shards. Wren, who had ducked behind the bar, shuffled towards them with her arms cradled over her head. The room exploded with shouts and screams and gunshots.

Pressed against the shelves under the bar, Özdo stared at Rook with wide eyes. "You weren't kidding when you said it could be dangerous!"

"Just stay down!" Rook shot her free hand forward. She wrenched the under-bar shelves from their brackets, sending stacks of glasses crashing to the floor. Then she shoved Özdo and Wren into the makeshift enclave. "Don't come out until I come back for you, or when you know this is all over." Rook withdrew her knife and shoved the long cane into Özdo's hands. "It's not much, but it's better than nothing."

Wren swallowed hard, and Özdo gave a jerky nod. Rook, her grip around the knife's ball handle as strong as the steel of the blade, pulled in a deep breath before bringing her eyes above the bar's edge.

A bullet sailed past close enough that it made her heart twist. She ducked down and hurried, bent-backed, to the swing door at the end of the bar. It was hard to make sense of the Skilled swirl of conflict before her. Avanish green, Jaguar gray, and Conventicle black melded together, shot through with growing spurts of red. What she could see clearest of all, though, was Mama Magpie in the center of it all. Her black lips parted as she screeched and brought down one solider after another. This was the Magpie of legend. This was Líbhas returned, so Rook's mother said. This was the magpie holding the Spirit of Tuachiad.

Emboldened by her leader's majesty, Rook grinned and threw herself into the fight. Her knife glinted gold in the yellow light from the chandelier. Flat-capped Shadowmen ducked around her, using their fists as much as their guns. Each man moved with a swift purpose, in stark contrast with the unskilled fumbling of some soldiers. Rook's suspicion rose even more. They should have been proficient fighters. The Avanish military was the pride of their nation, but these men were nothing to be proud of.

One of them had his gun outstretched, and Raven in his sights. With a growl, Rook leaped forward and sliced at his shoulder. The man screamed as his uniform ripped, wet flesh flashing underneath. It wouldn't kill him, but it was enough to ensure he wouldn't fire another shot for the foreseeable future.

"Thanks!" said Raven, before she whipped around to face another attacker.

Rook's victim crumpled, writhing in pain, and she got a better look at his insignia. Just as she'd thought, it wasn't the usual black lion of the Avanish military. It was red.

She didn't have time to ponder as another shot sailed towards her. Rook ducked, and the bullet winged overhead, burying itself in the wall over the bar.

The soldier who'd taken the shot cursed and leveled his weapon again. For a moment that lasted a lifetime, they stared at one another as the conflict swirled around them. He was young, his eyes Avanish gray, his hair light and fine. His arm trembled under the weight of the gun. Trembled? Rook narrowed her eyes.

Before he could curl his finger on the trigger, Rook's arm flashed forward with Skilled speed, and the knife flew from her hand. It buried itself in the soldier's arm, right to the hilt. He reeled, screeched, and dropped his gun. Rook launched forward and wrenched the knife out again, then made a grab for the fallen gun. The soldier kicked out and sent the weapon clattering across the floor. It disappeared in the maelstrom of warring feet.

At first the soldier glared at her, triumphant, but realization arrived like a steam train thundering on the overline. Under the threat of Rook's knife, his hand went to his belt. For a sickening second, Rook thought he would pull one of his grenades. Instead, he drew a blade of his own, and flashed it at her. She snorted. He wielded it like an amateur. Just like all the rest, he moved without the finesse of a trained killer. Something definitely wasn't right.

Rook lashed out and danced around him with ease. He failed to keep up with her and half-stumbled. Taking the opportunity, Rook wrapped an arm around his neck. With the blade of her knife held to his throat, she used her Skill to drag him behind the bar before he could fight back.

Even though she knew the layout of the room, she still slammed into the wall. The force of her blood-burning speed brought the last few bottles raining down. Rook flipped the man onto his back, the knifepoint poised in the dip of his throat. His breath came in shallow gasps, his eyes wide, and Rook realized how very young he was. He was no man. He was just a boy.

Everything came together. Their inexperience. Their mismatched uniforms. The lieutenant who was no military man.

"You're not real militia," Rook spat. "Who are you?"

His fear flickered, his expression sharpening with hatred. "We *are* real military." He jabbed a finger at the crest on his uniform. "We're the Stamchester Defense League."

"Never heard of you." Rook pressed her blade into his skin. His fear renewed. "Why are you here?"

The apple of his throat bobbed under her knife, but he attempted to steady his voice. "We're here to get rid of scum like you."

Rook's rage rose, and she grabbed a fistful of his hair, pulling it forward until the tip of her blade drew blood. He whimpered, assured of his own death as Rook pulled on her Skill. But instead of wrenching him onto her blade, she shoved him backward. His head collided with the liquor-stained floorboards, the impact knocking him out cold.

A shadow moved in her periphery and Rook raised her blade, ready to strike. Instead, her eyes widened. It was Özdo.

"I told you to stay under the bar!"

But Özdo wasn't looking at her. She fixed her eyes on the soldier. "Did you kill him?"

"No," Rook said, "but he wouldn't have hesitated to kill us. None of them would. Which is why you need to get back—"

The rest of Rook's words remained unsaid.

Shelves jumped from the walls as an explosion ripped through the building. The shattered remains of the bar's grand mirror disintegrated as the frame hit the floor, and then everything was white. Rook heard nothing but a horrendous buzz in her ears, saw nothing through the thick fog of dust and debris that choked the air. Blinded and deafened, she grasped at the space in front of her and the ground underneath her. First, she found the soft velvet of the soldier's uniform. Then her fingers tightened around the warmth of a laundry-calloused hand. When it squeezed back, Rook's chest flooded with relief even as she guttered in the explosion's aftermath. At least Özdo was alive.

Gradually the buzz in her ears receded to a hum. Though she choked on every breath, her throat burning from the dust, she spoke. "Are you all right?"

Özdo hacked out her response. "Just about. I think my limbs are all still attached."

Rook released her hand. She stilled her body and listened, not needing to sharpen her hearing to discern the aftermath of the explosion. Moans and cries accompanied the crumble of debris spilling from rooms overhead. Rook rose and peered over the bar. Though she Skilled her sight, it didn't help. It wasn't until the dust settled that she could take in the damage.

The Nest was no more. Tables and chairs were upended at best, blown apart at worst. Bodies littered the floor. Some of those were blown apart, too. Soldier viridian and Conventicle black alike lay coated in gritty white. Military plumed hats wilted on the floor alongside Rebel flat caps. There were fresh boot marks in the dust, all leading towards the street. Probably soldiers, Rook mused. In the middle of the Shambles, in the middle of a conflict, it was in their interests to flee. There would be no sympathy here for their injuries, only rage.

Something else felt strange, too. The air bit with cold and even though the dust settled, something like a new fog seemed to roll in. Rook blinked, forcing her mind to make sense of what she was seeing. It wasn't something like fog. It *was* fog. Her breathing stilled. The explosion had brought down the entire front of the Nest, exposing the inside to the outside world. She glanced up, following the line of ragged teeth that used to be walls, only to see the first bright red spits of fire rising. For the first time, she was grateful Magpie had never installed gas lighting in the Nest. If she had, they would all have been blown to bits.

In the distance, the whine of a siren started up, though Rook doubted the fire appliance would come anywhere near them. It was an Avanish service for Avanish people.

Özdo rose and let out a low whistle Rook could just hear above the ringing in her ears. "This is horrifying."

Rook nodded, her eyes roaming over the fallen bodies once again. Some of them writhed and squirmed, but some were still. Halos of dark blood seeped from their fallen bodies. She couldn't quite make out who was who, but was certain Kestrel wasn't among them. None of the bodies, dead or alive, were tall enough. That meant her friend was somewhere in the destruction, perhaps even buried beneath rubble.

A sudden panic came upon her, and she stumbled out into the remains of the bar. "I need to find Kes. And Magpie," she added, tripping over her own boots. "Magpie!"

Her shout echoed into the exposed street, where a crowd was gathering. Rook clambered over fallen masonry and roof beams rising like a ship's masts snapped in a gale. She scanned the destruction, looking for even the smallest flash of Magpie's black coat amongst it, but she saw nothing.

Özdo hurried after her and grabbed her arm as Rook stumbled again. She was so weak, so clumsy. What was wrong with her?

"Rook, stop. You're bleeding."

Özdo withdrew her hand to show the wet red. It was too bright against the chalky dust. Rook's brow furrowed. Where was she bleeding from? There was no pain anywhere.

"Are you sure that's from me and not you?" she asked. "I can't feel anything."

"You're in shock," Özdo replied, placing her hand on Rook's arm again. "You should sit down."

The idea drew an obnoxious laugh. "Where?" Rook asked, gesturing at the destroyed room.

Özdo pressed her dust-covered lips together. Despite the growing fuzz in her head, Rook slipped from Özdo's grasp once more and picked her way across the destruction. Figures crept in from the street, some curious, but most distraught. The fire appliance siren remained far enough away that Rook knew it wasn't coming for them.

As she crossed the room, a figure at her feet shifted. It turned its head, exposing the bleeding and bruised face of Raven.

Rook bent to help her sit up. Dust and debris fell away from Raven's stout form. "Are you hurt?"

Raven coughed and winced. "I'm hurt, but I don't know where. It feels like everywhere."

"Can you stand?"

"We'll soon see, I guess." Rook offered her hands, helping Raven to rise, but as soon as the other woman flexed her left ankle, she hissed and wobbled. "That would be a no."

As she tried to help Raven balance, a burning started in Rook's right side. She cursed. That was where Özdo's touch had come away red. That explained why her head was growing lighter and the gray was encroaching on the edge of her vision.

She swayed on her feet, reaching for the nearest wall, then realized she was in the middle of the room. Her hand touched something warm and steadying. Head swimming, she forced her head up. A pair of mismatched eyes gleamed down at her.

When she spoke, her words were slurred. "I thought you weren't coming back here?"

Pit shook his head, his tone sardonic. "Things change." As Rook slumped into him, his voice changed. "Where's Kes?"

"Haven't found her yet." Rook's own voice sounded far off, almost an echo. Her whole side burned. "She'll be okay. She must be. I'll never forgive her if she isn't."

"Same to you," another voice said, "and it seems like you aren't okay."

Even though she could see now see nothing but a pinprick in the center of her vision, Rook grinned. "Kestrel."

Relief flooded her, taking every drop of strength from her body. By now Pit was the only thing holding her up.

Kestrel spoke again, but Rook couldn't make out the words. Everything bucked and swirled, and then there was nothing but slick darkness.

TWELVE

The room was dark and dank. Its paperless walls showed cracks in the ancient brick. A single candle lantern hung from the roof of a windowless room, swinging in the aftermath of being lit. A stoop-backed man with a limp reached the battered wooden chair on the other side of the room and turned. He clapped a hand on the well-worn wood and beckoned them forward.

"Which one do you want done first?" he asked.

His voice was like the rasp of a boot on gravel. In contrast, Rook's father's words were deep and sweet. "Isianná," Sionn said as he pressed a hand into the small of his oldest daughter's back.

Isianná whimpered. Rook hooked an arm through her older sister's and held on tight. Isianná might have been the oldest, but she'd never been the bravest. That was Rook's destiny.

"I'll go first, Da." Her girlish voice echoed in the empty room. "Don't worry, Ishie. I'll show you how easy it'll be."

At only nine, she spoke to her ten-year-old sibling with an authority and knowledge she had no claim to. Rook had always been that way. She'd always made pains to talk with confidence befitting a girl twice, three times her age. She was always the sister in charge.

"Suit yourself," the stoop-backed man said, patting the chair back again, "but can we get on with this? I don't have all day."

Her father laid a brief touch to the top of her head. "That's my Rébh. Always brave."

Rook's face flushed with pride as she padded across the bare boards of the floor and sat as directed. Her father wrapped an arm around Isianná's shoulders. Isianná hunched in on herself, hid behind her long dark tresses, and leaned into their father's embrace. Sionn Artur stood tall beside her, strong and imposing as a mountain.

The stoop-backed man rolled Rook's right arm over to expose the fleshy inside of her elbow. He grabbed a short belt from a metal tray on a nearby table. Rook flinched. The man laughed.

"I'm not going to hit you, sweetpea. Didn't your da explain? I'm just going to type your blood, that's all."

"I explained it to them, but not well," her father said, one arm still tight around Isiannà's shoulders. "You know I've never been good with words, Cianúbh."

The man, Cianúbh, harrumphed in response as he tightened the belt around Rook's upper arm. "It's a good thing you're good with other things, Sionn," he said as he poked at Rook's arm for a vein, "but if you weren't so good at making bairns, you'd not be here right now."

Her father gave a dry laugh. "You're not wrong there, Cianúbh."

Rook's eyes widened as the stoop-backed man plucked a long silver object from the table. Her youthful courage flickered like the guttering candle swinging above her head.

"Now," Cianúbh said as he palpitated her arm again, "this needle's just out of the steam cupboard, so it's nice and clean. It will hurt, I won't lie to you, but not much. I'm sure you've done worse fighting with your sister."

"Ishie doesn't fight," Rook said. She held Cianúbh's gaze like an adult would. "Maird, yes, but—ouch!"

Rook flinched as the hollow steel needle passed into her arm. But the pain gave way to fascination as Cianúbh extracted a vial of red power from her veins.

At nine and ten, the girls were far younger than most of those who came for blood typing. Even Rook understood they were young for it. Typing identified your particular kind of blood, which was important for two reasons: knowing what you had to buy, and knowing what you had to sell. To use donor blood, you had to know what you needed. The wrong blood could cause significant harm, perhaps even death. To inject untyped blood into untyped veins was like playing with poison.

However, their father had brought his oldest daughters for the latter reason. Selling untyped blood was far less profitable. Typed blood fetched a higher price, and since his wife was pregnant with their seventh child, not including her waifs and strays, they needed more money. A man could only work as many hours as the day gave him. Thus, he'd explained to them, the family needed to sell more blood.

"We'll go nowhere near the Bloodhouse," he'd said at the wide-eyed horror on both girls' faces, "but we'll not go to the infirmary clinic, either. There's somewhere else we can go."

To go to the infirmary for typing meant the Avanish took a record of your blood type. Even at nine, Rook appreciated that the less the Avanish knew about you, the better. Thus, they'd ended up in Cianúbh's dingy makeshift clinic.

With her blood extracted and a stinging alcoholic concoction splashed onto the pinprick in the crook of her arm, Rook scowled and stood. Cianúbh turned to his table, his stoop-back toward them, and fiddled with whatever would show him her blood type. Intrigued, she peered around him, watching as he dropped an unknown liquid into the vial of her blood. Its dark red turned orange in the drop's wake.

"This one's a One, Sionn," he said. "Nothing special, but not bad. Lots of people are Ones. You'll get a decent price for hers."

Rook rankled at the unflattering description, but returned to her father's side as Isianná took her place on the chair. 'Don't worry,' she mouthed.

Cianúbh repeated the same steps as before with a new needle, extracting the blood, performing whatever alchemy it was that revealed the type. But when Isianná's blood changed color in the vial, he became unearthly still and clenched the glass tube in one hand. Rook squinted for a better look, but his thick fingers obscured the liquid.

Beside her, Rook's father straightened and stiffened. "What's wrong?"

It took a moment for Cianúbh to turn around. When he did, he held the vial of Isianná's blood aloft. It wasn't red any longer, but wasn't orange like Rook's had been. At the sight of it, Rook's father whistled long and low.

"By the Spirit of Tuachiad," he breathed.

"What is it?" Isianná asked, gripping the sides of her chair. A trickle of blood ran down the inside of her arm. "Am I bad? I'm sorry, Da. I didn't mean to be bad."

"Hush, bairn," Cianúbh said. He uncurled his fingers to reveal the green liquid swirling inside. "You're not bad. You're a Zero."

The trickling blood reached Isianná's wrist and slipped into her hand. "What does that mean?"

Rook knew what her sister didn't. She listened when people didn't realize. She understood the color's gravity.

"You're a universal donor, Isianná," her father said, reaching to wrap his fingers around the vial of green. "That means you're very, very rare."

Consciousness returned along with the deep aching of her side. But the blur cleared from her eyes, and Rook took in her surroundings. She was in her room, in her mother's home. Cold winter sun flickered as the breeze caught the edge of the faded curtains. As the fog of unconsciousness ebbed, memories flowed. The Nest. The militia. The explosion. Rook tried to sit upright, but her limbs wouldn't cooperate. She tried to use Skill, but from the aching weakness in her arms, she had no reserves to burn.

"Shh, don't get up," said a voice.

Rook tilted her head towards the source of the words. The world sharpened, and Kestrel's face came into focus. Her skin was blotchy and her eyes red-rimmed.

Rook struggled to sit up again and asked, "Why are you crying?"

The ache in her side grew to a pulse that forced her back down. Kestrel tutted, though her smile negated her faux annoyance.

"I'm not crying," she said as she smoothed back a sweat-dampened coil of Rook's hair. "I was crying, but now I'm not."

Rook made another attempt to rise, but this time Kestrel's firm hand kept her down. "I might cry over this fuss," Rook said. "I'm fine." Something strange flickered in Kestrel's expression. "What?"

Kestrel paused long enough before she spoke that Rook knew a blow was coming. "There's no pleasant way to say this, so I'll just say it. They got Magpie."

The aftermath of the explosion flashed through Rook's mind. The tightness in her chest returned. She hadn't seen Magpie amongst the rubble. It wasn't because she was lying dead or buried under debris. It was because she wasn't there.

"Who are 'they'?" Rook asked. "There seem to be more and more 'theys' appearing in the city. Dreidchain's police, the military, and now this Stamchester Defense League, whoever they are."

"'They' seem to be all the above." Kestrel's shoulders sagged as she deflated in her chair. "We still haven't figured out what happened, but Magpie's gone. We have it on good authority they dragged her kicking and screaming into the back of a police wagon. Where they took her, we don't know. All we know is that she's gone."

Rook pushed out a long breath. "At least that means she's still alive."

"For now, at least," Kestrel replied. "Dreidchain's wanted her for years. If he gets the chance, there's no doubt he'll hang her, just like Dál and Sénnarlann."

Pain and fear and loathing swirled inside Rook, burning her tongue like bile. "How did this happen?"

Kestrel passed a hand over her eyes. "I can't make sense of it. I always thought we were untouchable."

"We were," Rook said, "until we weren't. Magpie paid enough bribes to the Filth to keep us below consideration, but this new Stamchester Defense League is something different."

"We got too comfortable," Kestrel said, "and we paid for it."

Rook pressed her palms to her eyes until swirling lights appeared. "I don't want to ask this, but were any of ours killed?"

She concentrated on the darting colors behind her eyelids as Kestrel ticked off the list in a wavering voice. "Heron, Robin, and Swan. All shot. And when the walls came down, it killed Crane and Jay." Rook dug the heels of her hands further into her eye sockets. "The explosion injured Redshank and Greenshank, but they should survive. Whether Greenshank will walk again is questionable. It's likely she's broken her back. She hasn't been able to feel her legs since it happened, which is a small mercy. They look like they've been through a mincer. Crake is doing her best, but I don't think any amount of Skill healing is going to help." Rook pressed her lips together, pressure building within her as Kestrel continued. "There were lots of other injuries, and we haven't found Pelican and Raven. They might still be under the rubble. Though if they were alive when the wall came down, they're dead by now."

"By now?" Rook asked. "How long have I been out?"

"The attack happened three days ago. You've unconscious since." Kestrel's words grew thick. "I thought you might never wake again. Hence the tears, you ungrateful prick."

At that, the pressure within Rook released. But instead of screaming, she allowed herself to laugh. It was a strange sound, half-strangled and half-disbelieving. How could this have happened? How could the place she had considered her second home, a place she'd felt safe despite their lawlessness, have been destroyed? Worse than that, how could Magpie, a woman so fierce, be taken? And worst of all, how could so many of her friends have been killed?

"This can't be real," Rook said. A few hot tears joined her laughter. "Kes, please tell me this is all some sick nightmare."

Kestrel shifted in her seat, and Rook opened her eyes. Her friend plucked up one of her hands and pressed a kiss to the backs of her fingers. "I wish I could, Rook, but I can't."

Rook flexed her hand, grasping Kestrel's fingers in her own. "We can't let this go. We have to get Magpie back, and we need some kind of justice for the killings."

"That's the Jaguar's line of thought too," Kestrel said.

At the mention of that name, Rook's mood blackened. "Did we become a target because of him?"

"We're not sure, but it's likely that's why," Kestrel said. She let go of Rook's hand and passed her own over her eyes again, as if the weight of her words exhausted her. When she spoke, Rook focused on the magpie tattoo on her arm. "Pit disappeared after the explosion and said he was going to find out whatever he could, like who gave the order to come for us, what this Defense League is. I haven't heard from him since."

Rook tried to sit up again, propping herself on her elbows despite the burning pain in her side. She hadn't checked the damage yet, but it wouldn't be pretty. For the first time, she got a good look at Kestrel. Her skin was waxy, bereft of the make-up she always wore, and a mild growth of hair had appeared on her chin. That made Rook sit up all the way. She hadn't seen that in years.

"Kes, are you all right? I didn't even ask before now."

Kestrel kept her hands over her eyes. "I'm fine. Somehow I made it out unscathed. But it's been a terrible few days." Her voice caught in her throat. "So many of us got hurt or killed, and then when I wasn't sure you would wake up..." Her words dropped into a whisper. "I don't think I could have survived that, Rébh."

The sound of her proper name on Kestrel's tongue was so strange. Had she been able to, Rook would've scooped her friend into an embrace. Injured and pained as she was, all she could do was place a hand on her knee. Kestrel covered it with her own.

"I'm here, Faoiatín," Rook said. "I'm not going anywhere."

"You'd better not, or else I'll come after you beyond the grave to give you a right slap."

The levity broke the tension between them, and Rook laughed again. She turned her hand around to grasp Kestrel's. "We're sisters," she said. "Nothing can separate us."

It was another two days before Rook made it out of bed without excruciating pain. The wound in her side was long and jagged, but Crake, the closest to a surgeon the Conventicle had, had stitched it closed as best she could. While unconscious, Rook couldn't assist her healing by using her Skill. Now she was awake, and with the help of extra blood from her sisters, the injury was improving with the swiftness only Skill could bring. The pain reduced to a constant dull ache, but while burning blood brought healing, it also brought fatigue.

Regardless, she pushed through it and made her way to the parlor. Her younger sisters delighted in her presence and inability to move, and most of her time she had one head or another in her lap. The only one not pleased was Maird, who slunk from room to room with a permanent scowl.

"She's worried for you," their mother said, "but she can't express it."

Rook wasn't sure if that was true, but she withheld her eye roll out of respect for her mother.

On her third day out of bed, she insisted Kestrel take her along to the Jaguar's meeting.

"If you don't take me, I'll walk myself," she said as she pulled on her stolen Shadowman's coat. "If you hadn't wanted me to know about it, you shouldn't have mentioned it."

"You don't even know where you're going," Kestrel said as she helped ease Rook's arm into her sleeve, "so good luck walking there."

As Rook stepped into her boots, Maird hung by the front door, half-hiding behind her long black hair.

"Don't even ask," Rook said. "You're not coming with us, and that's that. End of story."

Her younger sister grunted and threw her hands into the air. "I have a right to leave this house if I want to!"

Rook scoffed. "You have a responsibility to stay here and look after Ma and the babies."

Maird tossed her head in frustration. "You're older than me! You should be the one staying here." Her tongue ran away with itself as she continued. "If Ishie was here, she'd let me go."

The residue of that name stuck in the air between them. Maird stopped short of clamping her hands over her mouth, but her face tightened with her misstep.

Rook straightened her back to make herself seem taller than she was. Oldest remaining sister she might've been, she was still shorter than Maird. "Well, Ishie isn't here, is she? So what I say goes. Understood?"

Tears glittered in Maird's eyes, though Rook suspected it was more to do with speaking their lost sister's name than the frustration of being denied permission to leave. Without another sounds, Maird turned on her heel and fled back into the parlor room.

With a sigh, Rook shook her head. "Let's get out of here."

At the street door, a cadre of capped and coated Shadowmen met them. The burly escort brought them to a waiting carriage, a huge black horse standing ready between the shafts.

"Where are we going?" Kestrel asked. She climbed in first, helping Rook in after.

"We'll keep that to ourselves," one of the Shadowmen replied. "Nothing personal, ladies, but the less we say and the less you know, the better."

Despite understanding the wisdom of it, being kept in the dark still stung. And dark it was, literally and figuratively, for an old newspaper covered the carriage's back and side windows. A thin haze of green gaslight filtered into the darkness, but that was all.

The carriage shifted as the two Shadowmen climbed aboard. One clicked his tongue and jerked the horse into motion, and they started on their way. For the first few turns, Rook tried to keep track of where they were, but disorientation was inevitable.

"Where do you think the Jaguar's den is?" Kestrel asked.

"No clue. We could be anywhere in the city by now."

Eventually they came to a stop. The carriage rocked as their escort descended again. When the door opened, one Shadowman stood with a hand outstretched.

"We're here, ladies. The Jaguar requests you join him for tea while we wait."

The strangeness of that notion almost made Rook laugh, but she kept her mouth closed. Big and burly as he was, the thought of the Jaguar offering them a hot drink in a porcelain cup jarred in her brain, but the humor soon gave way to curiosity. 'Wait' was interesting in its vagueness. Wait for what?

Though she scanned the street for distinguishing landmarks, there were none. Rook and Kestrel entered the nondescript building none the wiser about where they were. There was safety in that, but it still elicited frustration.

The Shadowmen escorted them through a narrow hallway and into a parlor room in great need of repair. Its green-striped wallpaper peeled and sagged, and the furnishings were a hodgepodge assortment of battered objects. The only new object was a wood and metal object standing on the sideboard. It consisted of a frame with two odd cones hanging from it.

It took Rook a moment to realize its significance. It was a telephone.

The Jaguar rose from a threadbare couch and welcomed them with a flourish.

"Welcome to my humble home," he said. "Please, make yourselves comfortable. I'm hoping our wait won't be long." He turned to one of the Shadowmen. "I think the ladies could do with a drink."

The man nodded and disappeared, leaving the three alone.

"Thank you for coming along today," the Jaguar said, taking some of his own tea. "I'm glad to see you"—he went to say the wrong name, then corrected himself—"Rook."

Rook regarded him for a moment before offering the mildest of smiles. "You've come a long way from playing Hunters and Jaguars with us on the street, Drucách. You're the only Saosuíasei I know with a telephone."

The Jaguar laughed. "Indeed. If you ever need me, just ask the operator for 2-7-0.5. We've all come a long way from the innocent children we once were.." His tone sobered. "Are you all right? I heard you got hurt."

"I did, but I'm all right now," Rook said.

Kestrel harrumphed and poked her uninjured side.

Before Rook could respond, a door swung open. She turned towards the approaching footsteps and grinned.

"Özdo!" The sight of the Undténsian woman sent a wave of relief through her.

Özdo set a tray on the table between the couches and grinned. "Not dead, then?" she asked, looking to the Jaguar for permission to pour.

Rook couldn't help but laugh. "Not dead yet." She watched as Özdo decanted a dark liquid from a teapot into three mismatched cups. From the froth it made, it was anything but tea. As Özdo passed out the cups, Rook raised an eyebrow. "I thought you didn't want to be a lady's maid?"

Beside her, Kestrel snorted into her cup. Across from them, the Jaguar raised an eyebrow of his own. "Lady's maid?"

"In my experience," Özdo said, "big cats are easier than little ladies. They're nicer to pet, at least." Kestrel half-choked on her drink again. "Mr. Jaguar here offered me asylum until I figure out what I'm going to do." Her humor slipped. "I don't think joining your Conventicle is much of an option anymore."

Rook gripped her cup, then brought it to her lips. It was beer. "We're down, but we're not out."

A gentle smile returned to the Jaguar's lips. "I'm glad to hear it."

Özdo withdrew a few steps and caught his eye. "Do you need anything else for now, Mr. Jaguar?"

Once again, he didn't correct the mode of address. "Nothing for now. Thank you."

She gave a curt nod and slipped out of the parlor again. The Jaguar watched her go, not turning again until she closed the door behind her. "You know," he said as he faced Rook and Kestrel again, "I think I'm going to marry her."

For a moment, the Jaguar disappeared, and the Drucách Tial of their youth sat before them. From his earnestness, Rook believed him.

She took another sip of her beer as, beside her, Kestrel tried to mop hers from her chest. Curiosity got the better of her, and Rook asked what she'd wondered about since she'd discovered Dru's new identity. "How on earth did you become the new Jaguar?"

The Jaguar lifted his cup in a silent toast to the sky. "Fiacónn Dál was my uncle on my mother's side. When the Avanish executed both him and Sénnarlann, most of their Shadowmen died with them. Most of the old guard are shells of what they used to be. I never wanted to follow in his footsteps, but there was no one else." The Jaguar's focus drifted to his own memories. "And when I saw their bodies hanging there, dangling off the Buxridge Bridge with no dignity, I knew I had to step up. Uncle Fiacónn and Ro loved our people as much as they loved each other. It's the least I can do to carry on their legacy. And," he added, his expression growing dark, "they didn't even let me bury them. The Avanish need to pay for that."

Kestrel set down her cup and reached across the table. She set her hand on his. "I'm so sorry, Dru."

The Jaguar lifted his other hand and pressed it over hers. "Uncle Fiacónn always told me to use my anger for good, which is why I asked you here."

"How so?" Rook asked.

The Jaguar sat back on his couch. "Our mutual friend has some news. I want to hear it alongside you."

At the mention of Pit, Kestrel straightened. "Is he here?"

"He will be," the Jaguar said. A knowing smile played on his lips. "That's who we're waiting on. I'm sure he'll be pleased to see you."

Kestrel flushed and looked away, burying her face in her cup.

It wasn't long before one of Jaguar's men appeared in the doorway to tell them Pit had arrived. Standing, the Jaguar gestured for them to proceed him from the room. They moved from the parlor into the dining room, which like the rest of the house had seen better days. There were two others in the room already. One was Pit, but the other was familiar too. It was Cian, the one who'd escorted Rook to Dreidchain's mansion. He tipped her a wink, this time his jaguar spots clear for all to see.

Beside him, Pit flashed a relieved smile. Rook returned it. Thank god he was all right. Of them all, he was playing the most dangerous game.

As they sat, the Jaguar made a round of introductions. "Ladies, this is Cian, my second. Cian, this is Rook and Kestrel." He gestured to Pit. "No introductions needed for you, my friend. You know us all, and we all know you. So," he continued, clasping his hands together, "please tell us what you found out about Mama Magpie."

Rook sucked in a sharp breath at the mention of Magpie. Her hopes rose. "Do you know where she is?"

Pit hesitated before he answered. "I do, and it's not good." He took a deep breath. "She's in Purgatory."

THIRTEEN

Rook slumped against the hard back of her seat. Her side flashed with pain. Purgatory. The worst of the five Stamchester prisons, its dank grimness reserved for the worst of criminals. On its man-made island at the convergence of the Eastraine and the Allen, no one had ever escaped its horrors. And no one entered on their own accord.

The Jaguar gave a solemn nod. "It would seem the governor, now the Magpie is in his possession, is keen for her to stay there."

Kestrel dug her fingernails into the thick fabric of her dress. "He's wanted her for years. Even before he was the governor and was still in the police, he obsessed over putting her behind bars."

Memories of Magpie's mentions of Dreidchain came back to Rook. "He sees me as a big ticket," she'd said more than once. "Dreidchain's the type who's always on the lookout for whatever will bring him the most fame and the most admiration. They'll laud whoever jails the Magpie as a city hero. Dreidchain wants to be that hero, so he'll never let me go." Though Magpie had never alluded to it, Rook always wondered if there was more than that. There were plenty of people like Magpie who ran gangs and rackets. There were plenty of avenues for Dreidchain to pursue his desire for fame. But, Rook mused, while there were plenty of others, many up to their elbows in beatings and blood, there was only one who was female. Perhaps that was the root of his obsession.

"We've got to get her out," Kestrel said. "She's done too much for us. We can't abandon her."

All eyes swung to the Jaguar. Whatever they might do depended on him.

"Agreed," he said with a firm nod. "I've known her since I was no age and barely tall enough to see over a bar top. I won't abandon her."

Rook cocked her head to the side, considering him. "I didn't realize you knew her before"—she made a sweeping gesture with one hand—"all this started."

A softness came over the Jaguar's face and he nodded again, this time more gently. "She helped my family out of a rough spot when I was a child. We were destitute, bound for the Bloodhouse or the bottom of the river, but Magpie provided for us. I've never forgotten it. She's an exceptional woman." Darkness consumed his face. "I'd kill every Avanish man in this city before I'd let her rot in Purgatory."

The disconnect between this Jaguar, all aggression and brass knuckles, and the playful Dru they'd known as a child jarred hard. Then again, Rook mused, there was a substantial difference between the Rook who climbed through windows and reacquired stolen property and the one who hushed her youngest sisters to sleep at night. The Jaguar, like everyone, had endless facets.

"So," Pit said, "what do we do?"

The Jaguar's expression brightened again, this time with a mischievous smirk. "Well, dear Pit, that's why I've brought you all together. We're going to orchestrate a little prison break."

Rook shared wide-eyed glances with both Pit and Kestrel. Cian grinned.

"A prison break?" Pit asked, his voice incredulous. "From Purgatory?"

"Correct, old friend." The Jaguar's face split with a full grin. "And we're going to do it tomorrow night."

"But how?" Kestrel asked. "Purgatory is impenetrable. No one gets in, and no one gets out."

The Jaguar lifted a finger and waved it to negate her point. "Incorrect. No one gets out, but plenty of people get in."

A cold ball formed in the bottom of Rook's stomach. "You're sending us in as prisoners."

"Correct," the Jaguar replied.

"That's insane," Kestrel said. "Once we're in there, we'll be under the control of the guards. We can't just walk in and do whatever we want. They'll lock us up, and then what use will we be?"

The Jaguar slid his gaze to Rook. "I'm counting on the Conventicle to provide us with a little help on that front. You must have some talented lock picks among your number."

"A lock pick is only useful if she has her tools," Kestrel countered. "It's not like they won't notice us bringing in a set of picks. Even if we hide them in our shoes, they'll strip us down for that very purpose." Something jolted in her at that thought, and she turned to Rook. "I can't go with you. They'll see..." Her face burned with shame and anger. "They'll see me."

In her moment of sorrow, Rook wanted nothing more than to embrace her friend. Her mind raced back to the incident after her theft from Teog Gria.

Disgusting he-she.

If Kestrel went into Purgatory, they would find out what was underneath her clothes and judge her upon it. They'd get separated. Even worse, they might kill Kes for being herself. Rook's stomach lurched. She'd never let that happen.

"No, Kes," she said, "you can't come. But I know who can. Someone who can smuggle tools and break any lock."

Kestrel's sorrow flickered to pleasant realization. "Of course!"

Rook grinned. "Of course."

The clocks across the city struck four when the small party set off across the Shambles. Pit had stayed behind with the Jaguar as Rook gathered her team. She'd had more volunteers than needed, and it had been difficult to beat the more enthusiastic ones back. Every surviving member of the Conventicle was willing, but not all were able. Redshank was the first picked, as Rook hadn't been able to say no to her. Rook was too familiar with the scald of fury surging through her over Greenshank's injuries.

Sparrow was the next choice, as while she was flitting and excitable, she was also one of the most proficient Bloodskillers among them all.

The last Rook chose was Crake. Crake was the most level-headed among them all, if also the least cheerful. Since cheer wasn't something they needed in Purgatory, that didn't matter, since it was Crake's specific brand of Skill they would need.

Rook mourned the weight of the bracer on her arm as she and the others disappeared into the back alleys of the Shambles. They were to meet the Jaguar and his men at the junction of Whiston Street and Furnam Road, and then the journey to rescue Magpie would begin. They walked the short distance without Skill. All of them had topped up as much as they could, but no one wanted to burn precious blood before they needed to. They couldn't wear their bracers, for if they appeared at the prison wearing them, they'd be the first things confiscated.

At Rook's side, Crake kept her hands jammed in the pockets of her overcoat. She was a tall and spindly woman, with hair cropped close to her skull. It was pale as milk, just like the rest of her, as if something had leeched all color from her body.

"Are you sure you're up to this?" Crake asked in a gruff growl.

"I'm sure," Rook said. "I'm no invalid, and it's not like we need to break in. It's getting out that'll be the challenge."

Crake replied with a grunt, but said nothing.

They made the last turn towards their meeting place. Of course, the plan wasn't as simple as Rook suggested. Getting in could prove more of a challenge if the prison guards asked too many questions. By reputation, they weren't men interested in the people they processed, which gave Rook some kind of hope they might pull this off.

They reached the meeting place and, though she knew it would be there, the sight of the huge black prison wagon still brought Rook up short. The van, drawn by four enormous draft horses, was windowless, and the rivets in the steel sides spoke of its weight and the need for a team of four to pull it. Bullet holes riddled its side, and even in the darkness Rook could see the shift in paint texture where its original identification number had been doctored.

From its driver's seat, two men in the dark uniform of the Stamchester police force stepped down. One of them was Pit. It was strange to see the silver buttons glittering across his chest in a strange constellation. The other was Cian, who gave them a grin. He'd replaced his usual flat cloth cap with the dark hat of a police officer, and once again, his jaguar spots had disappeared.

"Ready?" he asked.

Rook, Crake, Redshank and Kestrel nodded as one. "We're ready," Rook replied. "Let's bring Mama home."

Pit crossed to the back of the prison van and drew a set of iron keys from his pocket. The sight of him in the Avanish uniform made Rook's stomach churn.

He caught her discomfort as he unlocked the armored doors. "Once this is all over, I'm going to burn this uniform."

He made a stirrup with his hands to help her up. Rook hesitated, then accepted. "I'll provide the match."

The inside of the van was darker than night. Rook slid along the wooden bench to make room for Sparrow. Crake and Redshank sat across from them. Pit clambered in, picking another key from his bunch. The jangle of it and the chains he drew up from the floor made Rook's hair stand on end.

Cian appeared at the open doors as Pit shackled them to the floor of the van, one by one. "Remember, say nothing and do nothing until you're told," Cian said. "Let Pit and me do the talking."

"Understood," Rook said. She tapped the sole of Redshank's boot. "Right? Keep it cool."

"Understood," Redshank echoed.

The slam of the van's thick doors plunged them into darkness. The bullet holes only penetrated the outer layer. A small barred window, too high for the seated prisoners to see out, let in the only light. Flimsy moonbeams slipped inside, but they did nothing to lift the dim reality of confinement in a prison wagon. Cold discomfort seeped into the back of Rook's legs from the bench and crawled up her spine. At least she wasn't a true prisoner on her way to spend the rest of her days in Purgatory. She tried to imagine herself into Magpie's mindset, unsure whether this would be the last drive she would ever take. It wasn't the first time Mama Magpie had been to prison, but it was her first time in Purgatory. No one ever got out. It was a place of despair, where they locked you up for life. How long that was depended on your crime and sentence. Those the Avanish considered the worst of offenders didn't get life. They got death high on the gallows.

The van shifted on its suspension as Cian and Pit climbed onto the driver's bench. Rook shared a glance with Crake, who gave her a slow blink. Then, with a whistle and a jolt, the four-horse team pulled into action.

The chains clanked in a somber chorus as they made their way across the city. As they drew near, Crake sniffed hard. Her face creased with disgust. "We're nearly there."

Rook wrinkled her nose at the stench. The convergence of the Eastraine and Allen heralded itself in its own unique way.

The vibrations under the wagon's wheels changed as they left the smoothness of the packed dirt road and bumped onto the wooden surface of the bridge. Purgatory was connected to the riverbanks by wide road bridges. The bridge over the Allen had been there for decades, but the one over the Eastraine was new. There'd been much pomp and ceremony when the new bridge, so cleverly named the New Eastraine Bridge, had opened. While the bridge's roadway was wooden, the rest of it was of iron and steel, with a huge mechanism that made the whole thing to open, allowing tall ships to pass through. Many of the Conventicle had gone to observe its grand opening, though Rook had not. It had only been a few weeks prior when her father had drowned himself in waters too close to that place, and she'd known she couldn't face being near its dark embrace.

The wagon slowed as they approached the tall gates of Purgatory. While Rook couldn't see it now, she'd glimpsed the imposing brick and iron edifice from afar. The whole place was double-walled, and each hexagonal wing of the building rose four stories high. Six hexagons of four storeys of pain, of sorrow, all coming together to frame Purgatory's macabre centerpiece: the six-man gallows.

The horse team drew to a stop and there was a murmur of voices. Rook Skilled her hearing to catch what they said.

"We didn't think we had anyone coming in," an Avanish accent said.

It was Pit who replied. "These are more women from the Conventicle of Magpies. We're under orders to bring any of the Magpie's brood here on capture."

"How many of them?"

"A lucky four."

The Avanish man chuckled. "Right place, right time, eh? I'm sure you'll get a fat bonus for that catch."

"I hope so," said another voice. It took a moment for Rook to recognize it was Cian, speaking in perfect Avanish tones. "I'm sick of running around after them."

"Too right," the man replied. "Go on in and park up. I'll send word ahead that we have four new chicks for our nest." He chuckled again, this time at his own joke. "Bloody women naming themselves after birds. Who do they think they are?"

Rook pulled back her Skill as the wagon moved forward again. She glanced up at the barred window, though she knew it was futile. She'd see nothing more here than she had on the journey. Yet she still peered at the darkness through the bars, hoping to glimpse even a single star. Was that what Magpie was doing inside, if she was lucky enough to be near a window? Did she hold any hope that she would be free again? If she was the formidable woman Rook thought she was, Magpie was already formulating a plan of her own. If all went well now, she wouldn't need it.

The police wagon came to a stop. It rocked as Cian and Pit descended. Rook closed her eyes, waiting for them to unlock the door, and for their mission to begin.

FOURTEEN

Just as Rook had said, getting in was the simple part. With their Stamchester police uniforms, Jaguar and Pit gave the prison guards nothing to suspect. On their release from the van, the chains that bound them to the floor were replaced with manacles, both wrist and ankle. Rook glanced over her shoulder and caught Pit's eye. He gave her a near-imperceptible nod. From here on, until they escaped back across the bridge again, she and the others were alone.

Their new guards slung chains between them, connecting all four women in a solemn procession. Or at least it would've been solemn, if they'd been condemned to die there. As it was, they hadn't, and their single-file progress was a procession of determination.

A cadre of guards flanked them as they trooped deeper into the prison. Purgatory's inside was as grim as its outside. The walls of its narrow corridors had once been whitewashed, but now lingered under decades of grime. Green paint on the many iron gates and bars was brittle, flaking off as rust erupted from within. The noise of the men inside, for they were all men, was so thunderous Rook wanted to tone down her hearing with her Skill. But she knew it would be a waste of blood, even if it would have dulled the crassness slung their way.

"Twit-to-woo, little birdies."

"Bring those chicks over here so we can take a peek under their feathers."

Their guards did little to assuage the vulgar comments, though it didn't surprise any of them. Nor did their references to birds. Most women inside prison walls were vagrants, drunks, or accused of prostitution, but not in Purgatory. The Avanish reserved Purgatory for the worst, and the worst women in the city were those in the Conventicle.

Rook lost count of the number of gates they passed through, and try as she might, she couldn't orient herself to figure out which of the six wings they were in. Eventually the guards drew to a stop outside an empty holding cell flanked on one side by another, occupied by a large group of men. On seeing the four women, the men erupted into jeers and catcalls. Some rushed forward and thrust their arms through the bars like groping tentacles.

"Be grateful we're not throwing you in with this lot," one guard said as he released the chain that bound them in a line. It fell to the painted concrete floor with a thick clunk. "Every one of them would split you in two, given half a chance."

One by one, the guards shoved the little group into the cell. Rook was the last propelled inside. Before the guard slung her in, he snagged her by the elbow. "I'd split you in two given a quarter of a chance, you wee beauty. And I bet you'd even thank me for it."

Had circumstances been different and her focus not been on rescuing Magpie, Rook wouldn't have hesitated to headbutt him hard enough to break his skinny nose. Instead, she gave him her best blank stare. Unable to get the rise he desired, he shoved her into the cell with more force than necessary and swung the heavy barred door shut behind her.

The four women clustered far away from the men and their grabbing fingers. They put their heads together, speaking as low as they could.

"This is the bin, just like the Jaguar described," Rook said. "From here they'll take us to the cells. They keep men and women separate, so we'll likely end up near where they're holding Magpie."

Sparrow spoke in her quick voice. "So we just wait?"

"Yes," Crake replied. "There are too many guards and too many gates. Even if I burned all the blood I have to speed through picking the locks, they'd still catch us."

Rook nodded. "Right. We stick to the Jaguar's instructions. Let them throw us in the cells, and we'll go from there. Crake gets herself out using her lock picks, then releases the rest of us."

Redshank remained silent through the conversation, but the darkness in her eyes said everything. Rook slipped a hand onto her shoulder and guided her away from the baying men to find some privacy.

"I need your head in the game, Red," she said as they sat on the cracking paint of the concrete floor.

"It is," Redshank replied. "I promise."

Rook drew one knee up to her chest and allowed her other leg to stretch out. Alongside Redshank's longer limbs, she looked like a child. "I know what it's like to worry about a sibling. Some days I feel like all I do is think about Isiannà. Where is she? How is she doing? Will I ever see her again, and if I do, will she be the person I remember?"

Redshank allowed her head to loll against the bars. "I can't get the sight of Green out of my mind." She squeezed her eyes shut and gestured to her face. "Even when I close my eyes, I see her. I see the blood, her legs shredded and flattened and destroyed." She touched her ears. "And all I can hear is her screaming. She was in so much pain, Rook. And even now, she's still in pain if we don't give her enough laudanum." She let out a choked laugh and opened her eyes again. "We can only afford that for a little while longer. After that, we'll need more money."

Rook nodded. "We'll all do what we can. That's part of why we need to get Magpie back. She's our protector. She's always been like a second mother. We owe it to her to get her out, but we all know there's selfishness in what we're doing too. We need her."

"You're not wrong, Rook," Red replied. She drew both legs up and hugged them tight to her chest. Her knees muffled her words. "We're going to get her out, right?"

"We'll get her out," Rook said. Her conviction was honest. "It might take a few days, but we'll make it work. The guards don't know our intentions, and they won't suspect we're as Skilled as we are." She let out a hollow chuckle. "A man never thinks a woman can be more Skilled than he is."

Redshank allowed herself a thin laugh. "You're not wrong there either."

They waited for near two hours amid the baying abuse of the men before anyone returned. Four guards trooped to their cell, accompanied by a formidable-looking woman in a uniform more like Miss Vost's pinafore than a prison guard's. The men in the next cell renewed their jeering at the appearance of another female.

"I love a woman in uniform," one said.

Another jerked a thumb at Rook and the others. "Forget them! Take me into a cell and have your way with me!"

The woman, whose face was smooth and hard as granite, pointed to the cell. "Please extract one of them for me."

Two of the guards did as they were told and pulled the nearest body out. He was the man who'd spoken second.

"Bring him to me."

Again, the guards did her bidding. The prisoner was three heads taller than her, and he exposed two rows of crooked teeth when he leered anew and tried to speak more lewdness to her.

"That's it, my lovely. I want you to—"

He never got to finish his sentence. The woman withdrew a spiked baton from underneath her pinafore and shoved it into his most tender part with the force of a landslide. The man crumpled to the ground, sucking in a shuddering breath. His compatriots in the bin made a chorus of groans and squeaks and clutched at themselves, their faces bloodless with shock.

The woman turned to them and slid her baton back into the folds of her clothing. She clasped her hands behind her back and stood as prim and proper as a governess, as if she'd never held a weapon in her life.

"Now, gentlemen," she said in clipped Avanish tones, "we'll have no more of that nonsense, shall we?" The men shrank back into the far reaches of the holding cell, eliciting no further hoots, hollers, or crass words. The woman tapped the crumpled form of the injured man with her fine leather boot. "Please place him back inside."

The guards, whose faces were as pasty as the prisoners', once more did as she told them. The woman spun on her heel with military precision and turned her attention to the four women in the cell. Rook took in her sharp and solid features and the straightness of her stature. She was not someone to turn your back on.

"Ladies," she said, gesturing for a guard to open the cell door, "I am Matron Avery, and I look after all female prisoners here. You're to come with me at once. You will strip, bathe, and make yourselves available for a medical examination."

Though Jaguar had warned Rook of this, it still brought a queasy chill to her stomach. This was why Kestrel had to remain behind. If they hadn't figured out her anatomy by now, they would do so during an examination. Under other circumstances, stripping would've made Rook fear too. Many thieves, such as herself, kept lock picking kits in the heels of their boots. But they didn't need to worry about that. Crake had her own ways of concealing things.

"Come along," Matron Avery said as the prison guards opened the cell door and reattached their shackles. "We don't have all day."

This time they walked in single file, but the guards didn't chain them together. They headed through more gates and turns than Rook could count, and by the time they reached a flight of stairs, her head spun. But instead of walking upward as she expected, Avery directed them to descend. Rook's face tightened. There was a subterranean level to Purgatory? The Jaguar hadn't told them that. The same feeling of strangeness, of something not being right, returned. Regardless, they went down. What could they do?

The stench of fetid river water permeated through the ground. The air was damp, and rivulets of water ran down the irregular stone walls. This place felt ancient, as if it had been here far longer than the city of Stamchester.

When they arrived, they found their destination was a dim, green gaslit room. It was long, with bays of beds dressed with crisp white linen. With the cloth partitions drawn back, it was clear none of the beds were occupied. Rook's belly chilled further. Though she'd never been to prison before, this seemed highly unusual.

"Now, girls," Matron Avery said, "I'll assign each of you a bed. You will draw the partitions, remove your clothing including shoes, change into the gown provided, and lie down on the bed. There you will wait until the doctor comes to you. Do you understand?" Their reply was lackluster, but Avery accepted it. "Please remember that there are four prison guards in the room, plus more outside. Don't try anything clever." Her hand twitched beside her concealed truncheon. "You won't come out the better for it, I assure you. You don't know who you're dealing with."

The members of the Conventicle nodded their understanding, though they exchanged humorous glances when she turned away. Avery didn't know who she was dealing with either.

The matron plucked up a clipboard and pencil and set to work. She noted down the vital details of each woman beside the number of the bed they assigned to her. Rook found herself in bay three. Although she was certain she and the others could take down the guards and the matron without difficulty, they still didn't know where Magpie was being held. Until they did, they needed to play along.

She stripped off her frock coat, shirt, and trousers, and set her boots under the bed. The hospital gown was rough-spun undyed cotton, and its surface rasped along her skin. As she lay on the bed, she glanced at the pulled partition around her, half-certain she saw the glint of a peeping eye through the small gap between the heavy curtains. A guard, she thought with a sneer, trying to glimpse a naked woman. She stretched her legs out and laid her hands at her sides, watching where the curtains didn't quite meet, but the eye never returned.

It wasn't long before Matron Avery returned with her clipboard, this time at the side of a man Rook assumed to be the doctor. He was of middling height and age, with a bushy mustache that attached directly to her side whiskers. He wore a suit that had once been grand but now edged towards shabby, and he had a demeanor that gave the impression of permanent stress.

Matron Avery ran her finger along the page where she'd recorded Rook's details. "This one has given her name as Reb Artur." Rook grimaced at the Avanish mispronunciation of her name. *Rébh*, she thought. *It's Rébh.*

The immediate upward snap of the doctor's head interrupted her irritation. "Artur, is that what you said?"

Matron Avery scrunched her brows and double checked what she had written. "Yes. Reb Artur."

The doctor snapped his fingers, and a nurse appeared, rolling in a metal trolley filled with instruments and various solutions and liquids in bottles and flasks. Rook's mind clicked with understanding, bringing memories of when she was nine years old. She'd been through this before.

"I can tell you my blood type," she said. "I know it."

The doctor bristled under his mustache and took up her arm. There was something jerky about his movements, as if he was trying to contain a bubbling emotion. He turned her arm over, inspecting the needle marks on her skin. "I'm sure you can. It looks like you're a prolific Skiller, hmm?" He didn't wait for a reply, and instead held out a hand. The nurse placed a thin belt into his grip. "No doubt you use plenty of donor blood and you know what type you need. Regardless," he continued as he tightened the belt around her arm, "I need to see for myself."

His voice dropped on the last sentence, as if she was an unopened chest and he was about to reveal what treasures lay within. He clicked his fingers, and the nurse furnished him with a steel-needle syringe. Rook didn't flinch as he plunged it into one of her veins, extracting the vital red from within. The doctor bustled to the tray the nurse had wheeled in and turned his back to Rook, doing whatever it was he did to reveal her type. He held the vial of blood aloft, swirling it as the color changed. His shoulders slumped as the liquid turned orange.

"She's a One," he said, slamming the stoppered vial on the tray. "She mustn't be the right Artur. Dammit." He hung his head as he spoke to Matron Avery. "Are you sure she said Artur? I thought we were onto something."

Rook shot upward, a trickle of red running down her arm. "What do you mean, the right Artur?" she asked. All her mind's eye could see was Isianná's face. "What's the right kind?"

The doctor cast her a side-eyed glare. "It's none of your business. Remember your place, prisoner."

Curiosity and ire rising in tandem, Rook slid off the bed. Her bare feet hit the whitewashed floor.

"Guards!" Avery cried.

Rook stood with her elbows bent and her chest heaving, ready for a fight but wanting information. Panic loosened her tongue and words spilled she knew she shouldn't say. "I've been looking for my sister. She disappeared some time ago. Her name was Isianná and she was a Zero. Is that what you thought I'd be? Do you know where my sister is?"

The doctor turned to face her and squinted his eyes. They disappeared under his substantial eyebrows. "I can see it, you know. You look like her."

All sense escaped her. Their mission disappeared from her mind. Rook launched forward, screeching "Where is she?" Instead of words, her answer came in the form of Avery's baton striking across her shoulders. Rook lumbered under the blow and, thoughts and Skill slowed by pain, she found herself in the iron grip of two guards.

Forced to her knees, she glanced up at the doctor. "Please, tell me where she is. I need to know. I need to tell our mother!"

The doctor's face softened with a smile and for the briefest of moments, hope bloomed. But then he spoke. "I don't suppose you have any other sisters, do you? Even a brother would do." The entire room shook with Rook's fury. The doctor shook his head and gave a wry laugh. "She's not what we need. Take three pints from her and send it for storage. We can use it anyway. That'll subdue her enough to stop this nonsense. Let's move on to the others and get this over with."

Rook struggled so hard the guards summoned another of their fellows to keep her down. Eventually they shackled her to the bed as the nurse came in with the needle and waiting vials.

"Where is my sister?" she screamed again and again, until the claws of hypovolemic shock dug deep within her, and she couldn't speak around the sweating and the nausea and the pain.

One thought remained in her mind, even as weakness overcame her. From everything the doctor had said, he had known Ishie, perhaps even knew where she was.

That was Rook's confirmation. Isianná was *alive*.

FIFTEEN

All Rook could think of was Isianná. Her head filled with images of her sister, both the girl she'd known safe and sound at home, and a wraith in the horror Rook imagined for her. She might've been alive, but that didn't mean she wasn't in danger. Whoever was typing prisoners for blood was looking for Zeros, and they knew Isianná Artur was one. Ishie was the only Zero Rook had ever known. They were rare, and rarity was valuable. The question was whether Ishie was selling her blood, or if it was being stolen. The former couldn't be true. If Ishie was alive and well and making a fortune, she wouldn't have stayed away. She would have told at least Rook what she was up to. She would have sent money home. Rook dug her fingers into the flesh of her arms. The prison smock rasped against her skin. If Isianná was alive, and if this doctor knew of her, whatever the motivation, she was being held against her will.

Being subdued through a lack of blood was a novel experience, but even in her leaden state she had to admit it was an excellent strategy to control a prisoner. Rook had been impotent against the prison guards as they'd hauled her away, and she didn't know how long she'd languished on the thin pallet masquerading as a bed. As she drifted in and out of consciousness, her only comfort was that Crake too languished on another pallet. At least she wasn't alone in her weakness.

The cell was so tiny that had each woman reached out, they could have grasped one another's hands. When Rook hauled herself upright, her head spinning, Crake cracked open an eye and followed suit.

"How do you feel?"

Crake's voice broke through her thoughts and Rook scowled. "Like they've killed me, revived me, then killed me again." She winced at the croak in her voice.

Crake huffed in agreement and perched on the edge of the bed. "Are you ready to get back to work? It seemed like you lost your mind." Before Rook could explain, Crake held up a hand. "I heard what they said. They mentioned your sister. Have you got your wits about you enough to carry on?"

Rook almost bit back at the insinuation, though she didn't. With the state she'd descended into on the hospital bed, Crake was justified.

"I'm fine," she said, forcing any last hint of a croak from her voice. "Let's get it done. Magpie still needs us."

Crake held her gaze for a long moment, then nodded and reached one hand to the back of her neck. This was why Rook had brought her along. She started prodding her skin. Her fingertips landed on what she wanted at last and, with a grunt of pain, she Skilled her strength and pushed her nail through the skin. A crimson line of blood spilled down her white skin and below the collar of her prison smock. With a little work, something long and black emerged from the cut. Crake plucked it between her fingers and pulled. Rook smiled. It was her lock pick.

"Handy," she said.

Crake raised one eyebrow. "Necessary."

Rook gave a soft laugh. This was one reason Crake was the best lock pick in the business. Not only was she talented at breaking any lock, she had the means to bring equipment where others couldn't. Had she kept her kit in her boot, it would've been long gone with the rest of their clothing. It didn't take great Skill to pierce one's own skin. However, to hold something beneath it took more determination and pain than most could give.

"Doesn't that hurt?" Rook asked.

"Of course," Crake said as she wiped off the blood on her coarse sheet.

In authentic Crake style, she offered no further explanation. Rook considered the length of iron that had just been inside Crake's body, her eyes following the crook at its top. A cold shudder threatened to pass through her. What Crake did was something Rook could never do. Sometimes she wondered what else the woman hid under her skin.

"You don't have a knife in your arm or something, do you?" Rook asked.

"Knives are a no-no," Crake said as she kneeled in front of the locked door. "They do too much damage going out and in. Not worth it."

Rook blinked at the unexpected answer. Crake strained to see as far up and down the corridor as possible. Rook pressed her head against the cell bars and did the same. From both the sight of empty cells and the lack of other voices, they were the only residents of the wing. Whether that was because of a lack of female criminals or their status as members of the Conventicle painting them as more dangerous, Rook didn't know. Whatever the reason, it worked to their advantage.

As Crake worked the lock pick with her deft fingers, Rook gave a stage-whisper into the corridor. "Red? Sparrow? Are you there?"

At first only her own voice came back at her. Then came a low, "We're here." The click of a lock followed, and Rook turned to see Crake pull open the barred door.

"You did it," she said.

Crake flashed her a rare grin. "I always do."

Still slow enough to avoid unexpected creaks and groans, she pulled the door open the rest of the way. Rook Skilled her hearing, but found nothing other than Redshank and Sparrow's breathing. She stepped into the dark corridor to see her friends pressed against the bars in a cell down the line. She kept a lookout again as Crake set to releasing the others. Soon enough, all four stood in nothing but bare feet and prison smocks, illuminated by dull green gaslight.

"How far up are we?" Rook asked.

Sparrow flitted and jerked a thumb back at their cell. "Red lifted me up to the window. We're on the top floor, facing north, which means we're in the furthest block from the Old Allen Bridge."

"The new bridge is there if we need it," Rook said. "It'll bring us out on the wrong side of the river, but we'll make it work. For now, we need to find Magpie. We'll worry about where we're going once we get out."

The intention was, and always had been, to escape onto the outside of the building and climb. What none of them had counted on was having blood taken. They'd known it might take a few days to get out, but all had counted on having reserves for Skill. Rook closed her eyes and took a moment to take stock. She wasn't back to normal, and wouldn't be until her body had time to recover, or she had access to an infusion. Neither of those were options in the moment.

She opened her eyes and caught the other girls' attention. "We need to leave enough blood so we can Skill out of here. I don't know about you, but I'm more depleted than I've been in years. No Skilling unless absolutely necessary."

"Agreed," Redshank said. "The last thing we want is to find Magpie and then get caught. We'll all be for the noose if that happens."

Rook suppressed a shudder at Red's frankness, but there was no doubting the truth of her words. If the guards caught them, there would be no mercy and no hesitation. A phantom rope coiled around her neck, and she just stopped herself from touching her skin. She had too much to live for, even more now that she knew Ishie was out there somewhere. *Or in here somewhere*, she thought. *What if they're holding her right under my nose? What if I don't see it?*

She had no time for suppositions. Rook stilled her hands at her sides. It was bad enough she'd lost it when the doctor had said her sister's name. *The priority right now is Magpie*, she told herself. *Anything else is secondary.*

"We'll stick together as we search so we can look out for one another." Rook pulled every ounce of authority into her voice. It wasn't for the benefit of the others. It was only for herself. "We'll comb the block floor by floor, cell by cell. With luck, the rest of this wing is as empty as this part."

Redshank folded her arms, but nodded. "Agreed. Although considering the overflow of inmates in processing, I can only imagine they'll start filling up."

The wing proved unnerving in its emptiness. The small group roamed the corridors in eerie silence, peering through bars into every dark corner of the cells. They didn't know where Magpie might be or what state she would be in. If they'd beaten her or weakened her through continuous blood removal, she mightn't have the strength to cry out if she saw them. If unconscious, she wouldn't be able to see them at all.

Rook stopped short when she spied a lump lying in the corner of a cell. Magpie? Her hands were on the bars, ready to Skill them apart, when Crake called to her.

"Don't waste your power," the pale woman said. She waved her lock pick, the fingers grasping it still red with her own dried blood. "I'll get you in. Those bars are reinforced iron. You'd kill yourself trying to force them apart."

Rook stepped back and gestured for Crake to move in. As the other woman worked, she took the time to school herself. *Calm down, you idiot*, Rook thought. *Use the brains you were born with.*

She was inside the cell as soon as Crake picked the lock. Rook went to her knees beside the lump, her heart pounding, and reached for it. The cell stank of disinfectant, and whatever was underneath the threadbare covering was unnerving in its stillness.

As soon as she put pressure on the form, it collapsed. Rook cursed and rose again. "It's just a pile of moldy blankets." She stalked out of the cell and her temper threatened to spike, but she forced it down. "Let's move on."

They combed the corridors cell by cell, finding nothing but more ancient blankets and the stink of industrial cleaner.

"I don't understand why this place is so empty," Redshank said as they completed another corridor. "It doesn't make sense. Stamchester prisons are always full to the brim."

"The rest of the place seemed full enough," Sparrow said. "I don't like this one bit. And why is it so clean? The holding cell downstairs stank to the sky, but they've gone to a lot of trouble up here."

Rook grasped the cold concrete corner of the junction between two corridors and eased her head outward. Without Skill, she was more reliant on her natural sight and hearing, and that required far more care in her movements.

"There's something not right about this," she replied, keeping her voice low. The corridor was clear, and she gestured for the others to step forward. "It's almost like they've cleared the place out to make ready for something different. This place smells more like a sanitorium than a prison. Considering they typed us when we came in, I wonder if we were the unexpected beginning of a new project."

"What new project?" Redshank asked.

Rook pressed her lips together and shook her head, not quite believing the conclusion she had come to. "Maybe the authorities are going to take prisoners' blood."

"That's illegal!" Red's voice pitched too high and echoed down the corridor. She clamped her hand over her mouth before Crake could do it for her.

They all stilled, peering in different directions and waiting for the incoming guards. But no one came.

"I know it's illegal," Rook said when she was sure they weren't heard, "but since when have Governor Dreidchain and this city ever worried about what's legal and what's not for the Saosuíasei? Think about it. They can do what they want inside these walls. The people who come into this place don't get out. What if they don't limit inmates to criminals? The city got used to people disappearing and showing up dead because of Billy Drainer. If more people go missing and stay missing, we'll get used to that too." Isiannâ's face flashed in her mind. Her emotions rose in a turgid mix of fear and hope. "Maybe Dreidchain's going to imprison people here and take their blood over and over, just like in the Bloodhouses."

"What does he want with so much blood?" Sparrow asked, hopping from foot to foot as her ire rose.

Crake replied with a single word. "Power."

It commanded a response of silence. Rook drew her hands into fists to control her sudden rage. Crake was right. It all made sense. The building tensions in the city were coming to a head. Everyone could sense it. The inevitable conclusion? An all-out war, and war required blood. Dreidchain, clever, clever Dreidchain, was already three moves ahead.

"I don't think we're going to find Mama in this block," Rook said at length, "because I don't think she's ever been here. This isn't a women's wing. It's more like a blood wing. Magpie must be somewhere else, and that complicates things."

"We're going to need a disguise," Sparrow said as she plucked at her prison smock.

"I don't think different clothes will be enough," Rook replied. She glanced at her bare feet and drummed her toes on the cold floor. "Although boots would be a benefit. None of the guards are female. Even in uniform, they'll spot us right away."

"So what do we do?" Redshank asked.

Rook's mind whirled. Then an orb of light at the far end of the corridor drew her eye. The moon had passed into the frame of the barred window. Rook pointed and took to her feet.

"We go out, and we go up."

The foursome headed back up the corridor, no longer peeping in every cell but hurrying past as they moved towards the edge of the building. The stink of the converging rivers grew stronger as they approached the outer wall, competing with the burning stench of endless disinfectant.

When they reached the end of the corridor, Rook considered their options. The window bars were the same reinforced iron as the cells, but unlike the cells, there were no locks to pick. The bars were attached by a frame, not embedded in the brickwork. Had it been the latter, things would have been more difficult. But as Rook considered the sight before her, a plan formed.

"Crake," she said, "you told me trying to bend the bars alone could kill me. But if all four of us Skill together, we might just be able to wrench the entire frame out with none of us being too depleted. Thoughts?"

Crake considered, then gave a nod. "It might work. It's less dangerous, at least."

"Let's do it," Redshank said, reaching into the deep recess of the window.

It took some effort for all four to get a good grip. Sparrow, being small with short arms, struggled to reach.

"When we do this," Rook said, "we'll increase the Skill slowly. Too much too fast, and we'll jerk ourselves backward and create enough noise to bring every prison guard running. If we do it carefully, we'll conserve blood too. Ready?" She waited for the chorus of nods. "All right, on three. One, two, three!"

As soon as the strength in all their hands increased, the iron frame shuddered. Rook's arms burned with the Skill flowing through them. "We need more."

At her word, the women each willed their strength to rise. They jerked backward as the frame moved its first inch, sending a puff of mortar and brick dust into their faces.

"Steady," Rook said, "but a little more." The frame moved again, pulling bricks loose around it. "One more increase. Get ready to catch it when it comes free."

Blood burning within her, Rook willed her strength to build a fraction more. With a final jolt, the entire iron frame caved in, bringing parts of the wall with it. Rook shifted straight away, taking the weight of the bars in her arms. The others did the same, and together they lowered the frame to the floor.

"Well, that worked," Crake said.

"And it was less dangerous." Sparrow glanced at her feet. "Though not without injury. I think a brick landed on my foot. Ouch!"

She hopped on her uninjured appendage, gesturing at the reddening patch atop her other foot.

"Let's hope it won't stop you climbing." Rook stuck her head out the new hole in the wall, "because that's what we're about to do."

One by one, the members of the Conventicle clambered out of their makeshift exit. There were grooves between the bricks large enough for fingers and toes to grip, but they only made it onto the prison roof by virtue of their Skill. By the time she perched on the roof tiles, which were hard and glittered with the beginnings of frost, fatigue was encroaching along Rook's limbs. From the drawn features of her compatriots, she knew they suffered too.

"We can't keep going like this," Redshank said, her words beginning to labor. "By the time we reach Magpie, we'll have nothing left."

Rook shifted onto the apex of the prison roof, staring out at the darkness of the city interspersed with the glimmer of gas lamps. Redshank was right. They needed blood. The wind whipped up, passing through her prison smock as if it wasn't even there. A shiver ran unchecked along her spine.

"We need blood and we need clothing," she said, "and I know where we can find just that. We'll take back what they took from us. We'll go back to the infirmary."

Crake grunted. "Do we know where it is? All I could tell was that it was underground."

"We didn't walk for very long from the holding cells until the stairway," Sparrow said. Her quick eyes glinted in the moonlight. "We came in from the south and moved northwest, so if we climb down in that area, we'll be in the best position to figure out the rest of the way."

Rook's memory sparked. "There was an outer door in that stairwell. If we find that, we can get back in."

Redshank huffed in mock irritation. "I thought we were breaking out of this prison, not into it."

Crake didn't share in her humor. "If I can't pick the lock, we'll need to Skill our way in again. And once we're in, we'll have to fight whoever we come across. With all this blood burning on no reserves, we're getting into dangerous territory."

"I know," Rook said, "but it's that or we climb off this roof and right out of the prison, and leave Magpie here to rot. I don't think any of us wants to do that. Am I right?" She looked at each of the other women one by one, and each nodded back at her. "Then we give this a shot. We owe it to Mama."

SIXTEEN

They kept low as they made their way along the roofs, following Sparrow's sense of direction. There were no guards at this height, and the lookout towers on the perimeter wall were more decorative than functional. The tiles below their hands and feet were both rough and slippery, the texture cutting into their fingertips yet giving little grip.

Rook's stomach twisted as they made it to the leftmost point of the hexagon. Her left foot disappeared beneath her and she jerked sideways. She yelped as she slid down the steep roof side, the skin of her knees and fingers and palms ripping against the tiles. By instinct, she dug down hard with her Skill and the roof tiles cracked beneath her strength. Her head reeled and bright lights blinked in her vision as her body screamed at her to stop burning its vitality as more seeped from the new wounds in her skin. Regardless, she brought her fall under control just as her feet jutted out over the edge of the roof. Cracked tiles and debris slid past her, plunging to the prison grounds below. Rook scrambled a little way up again, clinging to the desperate hope no one had seen as hard as she clung to the broken tiles. No siren sounded. She let out a long breath. Perhaps they hadn't seen.

Crake edged her way down the slope and pulled Rook back to the apex again. "Are you all right?" she asked.

Even though her head swam and fatigue hummed in every inch of her body, Rook nodded. "I'll be fine once I get some of my blood back."

The pale woman kept a protective hand on Rook's shoulder as they made their way to where Sparrow and Redshank perched, waiting with wide and worried eyes.

Rook waved their concern away. "Is this where we want to be?"

Sparrow nodded. "To the best of my understanding, it is. We'll at least be near that door into the stairwell."

"Let's hope so," Rook replied, "and let's hope my little fall hasn't brought a patrol running." She peered over the edge of the roof again. "I can't see any movement, but that doesn't mean they aren't on their way."

She closed her eyes and steeled herself for the effort of Skilling to soften her landing. She was already in the dangerous territory Crake had alluded to. One miscalculation, and she would find herself in hypovolemic shock again and powerless to escape. She opened her eyes again at the touch of Crake's hand on her shoulder again.

"Climb on my back and I'll bring you down," she said. "If you use Skill, you'll burn out, and if you don't, you'll break your legs."

Though her natural pig-headed stubbornness threatened to make itself known, Rook forced it down and nodded. "I'm not going to fight you on that one."

"Good," Crake said, her tone deadpan, "because you're too weak to win."

If it was a joke, Rook couldn't tell. She had no time to consider it as Crake swept her into her arms and followed as Sparrow and Redshank leaped from the roof.

They were on the ground before Rook could blink. Crake grunted and stumbled, sliding Rook onto her own feet again. The other woman reached for the wall, leaning into the bricks. "You might win now," she said with the merest hint of mirth in her voice, "because after that landing, I'm not sure I have anything left."

"Don't give up yet, Crake." Rook steadied her friend on her feet. "We're nearly there. You still have your lock pick?" Crake withdrew the long black tool from her smock's pocket. Rook nodded. "Let's find this door and get our blood back."

Sparrow's sense of direction lived up to its legend. She'd brought them down within feet of the doorway, providing there wasn't more than one, of course. But, Rook thought as Crake set to work on the lock, they'd handle whatever faced them. They had no choice.

Within minutes Crake had pulled the doors back, revealing a set of descending stairs that looked much like those they'd been taken down before.

"I think this is the place, all right," Redshank said.

The four women disappeared into the darkness, the familiar stench of river damp and bleach rising once again. There were no prison guards in the corridor, though Rook hadn't thought there would be. The only guard they'd had was the men who'd escorted them. Otherwise, the corridors had been empty. That was until they reached the infirmary itself, of course. But while they might be weakened, they had the element of surprise. She had to believe it would be enough.

Rook peered around the edge of the wall. At the end of the long corridor, a gas lamp illuminated the doors to the infirmary. One prison guard lounged beside it with his eyes closed. Rook knew enough not to count him as an easy target. If he'd Skilled his hearing, he might already know they were there. She gestured to the others, placing one finger against her lips to signal silence. Sparrow pointed at herself, then at the guard. Rook nodded in return. Of all of them, Sparrow was the lightest on her feet.

The small woman darted forward, her bare soles making no sound on the concrete. In an instant, she disappeared. A second later, the guard slumped to the ground, his fall cushioned and his yell silenced by Sparrow's hands. She lowered his unconscious body to the floor and slid him into the darkest corner. Rook and the others slipped to her side.

"Nice work," Rook said, tipping Sparrow a wink.

The other woman smiled, then tilted to the side, just catching herself on the wall before she fell. "Hard work," she said. "I can't Skill anymore, not until I get a top-up."

Crake grunted and pressed her fist into the palm of her other hand. She cracked the knuckles. "Leave it to Red and me."

Redshank rose on the balls of her bare feet, vibrating with tension. "I'm going to enjoy this."

"Not too much," Rook said. "Don't push yourself too hard."

Red gave a wicked grin. "I don't need Skill to do serious damage."

Rook shook her head, returning the smile. "All right. There'll only be a handful of guards in there, plus any nurses. You two focus on knocking out the guards. Sparrow and I will back the nurses into a corner and tie them up if we can. Then we'll get our blood, our clothes, and find Magpie."

Crake nodded. "And then we'll get out of here."

The element of surprise served them well. By the time the doors exploded inward and collided with the walls inside, Crake and Redshank were already on top of the two guards. Only one nurse was present, for the beds were empty, and together Sparrow and Rook rushed her. She screeched as they grabbed her arms and forced her down onto the bed she'd been stripping. Rook seized a nearby rag and shoved it into her mouth, stifling her shrieks.

"Get the sheets," Rook said. Her head spun and new sweat formed on her brow from the effort, but still she pressed the nurse onto the bed. "We'll tie her to the bed."

Sparrow, her breathing labored, did as she was told. She tore the sheets into enough strips to bind the nurse by the arms, waist, legs and ankles. They worked to secure her, and the woman's face grew redder as her terror rose. Sympathy pricked unbidden in Rook's chest and though she tried to smother it, the feeling kept emerging.

She glanced up to see Crake and Red dragging the incapacitated guards into screened cubicles, likely to hide them in the beds. Rook leaned over the nurse and locked her gaze, placing a hand on the other woman's neck. "We don't want to hurt you. That's why we haven't knocked you out like the prison guards. We just want our clothes and our blood, and then we'll leave you alone. Do you understand me?"

The nurse's entire body shook with fear, and her eyes were as wide as porcelain plates. But she managed a jerky nod.

"Where's the blood you took from us?" Rook asked. "Is it still here?"

The nurse nodded and worked her mouth against the rag inside it. Though she hesitated to do so, Rook fished it from between her lips.

"It's in the refrigeration cupboard in the side room," she said, the words thick from the dryness of her mouth. "I'll help you infuse it. Please, don't kill me. It's not my fault what they're doing. I just do what I'm told."

Seizing the opportunity, Rook narrowed her eyes. "They're planning on taking blood from all the prisoners, aren't they?" She flexed her fingers at the base of the nurse's neck as if she intended to squeeze, although she didn't.

The intimidation worked, and the nurse squeaked. "Not just prisoners, but anyone they bring in off the streets. I heard the doctor say they're going to lift Saosuíasei who've done nothing wrong and put them in the north wing, and keep them there to take their blood. That's why they've cleared the place out."

Rook flexed her fingers again. "You have good ears. Did you hear where they're keeping the Magpie?"

Tears slid down the sides of the nurse's face and disappeared below her white cap. "She's here, in the back ward. They've been doing something to her." At that phrase, Rook's expression darkened. The nurse squeaked in panic again. "I swear I don't know what it is. I never work in the back ward. I promise! I swear! Please just don't hurt me!"

"How many people work in the back ward?" Rook asked.

"At the moment there'll only be one nurse, but there are four prison guards in there because it's the Magpie. They had two at first, but she was too much for them."

Rook released the nurse's neck and forced the rag back into her mouth. Sparrow secured it with another strip of cloth.

"You mean she was in this part of the prison the whole time?" she asked. "We could have got her from here?"

"We'd never have known," Rook countered. "And they took so much blood from us, we wouldn't have been in any fit state to get out of here with her."

Sparrow secured the cloth with a tight knot. "What are they doing to her?"

"Whatever it is, it won't be good. And neither is what Dreidchain's planning on doing, because you know all this"—Rook gestured at the rest of the prison—"is his idea. What does he want all this blood for?"

Crake approached them, looking wan and drawn. "Like I said before, power." She leaned against the bed, her entire body sagging with fatigue. "He's going to steal our blood, then use it to crush us once and for all. It's sick."

Rook and Sparrow left the writhing, sobbing nurse's bedside and pulled the curtains closed around the bed. Crake and Redshank had done the same around the unconscious guards.

"It's insane," Rook said, "but for now, let's steal some of that blood back. We don't have enough time for anything more than a vial each to take the edge off, but we'll deal with it. Magpie's here, right under our noses, but that also means there are four guards close by. We need to be quick, but still careful. Make sure you pick the right blood type, and don't scrimp on the cleanliness. The last thing we want is anyone getting sick, or even dying."

The other women nodded, and they headed for the side room. Every minute that ticked by felt like an hour as they injected their fresh supplies. Redshank and Sparrow disappeared to find their clothing. As her fatigue and weakness lifted, Rook's mind whirred into action. If there were four guards and one nurse, they were outnumbered. But the nurse would be no more a foe than the other had been, and once they freed Magpie, she might help them. *Might.* The nurse's words echoed in Rook's mind. *They've been doing something to her.* What was it? What sort of state was Magpie in? Even freed, would she be able to help them?

There was a thud as a pile of clothing appeared in front of her, along with a pair of familiar too-large men's boots.

"Our clothes hadn't gone for incineration yet, it seems," Sparrow said. "A lucky turn."

Rook nodded as she reached for her shirt. "Let's hope the luck keeps turning in our favor."

Dressed and with their blood supplies renewed, the members of the Conventicle were ready. It didn't take long to locate the door to what the nurse had called the back ward.

"We go for the guards first," Rook said. "We'll deal with anyone else afterwards. Are we all ready?"

Redshank said, "Ready and able," and balled her hands into fists.

Rook drew in a deep breath and faced the door to the other ward. "On the count of three, we go in. One, two, three!"

The hum of Skill in her veins was like a drug. Rook burst through the doors with the others at an unnatural speed and felled the prison guards one by one. She swept the legs out from under her victim before he could react and pinned him to the ground, switching her Skill from speed to strength in an instant.

"Where's the Magpie?" she said. The guard struggled, so she channeled her mother. She grabbed one of his ears and twisted. "Where's the Magpie?"

The prison guard keened like a child and writhed below her, but Rook's strength was too much. His hand grappled for the baton he'd dropped in the struggle, but Rook kicked it away.

She wrenched his ear again, threatening to rip it right off. "Don't make me ask you again."

The voice that answered wasn't his. "I'm here, Rook."

Mama Magpie's words were strained in a way Rook had never heard before. She released the guard's ear but kept him secured to the ground. "Mama?"

A figure rose in the bed furthest from her. Magpie's skin was bereft of makeup, her signature black lips now odd and pale. Dark circles lingered under her eyes like the opposite of crescent moons, and even from a distance, Rook could see her tremble.

"Hel—"

Before the guard under her could finish his word, Rook slammed a hand over his mouth. He renewed his struggle, bucking and trying to bite her. Fatigue was encroaching again, so Rook did what she knew would be most effective with least effort. She grabbed a fistful of his hair and slammed his head against the concrete floor. With a groan and a final keen, he grew limp.

Rook released him and ran to Magpie, vaguely aware of her compatriots incapacitating their victims too. Crake, who'd made short work of her guard, was binding a terrified nurse to the wooden chair behind her desk. Magpie had sunk back onto the bed. Her hair spread like a jagged black and white halo around her, and her breath came in quick gasps.

Rook grabbed her hand. "What have they done to you, Mama?"

"Nothing that will keep me down," Magpie replied, summoning a grin that spoke all the confidence Rook knew she had. Sparrow, Crake, and Redshank appeared at the bedside, each grasping for a piece of their beloved leader. Magpie managed a low chuckle. "Why did you come for me, you silly girls?"

"How could we not come for you?" Rook asked. "You're our mama."

"We'd never abandon you," Sparrow said, smoothing down a section of Magpie's wild hair.

Crake retracted her hand from Magpie's arm and glanced around. Rook followed suit, glancing at the felled guards littering the floor. "We need to get out of here, and fast," Crake said. "We don't know the routines in here. There could be a guard change at any moment."

Redshank slipped an arm around her shoulders as Magpie struggled to rise again. "What time is it?" she asked.

Rook's hand reached for her father's pocket watch, and there was a moment of panic before she realized she hadn't taken it into the prison. She bolted across the room to what she assumed was the nurse's station, ignoring the hoarse and muffled screeches of the bound nurse. Sure enough, there was a small carriage clock there.

"It's almost midnight," she said.

Magpie's already wan face paled. "There's a change at midnight, and they're never late." She swung her legs over the bed and stood, leaning on Redshank. "We need to leave now."

"Can you make it?" Sparrow asked.

Magpie grunted. "What choice do I have?"

Rook returned to them and, spying a pair of canvas slippers, dropped to the ground to place them onto Magpie's feet. "We move into the extraction plan now," she said. "We can get out into the yard the way we came in. Then we make a choice. We either go south towards the Old Allen Bridge, or north to the New Eastraine. Either way, we'll either need a lot of blood to fight our way out, or a lot of luck."

"Or both," Crake said, "but we don't have time to infuse."

"Grab as many vials from the refrigeration cupboard as you can," Rook said as she rose once more. "We might as well take what's ours."

Magpie's eyes widened. "Take nothing marked with a black label."

The fear that spread across her face told Rook everything. Whatever the doctors had done to her, it was something to do with that black label. Rage rose hot within her.

Sparrow and Redshank went to grab the blood as Crake slipped in to support Magpie. Rook shrugged off her frock coat and draped it around the older woman's shoulders. "What have they done to you?" she asked.

"Nothing that will keep me down," Magpie repeated, though this time her resolve lessened.

They crossed the room as Redshank and Sparrow finished loading a leather bag with blood. Rook glanced at the clock. Three minutes to midnight.

"Let's go," she said.

They passed the unconscious guards and the nurse, still tied to her chair and sobbing. When they moved into the outer room, all was quiet. No one stirred behind the drawn curtains. Time ticked by as they pulled the now-damaged doors open and moved into the dark corridor that would lead them to freedom. Magpie tried her best to quicken her pace, but kept stumbling and sagging against Crake. Rook's ire rose anew. Never in her life had she seen Magpie so weakened.

Voices and steady footfalls came from the far end of the corridor. Rook's throat tightened. "The change of guard. We need to get to that door."

Without hesitation, Crake adjusted her grip on Magpie and swept her into her arms. Too exhausted to fight, Magpie looped her arms around the pale woman's neck. The voices grew closer and Rook, Sparrow and Redshank took off at a run, ready to fight whatever was coming. Sparrow, the fastest of them, skidded to a halt as she reached the slanted doorway in the roof. The leather bag swung around her as she gestured to Red. "Give me a leg up."

Redshank made a stirrup with her hands and boosted the petite woman up. Sparrow shoved the doors, throwing them open once more with a resounding clang. Rook winced. The voices in the distance stopped for a moment, as if they were listening. Then their once steady steps broke into a run.

Sparrow clambered through the now-open door and reached downward. "Hurry!"

Crake reached them as the guards' whistles sounded. Rook leaped onto Redshank's hands and launched herself upward into Sparrow's waiting grip. She scrambled around, and together they grasped under Crake's arms as Red pushed from underneath. Their arms burned with Skill she didn't have to spare, but they pulled Crake and Magpie upward, all four landing in a tangle of limbs. Rook righted herself and went to grab for Redshank, only for the woman to launch herself upward in an unbelievable jump. She crashed to the gravel in an exhausted pile.

Rook kneeled beside the open doors as four prison guards appeared below, bellowing and blowing their whistles. She flashed them a salute as she slammed the doors shut, blocking them out.

She went to Redshank's side and pulled her up. "Can you walk?"

Red gasped in reply. "I'll try."

Crake had Magpie in her arms again. "North or south, Rook?"

There was no time for hesitation. Rook pointed. "North."

They took off running as fast as they could, and within seconds the door behind them burst open. The guards leaped out, the prison sirens sounding. Rook swore as they sprinted as fast as Unskilled legs could carry them. They needed more blood. The guards would be upon them in a matter of seconds, full of reserves and ready to capture them. The southern gate to the Old Allen Bridge was too far, but the northern gate was also too far. Feet wouldn't cut it.

An idea flashed in her mind, as bright as electric light. They needed wheels. There was no time to explain before she bolted off, burning blood she didn't have to spare. It was a gamble, but they had no choice.

She sped through the prison compound, the world around her whirling in a cacophony of sirens and shouts, until she came upon what she needed. She stopped and blinked. Well, almost what she needed. Rook had hoped to find a horse and cart waiting somewhere. Instead, what she found was something much better.

A motor car.

It was open-topped and gleamed in the darkness. Its owner sat in the driving seat, pulling on a pair of leather gloves. Rook rushed towards him and clamped her hands around his throat. His eyes widened in fear and recognition. It was the doctor.

"Start this thing now," she said, "or I'll cut your fat throat."

She had nothing to cut him with, but he wasn't to know that. Terrified and spluttering, the doctor reached for the ignition and turned. It took what felt like a century for the contraption's engine to turn over, but the motor car burst into life, humming and groaning and vibrating in anticipation. Rook released the doctor's neck and for a moment, his features smoothed in relief. Then she reared up and kicked out, sending him flying into the gravel and dirt. Rook glanced at the controls of the machine, only now appreciating the simplicity of a horse's reins.

"How do you make this thing move?"

She grasped the stick shift at her side and shoved it upward. She pressed a pedal. The car revved, but nothing else happened. She pressed another pedal and shoved the stick again. This time it clicked, and Rook grinned. She pressed the accelerator again. The car jolted forward.

Its engine roared under her clumsy control, and she abandoned the stick. Now it was moving. That was all that mattered. She clamped both hands on the leather-coated wheel and whirled the car around, sending gravel flying under her wheels. She pressed the pedal hard and flew through the prison ground, slamming on the third pedal as she reached her friends.

Crake flung Magpie into the rear seat and pulled herself in afterward as Sparrow and Redshank clambered aboard. The prison guards were almost upon them.

"Do you know how to drive this thing?" Sparrow squeaked.

"Nope," Rook replied.

She jammed her foot hard on the accelerator, and they took off again. The guards might keep up with their speed, but they'd be fools to challenge them. No matter how Skilled, flesh would always lose in a battle with metal.

The car growled louder and louder as they sped. All Rook knew was that they needed to go north. By this time running prison guards flanked them, and when she glanced over her shoulder, she saw several horse-drawn wagons were now in their wake.

The New Eastraine Bridge came into view. The guards had closed the wooden gates in the brick wall and were waving for her to stop. She kept her foot down.

A shot sounded. Something clanged against the side of the car and Rook jolted, seizing the steering wheel as she tried to bring the machine under control. They were firing on them.

"Get down!" she screamed.

She hunched as far as she could while still peering over the wheel, and kept her foot flat to the floor. The car roared, and smoke rose from under its bonnet, but still Rook kept going, even as the guards and their gates grew ever closer.

The motor car thundered towards them. When they realized she wouldn't stop, the men leaped aside like struck skittles. The gates disintegrated as the car smashed through them. They jolted and bumped along the New Eastraine Bridge, hammering towards the outer wall.

They smashed through the second gate. Smoke billowed from the engine as they shot over the fetid water, and for a moment Rook was sure all four wheels lifted from the ground. Leaving the prison behind, Rook let out a shriek of delight as they disappeared into Eastraine's End. It was the wrong side of the river, but they were free.

SEVENTEEN

Rook abandoned the doctor's motor car in a dark alley, and they took off on foot as fast as their depleted bodies could. By the time the group slumped in a narrow alley, disturbing a nest of feral cats that shrieked and hissed at their presence, Rook had nothing more to give. Sparrow kneeled and rummaged in the leather bag as the rest leaned against the harsh brick walls.

"It's not ideal to do this in an alleyway without a bracer," Sparrow said as she set out vials of blood, "but we'll never get home without some fuel."

Rook shut her eyes and took a few steadying breaths as she steeled herself to get up. Sparrow was right. While the hollow steel needle had brought the ability to inject new stores of blood, it came with a danger and the potential for a deadly consequence. It had become clear within a few years of blood transfusion that injecting the wrong type wasn't the only danger. Without rigorous cleanliness, the use of needles spread disease at alarming speed. The sharing of equipment such as syringes and needles had been illegal for many years.

Rook pried her eyes open again and pulled up her sleeve. At least her skin was clean. Whether the syringe needle Sparrow gave her was clean also was unknown. You didn't need to see the dirt for it to be there. But knowing they wouldn't be able to Skill their way to safety without taking on a fresh supply, she accepted the blood and made the plunge.

The familiar warmth of strength returned to her body. Rook sank against the brickwork and sighed. She took another few measured breaths.

"Might as well use this up," Sparrow said, gesturing to the bag. "In a few hours it'll be useless."

She was right. Without refrigeration, the blood would turn bad. That, Rook knew, was just another avenue to sickness and probable death.

The members of the Conventicle took on as much fuel as they could in the time they had. Rook helped Magpie with her infusion, though the new blood did little to aid her fatigue. A chill passed along Rook's spine at that. What if whatever they'd done to her caused permanent damage? What if Magpie lost her ability to Skill? She locked eyes with Magpie for a moment, and though the older woman said nothing, Rook saw the fear in her eyes. That elicited another chill. Magpie was not weak. Yet now, she was vulnerable.

Determination renewed within Rook. She discarded the needle kit she'd used on Magpie and clapped her hands. "Okay. We need to get back to the Shambles."

"I'd say we're at least two miles from the nearest bridge," Sparrow said. She flicked her gaze to Magpie, then back at Rook. "I'm not sure if we can Skill our way that far on what we have. Remember, we're still running at a loss."

"True," Rook replied. She touched her forefinger to her chin in thought. Then it came to her. "Of course!" The rest of them stared at her. "We'll call 2-7-0-5." They still stared, and she laughed. "It's a telephone number. The Jaguar has a telephone in his house. Kestrel and I saw it when we were there before. We can ask him to send a wagon for us."

Redshank frowned. "I have to ask, does anyone know how to use a telephone?"

Rook waved her off. "I drove a car today. I think I can figure out a telephone."

Crake gave the tiniest nod, though her face still pulled in a scowl. "It'll be difficult to find somewhere with a telephone, break in, use it, and get out again without being caught. Then more time before the wagon gets to us. In the meantime, they might find us if we don't keep moving."

"So we keep moving," Rook said. "You and I will find a telephone. You still have your lock picks, right?" Crake patted her left breast pocket. "Good. I'll ask for the wagon to meet us somewhere we can get to in the time it'll take for it to get to us. That way we keep moving." She pondered the details. "Buxridge Bridge. That's the best place. We'll meet there in about an hour. Do you think you can make it by then?"

Sparrow shifted from foot to foot. "It's possible. But what if we get delayed or diverted? Considering how much Dreidchain wanted Magpie, he'll fill the city with soldiers to look for us."

Rook gritted her teeth. Sparrow was right. "We'll just have to hope. I don't know what else we can do."

With that settled, Redshank and Sparrow flanked Magpie, and the three began their slow progress south. Crake and Rook set off north towards Banker's Square.

"There's bound to be a telephone in one of these office buildings," Rook said.

Crake nodded. "Most likely, but there also may be a night watchman inside, or a guard dog. Not to mention that, as Sparrow said, the entire city garrison will be after us. And that we'll soon lose the protection of darkness. The sun's going to rise in a few hours."

Rook wanted to bite back at Crake's negativity, but she knew the other woman was right. They needed to move fast. "We'll take on whatever comes."

They chose their building by how expensive it looked from the outside. Satisfied that it was affluent enough to be part of the city's telephone network, Rook and Crake slipped through a little archway that led to an interior courtyard. Rook Skilled her sight enough to see in the darkness and waved at Crake to follow. They approached a door which, if she'd got the layout of the building right, would lead them into their chosen target. Crake set to work, and within minutes the door swung open.

The interior of the building was in complete darkness. Though she knew she'd regret it, Rook Skilled her sight a little more. The hum of blood burning grew stronger in her veins. The long corridor revealed itself, and the two women crept along it, peering through every open door, hoping to find an office with a telephone. There were plenty of desks with piles of paperwork upon them, but nothing more.

Rook cursed. "Dammit."

"Let's go up," Crake said. "Perhaps there's a telephone in a room upstairs. It's something you'd find in the office of a higher-up, and those sorts of people like to reflect their status in their distance from the street."

Rook huffed a laugh. "Heaven forbid they have to dwell in the gutters with the rest of us common folk."

They ascended the stairway without incident. Neither night watchman nor dog made their presence known. And sure enough, in one of the more affluent offices upstairs, the item they desired sat upon a polished desk. Beside it was a small gas lamp, and though it was a risk, Rook turned it on, just a little. While someone might see the gleam from the street, its light would allow her to ease off on her Skill. It illuminated the clock beside it, which ticked to one o'clock as she watched. If all went well, Sparrow, Redshank, and Magpie would be halfway to the bridge by now.

Rook sat on the plush leather chair behind the desk and, sure enough, there was the telephone. The contraption was a tall frame upon which hung two bell-shaped objects. She knew enough to know that you held one to your ear and one to your mouth, though which was which was a guess. Her hands hovered over the thing, half-expecting it to bite her. She took a steadying breath, then picked up the receivers.

Nothing happened for a long moment. Then something low and tinny sounded, and she was about to Skill her hearing when she realized there was no need. Instead, she swapped the receiver at her mouth for the one at her ear, and the operator's voice sounded loud and clear.

"Hello? Hello?"

"Yes, uh, hello," Rook said.

The operator's voice was quick and officious. "Number, please."

Rook's tongue stumbled over the unfamiliar process. "Of course. Uh, it's 2-7-0-5."

"Thank you. Please hold."

The operator's voice disappeared. It seemed to take a century before anything else happened, but the operator returned. "2-7-0-5 would like to know who's calling, please."

"Uh." Rook's voice faltered again. "Tell them it's Rook."

"Rook?" the operator asked. "Did I hear that right?"

She cursed herself for using her unusual Conventicle name and swallowed. There was no going back. "Yes, that's correct."

There was a pause before the operator said, "One moment please." Another century passed before she came back again. "Putting you through to 2-7-0-5 now. Thank you."

Rook was about to thank her in return, but the line switched before she got the words out.

A new voice sounded in her ear. It was the Jaguar. "Rook? Is that you?"

Rook breathed out in relief. "Yes, it's me. We got Magpie out. I don't have time to explain it all, but we need you to send a wagon to meet us at Buxridge Bridge in half an hour."

Instead of pressing for more information, the Jaguar responded, "Will do. Good luck."

The line went silent again, and Rook replaced the receivers on the telephone stand. "Well, that worked."

"Color me surprised," Crake replied, though there was a hint of a smile on her face.

Rook turned the gas lamp off and rose from the leather chair. She Skilled her vision again and paused for a moment, glancing at the surrounding wealth. No doubt this was the office of a plump and wealthy Avanish businessman, someone like one of Dreidchain's eminent men.

Her hands twitched with the desire to swing an arm across the desk's shining top and send everything clattering to the floor. Before she could move, there was a sound from the floor below.

"Whoever you are, I warn you, I'm armed! Come down with your hands up, or I'll release the dogs."

Rook mouthed a curse. The light. She Skilled her hearing a little and detected the telltale growl of an animal, perhaps more than one. She glanced at Crake and whispered, "He's not lying."

"I know you're up there!" the man called. "I say again, I have a gun and dogs. Come down at once."

Rook gestured toward the window. "I think that's our way out."

Crake flashed her lock picks and set to work.

Below, the night watchman lost patience. "Go, boys, go!" he shouted, and straight away the whole office building shook with the thundering of several sets of heavy paws. Rook flew across the room and slammed the door shut just as a set of vicious teeth flashed in front of her. The dog and its compatriot barked and howled, throwing themselves against the door. It bulged beneath their substantial strength, its handle jolting as their paws caught it. Rook made to drag the desk chair in front of it when there was a resounding click, followed by the rolling swish of Crake opening the sash window.

"Come on!" the pale woman shouted, before disappearing from view.

Rook vaulted across the office as the dogs broke down the door, sending it crashing into the wall. The animals launched forward, their jaws snapping and saliva flying from their dewlaps, and just as Rook grabbed the windowsill, something tried to pull her back. For a moment she steeled herself for the pain of the dog's bite, but nothing came. She jerked her head around to see the creatures had their teeth not around her skin, but clamped onto the tails of her frock coat. In one deft movement she released the windowsill and threw her arms back, allowing the animals to wrench the clothes from her back. The dogs shot backwards with the sudden release of their own strength, crashing into a heap at the feet of the night watchman who'd made it to the door.

"Stop!" He fired off a shot.

The bullet buried itself in the window frame beside her head, sending splinters of wood in all directions. Rook didn't know if he'd intended it as a warning or if he'd meant it to go through her brain. Whatever his intent, she didn't give him the chance to try again, but launched herself downward.

She and Crake took off running as soon as her feet hit the pavement. They kept pace with one another, Skill for Skill, but fatigue set in like a dark shadow and Rook slowed.

"I can't keep this up," she panted.

"Nor I," Crake replied.

They slowed to a regular run, then to a trot. In the distance, police whistles sounded. Rook swore again, aloud this time, and shook her head. The heat was on them.

"We need to get off the street," she said. She pointed upward. "Fancy a spot of roof-jumping?"

Crake sighed, though she nodded. "At least it'll take less blood."

Rook allowed herself one Skilled jump and scrambled onto the sloped roof of a tall brownstone. Since the buildings were so close together, they could make their way across the city this way both without being seen and, as Crake said, without as much blood. If they only needed to Skill their way across wider gaps, they might just make it without collapsing.

The sun rose as they made their way towards Buxridge Bridge, the streets below filled with the tromp of passing police and military patrols. But the many boots passed by without ever looking up. The sky above the city turned pink and orange with the dawn. Rook took it in. Gooseflesh trailed along her skin as the wind passed through the thin material of her shirt, no longer protected by her coat, though the cold wasn't the only thing eliciting her response. She realized it was strange, this sudden vision of beauty above the foul corruption of the city. Even the ever-belching smokestacks of the factories in Blackout Row seemed less at that moment. Perhaps it was a good omen. Rook shook her head, embarrassed at her foolishness. There was no such thing as a good omen, not in Stamchester.

Her moment of pause was short-lived as Crake touched her elbow. "We need to keep moving."

Rook nodded, and they continued.

It took another few jumps to reach their meeting place. Exhausted, Rook turned her face downwards, scanning the streets for any sign of either Magpie and the others or Jaguar and his men. From her vantage point, she could see straight down to the river and street below. There was no sign of the others.

"I hope Sparrow and Redshank can get Magpie here in good time," she said. She folded her arms and sandwiched her hands between them and her chest. It kept her warm and stopped her wringing them together.

"They'll get here," Crake replied, "and even if they don't, we can take the Jaguar's wagon and go looking for them."

It wasn't as simple as that, and they both knew it. The militia would stop any wagon on the road, and it would become very clear, very quickly, that they had no legitimate reason to be traveling at such an early hour.

The sound of someone running echoed up from the street. Rook and Crake shared a glance before running to different sides of the building, looking for the source of the noise. There was only one set of feet moving at speed, which meant it wasn't a soldier or policeman, as they always moved in twos or more. The figure drew up short right under Rook, glancing around and hopping from foot to foot. Rook recognized that behavior straight away. It was Sparrow.

She steeled herself for her drop to the street. She wasn't sure if she had enough blood left to burn without pitching herself over the edge into hypovolemic shock, but she didn't have a choice. Sparrow's movements were even more frantic than usual, and it was clear she couldn't wait around. That meant either Magpie or Redshank—or both—were in trouble. They'd need to act now.

Just as she was about to launch herself downward, Rook stilled. The sound of wheels and hooves clattered in the distance, but grew louder with great speed. A taxi carriage raced off the Buxridge Bridge and took a corner so fast it tipped onto just two wheels. The horses jolted and shrieked at the disturbance, but the driver pulled them under control again. He pulled up beside Sparrow and tilted his hat off his face. Rook grinned. It was Pit.

"Crake! They're here!" she called, beckoning the other woman back across the roof.

Waiting no longer, Rook jumped downward, but when she hit the ground, the landing was disastrous. Her Skill depleted, the impact of the packed dirt road on her legs was agonizing. She cried out as pain jolted upward through her pelvis and spine all the way to her teeth, and she collapsed in an inelegant pile of skin and bone. She was aware of a pale shape appearing beside her. It must have been Crake, but her eyes wouldn't focus through the pain.

Pit, who had leaped from the carriage's driver's seat at the new threat, realized who she was and dropped to his knees. "Rook, are you all right?"

"Never mind," Rook said, her voice thin with pain. "Sparrow..."

She wasn't able to finish her sentence, but she didn't need to. Sparrow flitted and jerked a thumb over one shoulder. "Redshank has collapsed, and I can't move her and Magpie by myself. We need to bring the carriage to them."

"How far away are they?" Pit asked as he helped Rook to her feet.

"Only half a mile or so," Sparrow replied.

"You hop into the front with me," Pit said. "Rook, you and Crake get in the back."

As the pain subsided and her self-control returned, Rook extricated herself from his grip.

"Are you okay?" Pit asked, his brown and green eyes round with concern.

"I'm not the one we need to worry about," she replied as she pulled open the carriage door. "Magpie's in a bad way."

Pit's expression darkened, and he nodded before wrenching himself into the driver's seat to perch beside Sparrow. Rook ushered an exhausted Crake inside and followed her, slamming the door shut behind them. As soon as the latch clicked, Pit urged the horses into a gallop. It seemed like only seconds before they reached the spot where Redshank and Magpie had collapsed. As soon as they pulled their compatriots into the carriage, the horses reared as Pit urged them on again. The wheels bumped over every stone and rut on the road, and Rook pulled Magpie's head into her lap for comfort.

The older woman was paler than Rook had ever seen, her lips cracked and bleeding from dehydration. *What have they done to you?* she thought once more.

Magpie's response echoed in her head.

Nothing that will keep me down.

For the first time in her life, Rook suspected Magpie was dead wrong.

EIGHTEEN

It would've been nice to take some time to rest and regroup after the debacle in Purgatory. It would've been nice if the city government wasn't trying to kill them all. But even as young as she was, Rook understood enough to know that what was nice and what happened in reality were two distinct things. Only a handful of hours passed before they were all together in the Jaguar's dingy parlor again, this time with Magpie as a welcome, if exhausted, guest.

Rook sipped beer from a cup and saucer as Magpie, reclining on a sofa and covered in blankets, recounted her tale. Kestrel sat beside her, gripping her own chipped cup, hung on every one of their mama's words. The Jaguar sat in a beaten armchair. He said nothing and drank nothing and gave Magpie his undivided attention.

"It was normal at first," the older woman said as she waved a weak hand, "all much the same as the last time I darkened the door of a prison, except this time they kept a heavier guard on me." She managed a chuckle. Then her expression grew cold. "But it didn't stay normal for long. Instead of taking me to the cells, they took me somewhere under the prison."

Rook nodded. As Magpie recounted this part of her tale, it rang in harmony with what had happened to them. Taken underground, blood typed, drained. The stories diverged when Magpie turned to what happened afterward.

"When I woke up, I wasn't in a cell as I thought I would be. I was still in the infirmary, or laboratory, whatever they'd like to call it. To me, it was more like a torture chamber." A sickly feeling twisted in Rook's stomach as Magpie went on. "They'd taken my blood, as I knew they would, but then they injected me with more. In my naivety, I scoffed at them. Why would they give me back what they had taken, only to strengthen me when they wanted me weak?" Magpie waved her hand again. "What an idiot I was to think that."

In the beat of pause that followed her words, the Jaguar leaned forward. "What did they do?"

Magpie let her arm drop. It fell with the thud of an unconscious body hitting the dirt. "This is where things become hazy. The doctors and nurses didn't tell me what they'd done, but sometimes I was more aware of my surroundings than they thought. I overheard things." She shuddered under the many blankets piled atop her. "For much of the time, I was ill. They put something in the blood they returned to me. I've never felt so sick." Magpie shuddered again as the memory of her experiences returned. "Whatever their goal was, they didn't reach it. When I could overhear what they said around me, I heard some horrendous things. There were voices other than the doctor and nurses, voices I didn't recognize. But some I know I've heard before. The information is all in pieces."

"What have you made of it all?" the Jaguar asked. He drew his brows low over his dark eyes.

Magpie stared at the ceiling for some time. Rook watched as she gathered her thoughts and steeled herself for what she was to say. That made the sickness in Rook's stomach twist all the more.

"They're trying to control people."

The Jaguar huffed. "They control us enough as it is. They have their laws and their police, and now this Stamchester Defense League."

Magpie snapped her head towards him. Her eyes, which before filled with sorrow, were now bright with rage. "No. Not like that."

"How, then?"

But reality unfolded itself in front of Rook before Magpie spoke another word. It all made sense now. The underground infirmary. Blood typing. The cleared wing of the prison ready for new Saosuíasei victims.

"They want to control us through our blood," Rook said in a voice tinged with disbelief.

"Yes," Magpie said. Despair softened the hardness of her stare. "They're looking for ways to use blood to manipulate our thoughts and actions. It's all under Dreidchain's auspices. His doctors and scientists seem convinced there's a way to bring a person under another's influence using blood. From what I gathered, if a person is Skilled enough and someone else injects their blood, there's some way the donor can exert their will over that other person." There was a beat of silence as the weight of her words fell upon them. Then she followed it with another blow. "They said they've managed it once before."

The Jaguar sank back in his seat, his gaze turning inward as he contemplated the heavy reality of Magpie's words.

"This changes everything," he said. "If they can control us through our blood, we've lost. We'll never be able to combat that."

A strange tinkling sound erupted. Everyone looked at Rook. It took her a moment to realize the sound was her teacup rattling on the saucer. She pressed them together to stop her trembling, clutching the chipped porcelain so hard it made her knuckles grow pale. Her face tightened in a scowl. She was never this nervous, never this weak.

"That's why they've cleared the prison wing," she said. "They're going to bring people in, inject them, and ultimately control them."

"It'll only work if they can make it permanent," Magpie said. Although it was a struggle, she rose to a sitting position. "And it will only work if the person's Skill is powerful enough."

"And if they're a Zero," the Jaguar said. "They need a strong universal donor. That's why they're typing everyone."

Rook's scowl went slack. They needed a Zero. Her mind flew back to her interaction with the doctor.

She mustn't be the right Artur.

I can see it, you know. You look like her.

They wanted Zeroes. The doctor had known about her sister.

They had her. They were using her. They had to be.

The thought of her sister drained of her blood, being used for whatever nefarious purposes made horror rise within her. It was so hot and so clammy it made her want to claw out of her own skin, yet there was a fringe of relief to it. If they were using her, it meant Ishie was alive.

A crash sent Rook leaping to her feet. She scrambled to hold tight to her cup and saucer, but found her hands empty. She looked down to see them smashed to pieces in a spreading sea of spilled tea. Some shards ground under her boot.

"I'm sorry," she said, her face flushing from embarrassment and rage. She was *never* this weak.

The Jaguar held up a placating hand. "It's fine, Rook."

Magpie, still sitting up, reached a trembling hand towards her. But her strength failed, and she fell backwards onto the sofa cushions again. "I know what you're thinking. They might have your sister somewhere, and they're looking for more Zeroes."

Rook slumped into her seat. Kestrel slipped a comforting arm around her waist, and Rook leaned more into the embrace than she had before. She'd considered herself to be a pillar of strength, though now she felt more water than concrete.

"That doctor, whoever he was, said he knew my sister." To her own ears, her voice was pitiful. "He got so excited when he found out I was an Artur. He thought I would be another Zero, but I'm not. But I know he's met her." She gave a hollow laugh. "He even said I look like her."

Kestrel tightened her hold. "You do."

Magpie nodded. The Jaguar pursed his lips. "You have other siblings, don't you?" he asked.

Dread pooled in Rook's stomach. "Yes. There are ten of us in total. Well, ten my mother gave birth to." She glanced up at Kestrel with a half-smile. "Mother has lots more children than she's birthed." Her sisters' faces flashed before her eyes, and her smile disappeared. "They're all in danger, aren't they?"

"I'd say so," the Jaguar said. "Have the rest been typed?"

Rook shook her head. "Mother said they were too young to start Skilling so much they might need donor blood, and Father was the one who got us typed so he could sell what we could give. Mother never wanted that."

The Jaguar gave a curt nod and rose from his seat. "Your family is in danger, even more than the rest of us. We need to get your mother and sisters into hiding. I don't doubt for one moment Dreidchain won't send his men to look for your family. Why he hasn't up to now, we'll never know, but it's imperative that we get them somewhere safe. I don't know how blood works, but I do know types run in families. While Zeroes are rare, they appear in family lines. If you have one sister who's a Zero, there's every chance at least one more of your siblings will be too. I'll set up a safe house for now, but we need to get them out of the city."

Rook pressed her lips together in a tight line. "Mother is very ill, Dru. She hasn't left our apartment in as long as I can remember. She can't walk. And she'll be so frightened. It'll be frightening for the little ones, too."

The smile the Jaguar gave was broad and reassuring. "I'll send my most gentle of men, don't worry about that. We'll get her and your sisters to safety. Then we'll plan from there."

Rook rose, and Kestrel followed suit. "I'll tell her. We'll gather up what we can carry." She turned her attention to Magpie. "What about you, Mama? You need to rest somewhere safe until you get your strength back."

"The Jaguar will take care of me until I get on my feet again," Magpie said. There was a hollowness to her words that betrayed her. Rook didn't believe she would ever recover, but now wasn't the time to challenge her on it. "I might just join your mother for a while, if we can get out of the city. I haven't left this cesspit in years." She reached for Rook again, her arm trembling, and Rook was quick to lean into the embrace. Kestrel did the same. "Take care of the Conventicle for me, you two. Look after all the girls." Her eyes gleamed with pride. "The Conventicle's mission has always been, and will always be, the same: to protect Saosuíasei women. Every one of us is under threat from Dreidchain and his ilk. Now is the time to turn our attention away from retrieving money and trinkets. We need to take our lead from the Shadow."

Rook turned from Magpie to the Jaguar. He nodded again. "It would be an honor to count the Conventicle among our ranks."

"We'll work with you, but remember one thing." Rook held Magpie's gaze. "We're the Conventicle of Magpies above everything else."

Jaguar gave a lopsided grin and tipped his head in agreement. "I can live with that."

Rook and Kestrel, armed with their customary weapons of cane and pistols, slipped into the night, winding their way through the Shambles. Mist surrounded them, so thick they could see a mere six feet in front. The city was silent apart from the eerie whistle of the wind passing through the narrow streets and alleyways, and the hurrying of their footsteps on the frozen ground.

"Mother won't want to leave," Rook said. Her words whirled into the mist. "It's going to be a job to explain this all to her."

"But she'll understand, and she'll agree to go," Kestrel said. "You got your stubbornness from your da, not your ma."

Rook's sharp laugh shot through the frozen air. "I did at that." She sobered as her next thought came to her. "I don't know what to tell her about Ishie. We don't know what's happened. We don't know where she is, or if she's alive, though in my heart I know she is. How do I explain it to Ma? We think Ishie is alive, but we don't know where she is, but we think she's being held somewhere and having her blood taken by force." She heaved a brief sigh. "Part of me thinks it might be easier not to mention any of this to her. All it'll do is cause more worry."

Kestrel blew out a breath and nodded. "I know what you mean, but she's going to want to know why your family needs to move. Your ma isn't stupid. She's going to sense the missing details, and she'll want to know. She might not be as stubborn as your da was, but she can dig her heels in when she wants to. And while she can't stop us from uprooting her and your sisters, she can make the job a lot harder than it needs to be. I don't want to sling her over my shoulder and force her out while she clings to the doorframe. Tell her at least part of the truth."

The thought of her mother being ripped from her home while screeching for the truth sent a shudder up Rook's spine. No, she couldn't make her mother suffer that indignity, not to mention the fact she rarely kept anything from her. Mónnuad Artur was so good at sniffing out lies and half-truths there'd been no point in trying to keep secrets. She had the strongest 'Mother Knows' sense Rook had ever heard of. Perhaps it was a strange Skill. Of course, that was impossible. Bloodskills came from physical things like strength or speed. Although considering the revelations from inside Purgatory, Rook thought as they slipped down a narrow lane, anything was possible.

They continued through the weaving criss-cross of the Shambles. Its narrow lanes and winding streets had resisted Avanish redevelopment for years, although with the razing of the Scar, the sense of impending destruction loomed as low and thick as the fog. As soon as Dreidchain could, he would send his bulldozers and traction engines in to flatten every inch of Saosuíasei territory. The Governor of Stamchester, whether it was Dreidchain or whoever came after him, wouldn't stop until every street in the city was under Avanish control, and every Saosuíasei was exterminated.

"How can anyone hate us just for who we are?" Rook asked. The question wasn't for Kestrel. It was more for the city itself.

After a beat of silence, Kestrel replied. "People hate what they don't understand and what they think is lesser than themselves. The Avanish have always thought of us as less than them, right back from when they marched onto our islands and took what they wanted. They didn't ask. They didn't think to ask, because they didn't think they needed to. The predator takes what he wants. The prey is at his mercy."

Rook gritted her teeth. "I'm done with being anyone's prey."

The world, being what it was, decided it was time to test Rook's words. From the darkness of a side street, a figure stepped into a pool of green gaslight. It was a figure they'd seen before, and one that brought their boots to a sudden stop on the icy ground. A shapeless sack of a face hid beneath the brim of a tall top hat. Rook's hand clenched the ball handle of her cane, and Kestrel drew her pistol before anyone could speak.

Billy Drainer.

"Don't start with me," Rook said, still gritting her teeth. "Tonight is not the night for this."

"I'd listen to her," Kestrel added. "She's just escaped from Purgatory."

Drainer remained silent in the pool of light, with only his eyes visible through the deep shadow cast over his face. His hands were bereft of weaponry, but that didn't mean there wasn't something lingering in the deep folds of his coat.

"Move aside," Rook said. "I haven't killed before, but I'll make an exception for you."

Drainer's head moved as if in a tiny flinch, but otherwise he remained where he was, his hands still empty.

"You're in danger," he said. His voice sounded as odd, yet familiar as it had before.

Rook's cackling laugh echoed into the mist. "No shit."

"Watch your mouth."

There was something in the snap of Drainer's tone that made Rook's grip on her cane loosen. The words cut at her, and it took everything she had not to snap at him, "You're not my father! My father is dead." But she kept her cool and tightened her grip once again.

"Make me," she said, then went to step forward.

Kestrel's firm hand on her shoulder steadied her.

"You know who we are," Kestrel said. "You called me by my name the last time we met. But we don't know who you are. You say we're in danger. Why?"

"Not you," Drainer said. He lifted a finger and pointed at Rook. "You."

Rook bared her teeth in a snarl. "Stop with the theatrics and tell me why. We're all in danger. There's you, for a start, and then there's the looming threat of extermination by the Avanish. So please, tell me why I'm in more danger than anyone else."

Drainer let his arm drift down again. He straightened his back as if steeling himself for something great. It took every mote of strength Rook had not to end the idiocy and stab him through the throat. The violence of her mind unsettled her, but she shook it away.

"You say you were in Purgatory?" Drainer gave a dry laugh. "Governor Dreidchain will be most displeased when he finds out he almost had you. Whoever let you go is a dead man."

Rook scoffed. "Yes, because I'm that special."

"You are," Drainer said, all humor gone from his voice, "because of who you are. He wants you so he can exert ultimate control over *her*."

All arrogance fled Rook's body. "Her?" she asked, though she already knew who he meant.

"Your sister." Drainer spoke with a certainty no one could deny. "Dreidchain wants you, because Isianná will do whatever he says in order to keep you safe."

"How do you know my sister?" Rook asked, barely able to hear herself over the sudden thundering of her own heart. "How do you know me? Us? Who are you? If you're working for him, why don't you take me yourself?"

As she stepped forward, Drainer stepped back. "Get yourself and your sisters to safety. And your mother. Get them all far, far away. I've done everything I can, but it's not enough."

"What? Who are you?"

Rook's words tumbled into emptiness as Billy Drainer pulled on his Skill and disappeared into the darkness. Her eyes filling with tears, Rook went to plunge her own spare vial of blood into her arm, her mind set on a half-baked plan to scour every nook and cranny of the city until she found him again, but Kestrel's strong grip fell on her shoulder once more.

Rook let out a strangled breath and slammed her cane on the ground.

"What the hell is happening?"

The only answer was the echo of her cane's strike.

NINETEEN

Billy Drainer's words played over and over in Rook's mind.
"*Get yourself and your sisters to safety. And your mother. Get them all far, far away. I've done everything I can, but it's not enough.*"

The crack of his voice on the word 'mother' sounded louder and louder each time. It couldn't be. It wasn't possible. Yet fear and doubt pressed on her like a set of threatening jaws.

"It can't be." Her voice was little more than a whisper. Tears beaded in her eyes.

"What did you say?" Kestrel asked.

Instead of answering, Rook shook her head, pushing away the pain. But it was impossible, and the first hot tear tracked down her face. No. Rook never cried. Kestrel couldn't see her like that.

With no warning, she Skilled into the misty darkness, leaving her friend far behind. Her body disconnected from her mind as she tried to push herself harder, to force the pain away. The memory of their ordeal in Purgatory seemed too distant to comprehend. Sense evaded her, and all she could think of was the face behind that shapeless sacking mask. It was impossible. Impossible. But what if it wasn't? What if the insane notion that gnawed and gnawed at her mind was the truth?

In her turmoil, she lost control. Her Skill stopped cold. Her worn boots slid on the frozen ground and her legs disappeared from under her. Rook squawked as she careened into a wall, coming to a halt in a crumpled mess of limbs. For a moment she couldn't move, as if an invisible hand of exhaustion pressed her down. She closed her eyes and took a few shuddering breaths. A distant clock chimed an ungodly hour. All she could do was try to breathe.

With a grunt, Rook tried to right herself. She pulled on her Skill, but the power wasn't there. She flipped herself onto her stomach, sucking air into her weary lungs, and reached for her cane. It evaded her reach at an infuriating distance, and she grunted again as she tried to slide towards it on her belly. Footsteps encroached upon her, growing louder, and part of her wished it was Drainer returning. At least then she could ask him the question she craved the answer to.

But the footsteps weren't those of a man's heavy boots. Instead, the sounds were made by the hammering of hard-soled women's heels on the frozen ground. Kestrel came to a stop at Rook's side and kneeled down, her many layers of skirts blooming around her.

"Why must you be so infuriatingly idiotic?" she asked as she looped one arm under Rook's shoulders and grabbed her cane with her other hand.

Rook sagged into her friend's embrace in equal parts of exhaustion and relief. "If you ever find out the answer, do tell me."

They started the last stretch of their journey. Between the tall tenement blocks, the clouds parted, revealing a sliver of silver moon.

"What made you take off like that?" Kestrel asked.

Rook's tongue stilled, unsure how to form the words. How could she explain her suspicions, her idiotic suspicions, without sounding like a lunatic?

"Rook?"

"I don't know how to say this without sounding insane, Kes."

Kestrel stopped and stepped in front of Rook, sliding her hands onto the shorter woman's shoulders. "Just spit it out."

The crescent of the moon reflected in Kestrel's dark eyes. Rook shook her head and licked her lips as she willed the words to come.

"I think Billy Drainer might be my father."

Kestrel's face slackened in shock, and her grip on Rook's shoulders loosened. "But he's dead. You remember that, right? Did you hit your head when you fell down back there?"

She tried to check Rook's scalp for abrasions, but Rook batted her hands away. "I told you I'd sound insane."

"You didn't lie about that." Kestrel's plucked eyebrows tilted upwards. "Why do you think that?"

Rook pursed her lips as a well of disappointment rose within her. Part of her had wanted, or perhaps needed, Kestrel to agree with her bizarre idea without question. Of course, Kestrel was a sensible woman. Why on earth would she agree with such a thing?

Rook shoved her hands in her coat pockets, her face growing hot, and walked again. "I'll explain when we get home. I want to ask Ma."

"Are you sure now is the time to broach this subject with her?" Kestrel asked, hurrying after her. "We're just about to tell her she and the rest of the family need to up and leave because any of the untyped girls could be a Zero. Don't you think she'll have enough to contend with?"

With a sigh that showed itself as a cloud even within the mist, Rook nodded. "You're right. I don't want to drag up Da's death in the middle of everything else. But there's something about him, Kes. Something about his voice, the way he spoke to me, the fact he knew not just our names, but Isianná's name too. And he mentioned Ma and our other sisters. But he can't be Da. Just like you said, he's dead. Dead men don't roam the streets killing people and draining their blood."

As she placed her foot on the first step of the apartment building's stoop, Kestrel stopped. She turned and held Rook's gaze.

"Since finding out the lengths Dreidchain and the Avanish will go to in order to exterminate us, it wouldn't surprise me if dead men started roaming the streets." She turned away for a moment, a lock of dark hair slipping from underneath her hat. "If I die, I'd welcome the chance to come back and wreak some revenge."

Mónnuad Artur took the news as well as anyone could have expected. Regardless of the fear that lingered in her eyes, she agreed. A considerate neighbor to the end, she wouldn't allow her daughters to pack until a reasonable hour. Rook didn't know whether to laugh or cry at her mother's powerful sense of duty.

Propped up in bed with a steaming mug of tea in her hands, Mónnuad shook her head. "Do you think she's alive?"

Rook, perched on the couch, managed a tiny nod. "Yes, Ma, I do."

Beside her, Maird squeezed her arm. The reality of a looming threat seemed to tame her rebelliousness. "And you think there's a chance they could want the rest of us as well?"

"It's not just a chance, but a definite," Rook said. "Whatever is happening, and I don't know what it is, is bad. They need Zeroes, and we're a family known to have one. It's only a matter of time before they come looking for the rest of Isianná's sisters. Considering how excited the doctor got when he typed me, I don't doubt it for a second."

Mónnuad clutched her mug tighter. "Where are we to go?"

"You're going into hiding with the Shadow of Jaguars," Rook said. "Dreidchain knows the Arturs are associated with the Conventicle. They'll come looking for us wherever they know Mama Magpie has connections. The Jaguar is going to bring you to a safe house tomorrow, but you won't stay there for long. He wants you all out of the city, and I agree."

A sudden hardness glinted in her mother's eyes. "If we must, we must."

Maird released her arm and drew back. "You said 'you,' not 'we.' Aren't you coming with us?"

Rook shook her head. "No, Maird. I have to stay here and fight."

"Then I want to stay!" Maird shrieked, her defiant nature rearing its head once more.

As she jammed a finger to her lips for quiet, Rook shook her head. "No, Maird. And shut up before you wake the little ones."

Maird pouted in a manner more suited to their younger sisters. Before she could utter another word of defiance, Rook jabbed a finger towards her.

"This is why you can't join the Conventicle, especially now," she said, keeping her tone hushed but pointed. "You don't think. You're too hot-headed. With all the conflict happening now, you'd be dead within a week."

Maird's pout turned into a venomous scowl. "That's not true. You just don't want me to be as good as you!"

"That's ridiculous," Rook spat, her volume rising. "I just want you to stay safe and not, I don't know, die!"

"Girls!" Mónnuad's single word silenced them like a thunderclap. "That's enough. What would your father say if he could see you bickering? He'd knock your heads together, and I wish he was here to do it, because I can't. May God have mercy on him."

The chastisement made Rook's face grow hot, but the embarrassment slid away as a wave of memory and curiosity took over. Though she remembered what Kestrel said, that mentioning her father now wasn't the best plan, the query was on the tip of her tongue. But she silenced herself. Her mother was clear in her belief he was dead. She'd never wavered from that point, or given any sign her husband was still alive. To bring him up now, alongside the rest of the distress, would be cruel.

"I'm sorry, Ma," Rook said. She jabbed Maird's side, and her younger sister followed with a mumbled 'sorry' of her own. "The last thing we need to do right now is fight. We need to stick together."

"Correct." Mónnuad leaned towards her little bedside table to set aside her still-steaming tea. "Maird, I want you to stay with me, and that's the end of the discussion. Your sister is right; it's too dangerous, and you're not trained like she is. Perhaps when this is all over you'll get the chance, but right now your place is with me, and to help look after your little sisters." Maird's pout returned at that, but she said nothing. Mónnuad looked to Rook. "Are you sure you won't come with us?"

Rook shook her head. "I have to stay here, Ma. Magpie's aligned the Conventicle to the Shadow, and she's named Kes and me as her replacements until she's well enough to take back the reins."

At that, Maird leaped to her feet and stomped from the room, jealously emitting from her like heat from flames. Rook went to follow, but Mónnuad waved her off.

"Leave her be, Rébh. If let alone, she'll calm down."

Rook flopped on the sofa and covered her face with her hands, letting out a long breath. "Everything is changing so fast. The sooner you're out of here, the better. Bad things are coming for us."

"That's what your grandmother said before the Avanish took us from the Old Country," Mónnuad said. When Rook uncovered her eyes, she saw a grief-laden smile on her mother's face. "Bad things were coming for us. She and your grandfather came across the sea with me in my mother's belly. The Avanish tried to convince them life would be better across the sea, but your grandmother knew the truth." She raised her eyes to the whitewashed ceiling. "I wish my mother was here now. She kept control of everything, kept our family afloat." Her smile flickered to one of fondness. "You're more like her than even I am."

"I don't remember her, or my grandad," Rook said. She stared at the palms of her hands, wondering if the creases and lines matched those her grandmother had had.

Mónnuad reached for her, and Rook went to her mother's bedside. "I don't want to lose you, Rébh," she said, "but I know I can't keep you with me. But I also know," she said, pressing Rook's palm to her face, "that you'll be fine. I kept trying to convince myself that Isiannǎ was gone forever, but in the back of my mind, I knew she was still alive. And I know now that you'll find her."

Rook closed her eyes as she savored her mother's touch. "You're always full of hope, Ma."

Mónnuad nodded and released her daughter's hand. "Your father had no such hope, and it drove him into the Allen. Though I never had a body to bury, unlike Isiannǎ, I know he's gone."

It took every inch of Rook's self-control not to blurt out, "I don't think Da is dead!" But what good would that do? What was the explanation? "I don't think Da is dead because I think he's the killer who's been stalking the Saosuíasei under the orders of Governor Dreidchain!" How could that bring her mother anything but fresh pain?

Instead, Rook stayed silent as her mother reached again for her tea.

At first light, a carriage and a wagon appeared in front of the tenement building. Within minutes a band of Shadowmen started to pack up the only home Mónnuad Artur had known. Rook found herself with an armful of younger sisters as they struggled to comprehend what was happening.

"Where are we going again?" second youngest Faibh asked as she clung to Rook's neck with a death grip.

Shifting Ibheis on her other hip, Rook gave Faibh a squeeze. "You're going on a trip, Faibh. It'll all be okay."

"Are you coming with us?"

Rook tilted her head to rest on Faibh's dark mop of hair. "I have to stay behind and help Mama Magpie, remember? That's my job."

Ibheis tightened her grip on her sister. "But you have to come too!"

"Yeah!" Faibh agreed.

Rook pressed herself to the side of the narrow hallway as two Shadowmen shouldered past them, bearing bags shoved full of children's clothing. "I can't come with you, but I'll come find you when it's"—she stopped herself before she could say 'safe,' then continued—"when it's time to come back again."

The two youngest keened, pressing their faces into Rook's neck.

"It'll all be okay," Rook said, stopping short of adding in 'I promise.' She'd never been in the business of telling lies.

It only took an hour for the Shadowmen to pack what few possessions the Arturs had. With the youngest girls bundled into the carriage, with Maird and Caió perched in the back of the wagon with the bags and boxes, all that remained was for the last passenger to embark.

Mónnuad waved off any help from the Shadowmen, instead beckoning Rook and Kestrel to her bed. She slid her spindly legs over the side and, for the first time in years, she slipped her thin feet inside a pair of boots. She leaned into Kestrel as Rook slipped a heavy coat about her shoulders. Mónnuad didn't miss that it was her late husband's coat. She clutched one lapel and pulled the garment to herself, as if remembering the embrace of the man she had loved.

Though her body trembled with effort, Mónnuad's voice was steady as she said, "It's time to go."

Flanked by two of her daughters, one she had birthed and one she had taken in, Mónnuad Artur walked out of her apartment for the last time. Her legs threatened to give way beneath her, but despite this, she continued. At the top of the stairs Kestrel bent to slip her hands under Mónnuad's legs, intent on carrying her, but the older woman would have none of it.

"I'll be all right," she said in a tone that permitted no argument.

A small smile curled on Rook's lips. Perhaps she'd received some of her stubbornness from her mother, too.

As they made their way down the flights of stairs, neighbors appeared at their doors. Couples whispered to one another, and if it wouldn't have been a waste of blood, Rook would have Skilled her hearing to listen to whatever gossip they had to say. Only one of the bottom floor neighbors, Mrs. Dimh, spoke to them.

"What's all this, Mónnuad?" she asked. "I've not seen you down these stairs in many a year."

Quick as ever she'd been in her youth, Mónnuad said, "I'm being treated to a holiday, Breanna. Can you believe it? Dear Rébh has arranged for us all to take a little trip."

Mrs. Dimh leaned on her broom. "Ah, Mónnuad, you have good kids around you. If any one of mine would even bother to come and see me, I'd be laughing."

"I'll see you later!" Mónnuad said, and a few more steps brought them outside onto the stoop.

Rook chuckled and whispered, "Ma, did I hear you tell a lie?"

Mónnuad clucked her tongue. "No. What I did is called a deflection, my dear. You've arranged a trip for us, haven't you? I just made the circumstances seem a little more pleasant than they are."

"Did I ever tell you I love you, Ma?" Rook said with another laugh.

"You have," Mónnuad said as they started their shuffling way down the steps, "but I never tire of hearing it."

Despite herself, a lump rose in Rook's throat as she settled her mother into a comfortable position along the bench seat of the carriage. "Are you going to be all right?" she asked.

Mónnuad, her limbs shaking from the effort of making it down the stairs, cupped Rook's face with one hand. "Don't worry about me, Rébh. Look after yourself, and Faoiatín. Cling to each other. The Avanish are cruel on their best days." She dropped her voice to a whisper. "But worse days are coming. Don't underestimate the lengths they'll go to."

Rook leaned in to press her lips to her mother's wrinkled cheek, then found herself in the middle of a tangle of siblings.

"We'll miss you, Rébh!"

"Stay safe!"

"Tell Maird to not be horrible to us!"

With a laugh at the last comment, Rook extricated herself from the entanglement of limbs and retreated from the carriage. One of the Shadowmen shut the door before climbing into the driver's seat. Maird and Caió peered from underneath the wagon's canopy.

"The girls asked me to tell you not to be horrible to them, Maird," Rook called across.

Maird's face darkened like a stormy sky, but Caió laughed and clapped her sister's shoulder. "I'll keep her in line!" she called back.

Rook gave the girls a final wave and turned to the driver of the carriage.

"Drive slow," Rook said. "As you've seen, my ma isn't well."

The Shadowman tipped his flat cap to her. "I'll treat your mother and those girls as precious cargo. They'll be safe."

As the last word exited his mouth, a deep and familiar boom sounded. It was distant, but not distant enough. Rook snapped her head to the side, locking eyes with Kestrel.

"That was an explosion," she said.

Rook turned back to the driver and stepped away. "Forget what I said about driving slow. Get them out of here, now!"

With a curt nod, the Shadowman jerked his two-horse team into action, shouting something to the driver of the wagon. His words were lost as another boom sounded, shaking the glass in every window in the street. The carriage and wagon rattled off down the street, and the last thing Rook saw before they turned out of sight was little Ibheis' face peering out of the rear window.

"Whatever god might be out there," Rook said, "please keep them safe."

The only response she received was another explosion.

TWENTY

The detonation's aftermath yawned into an eerie silence. Rook and Kestrel stood facing one another, waiting. Darkness billowed in the distance. The fat smudge of smoke and the debris of what was once a Saosuíasei building blotted out the growing dawn. Then shouts trickled through the odd tranquillity. Rook swore.

"They didn't give us much time, did they?" she asked.

The muscles of Kestrel's jaw clenched. "They never give us anything. We need to find the rest of the Conventicle, and the Shadow. If this is an all-out attack at last, we need a plan."

They needed a miracle, Rook knew, though she kept the sentiment to herself.

Around them, people emerged from their brownstones and tenements. Mrs. Dimh stepped onto the stoop, clutching her arms tight to her chest. "Rébh, what's happening now?"

"Get back inside, Mrs. Dimh. Don't set foot on the street until this is all over."

The older woman's eyes widened. With every word, she grew more frantic. "Until what's all over? Is this why you got your mother out? In the name of god, girl, if you knew something was about to happen, you should have told us all!"

"Get back inside!" Rook said, ushering Mrs. Dimh into the building. "There's no time. Barricade yourself in, hide under a table, do whatever you can to stay safe."

She propelled the woman into the arms of another neighbor and retreated before yet another neighbor drew her in again. Men from the apartments streamed around them onto the street, mingling with those from other buildings. A rumble of conversation rose. No one knew quite what was happening, but all were aware it was nothing good.

Another explosion, far closer this time, drowned them out. Rook shot one arm out to keep her balance and brought the other to her head to keep her hat in place as the entire world shook beneath her. More smoke surged into the sky, and the wind brought its choking taint.

She shared another look with Kestrel, then took off at a run.

As they pounded through streets filling with Saosuíasei men and smoke, all Rook could think of was her family. *I hope they got out. Please let them have escaped.* They hurtled around a corner, without skill but still swiftly, heading to the Jaguar's lair. They turned again, and the sight that greeted them stopped them cold.

Columns of vermillion marched towards them, with hands clutching firearms and knives hanging from their belts.

"This is it," Rook said as she motioned for the others to retreat. "This is the real reason Dreidchain created the Stamchester Defense League. He's sending in an army without sending in *the* army."

The League tromped towards them, as much in formation as any real military platoon.

Kestrel blew out a breath. "I wouldn't be so sure they're not the Avanish military, but I don't want to get close enough to tell for sure."

The men's progress was unwavering, neither slowing nor speeding up at the sight of the women. Rook clutched her cane as she walked backwards, reluctant to turn her back on the green march coming towards them.

"We'll go down Drummer's Lane," Kestrel said, grabbing Rook's elbow. "Come on!"

Rook ducked into the narrow passage as the first shot rang out.

"Should we Skill our way out of this?" Kestrel asked, panting from exertion and adrenaline.

"Let's see if we can outrun them without." Rook's words were tight. "It's too close-quarters in here. And I don't know about you, but I don't have any spare vials on me."

They continued down Drummer's Lane, ducking under dripping lines of strung up laundry and ignoring the shouts from above. The reason they were running would become clear to any onlooker within seconds. Sure enough, a knot of vermillion soldiers galloped into the alley, their silver buckles and boots jangling and slamming.

They were nearing the other end of the alley when another line of soldiers blocked their exit and raised their weapons.

"Now it's time to Skill ourselves out," Rook said. She skidded to a halt and pointed to the brightening sky. "Up we go."

She shared Kestrel's wicked smile as they engaged their bracers. The rush of fresh blood made Rook's head spin, but her mind was sharp and she knew what to do.

Together the friends leapt upwards, flinging themselves higher on makeshift hand and footholds and laundry lines. A rain of sopping clothing fell upon the soldiers, and Rook and Kestrel crested the tenement building as the men flailed below. The girls grinned, but the victory was short-lived as four soldiers Skilled themselves onto the apex of the roof and drew their weapons.

Rook withdrew her dagger with a *shing*. "All right, boys, let's play."

She and Kestrel had fought together enough times to need no prior planning. They did as they had always done before, moving in perfect synchronicity to separate the group of enemies. Two remained on Rook, with the other two on Kestrel.

Shots rang out from behind her as Rook Skilled herself above the soldiers' heads in a backflip too fast to see. As the one nearest to her turned, she lunged at him, not with her knife but with her leg. Before he realized what was happening, her foot collided with the flat hardness of his sternum, and the impact propelled him backwards onto the pitch of the roof. He slid over the edge with a yelping cry, and that was the last attention Rook paid him, for there were another two to contend with.

One of them discharged his pistol, and the bullet shot past Rook's ear. She dodged to the right, taking a few skipping steps down the slope of the roof. The second soldier fired. This time the bullet buried itself in the clay roof tiles at her feet.

"The next one will go right between your eyes if you don't surrender!" said the first soldier.

Rook shook her head. "Conventicle girls never surrender."

Skill thrummed through her veins as she shot forward faster than either soldier could counter. Rook ducked down and slashed at the back of the first soldier's legs. He screeched and slammed onto the roof, sending shards of roof tiles scattering as blood welled from his wounds. His pistol clattered from his hand and slid, coming to rest a few feet from the lip of the roof. Rook's first instinct was to lunge for it, but the other soldier appeared at her side and before she could react, the butt of his pistol collided with the side of her head.

Stars erupted behind her eyes as she stumbled away, clutching her face, waiting for the killing shot to ring out. Her mother's face appeared in her mind's eye. If she was the only one of her family to die that day, at least there was some hope left in the world.

But the shot never came. Rook tried to regain her balance and blinked, trying to clear her vision. The world was double, and the ringing in her ear overpowered everything else, but somehow Rook righted herself. Why hadn't the soldier finished with her? She squinted at the blurred figures entangled before her, one black and one green. Kestrel?

Her friend's hands steadied her as the two figures fought before them. "Rook, are you okay?"

"I'm fine. I took a blow to the head." She shook her head again, and some clarity returned to her vision. "If you're here, who's that?"

When she saw it, she didn't need Kestrel to answer. That shapeless sacking face belonged to one person and one person only.

"Drainer!"

The killer locked arm-in-arm with the soldier, the two wrestling for dominance as their boots dislodged tile after tile. But the opportunity to watch was short-lived.

As Rook and Kestrel watched the dreaded figure now rush to their aid, the fallen soldier snatched up his gun. It discharged with a deafening crack. Just as Rook turned towards him, the bullet sliced through her hat, knocking it clean off her head.

In unison, she and Kestrel flew towards the soldier. Rook snatched the gun from his hand, and Kestrel held him down. The click of the gun cocking rang out. The soldier swallowed as Rook pointed the barrel at his head.

"What was that you were saying about between the eyes?" she asked. His mouth quivered in response. "You wear the uniform of the Stamchester Defense League, but you're not like the others. You behave like trained soldiers. Who are you, and what's your purpose?"

Some of his courage returned at the reminder of his trained status, and he curled his lips into a sneer.

Undeterred, Rook went on. "Don't think I won't shoot you."

"You'll get covered in blood and gore at this close range, sweet bird," the soldier said. "You don't have the courage."

Rook moved her finger onto the trigger. "And you don't have the brains, *sweet bird*. Tell me what I want to know or I'll put a bullet right into that hollow head of yours."

Her heart pounded in her ears as the words tumbled from her mouth. Rook was not a killer. Life was one of the few things she hadn't taken in her career with the Conventicle. Mama Magpie had always been clear. Killing wasn't their business. Yet in that moment, Rook didn't doubt she would pull the trigger. Things were changing in the city, and perhaps things were changing in her too.

The soldier shifted under Kestrel's strength. Rook asked again, "Who are you?"

Despite the danger and his bleeding limbs, a strange serenity passed over the soldier's face. It was as if he'd accepted this was the moment he was going to die. Rook pulled on that serenity. So be it. If this was his moment to die, it was her moment to become a killer.

Her finger flexed.

Then something knocked the gun from her hand.

"What the—?"

Seizing his opportunity, the soldier pulled out of Kestrel's loosened grip, propelled himself to the edge of the roof, and disappeared. Rook spun on her heel and wielded her knife again, ready to attack the new soldier who'd come to his comrade's aid.

However, the figure before her wasn't a soldier clad in blood-streaked vermillion. Rook's jaw hung open, more stunned now than when the pistol had struck her, as she realised it hadn't been another soldier.

Billy Drainer had knocked the gun from her hand.

The sound of the surrounding conflict faded away, and to Rook there was nothing but whiteness around them. Not even Kestrel was there. It was only herself and this gruesome killer, face to face on the apex of a crumbling roof.

"What did you do that for?" she asked, rubbing her hand where Drainer had struck her. "I should've known better than to think, even for a moment, you had any loyalty left for the Saosuíasei. You're not even just as bad as the Avanish. You're worse."

Drainer flinched as if the words had sliced him. When he spoke, his artificially deep voice wavered. "I am worse. I know that. But I couldn't let you kill that soldier. Once you take a life, there's no going back. You can't undo a death, no matter how Skilled you are."

Unbidden tears sprang into Rook's eyes, a product of her betrayed frustration. "Why the hell do you care about that? You kill people every day, sometimes more than one innocent person. And you're concerned about *me* killing *one* person?"

Though she couldn't see his expression under his sacking mask, she saw the crumpling of his eyes. His dark, Saosuíasei eyes. "I care very much, Rébh. That's what started all this." Drainer gestured at himself with bloodied hands. "I've damned myself because of the Avanish. And I'll damn myself to darkness before I let you do the same."

His voice. Those words. It was all so familiar. He must be. He *must* be. But her father was dead.

Wasn't he?

Rook dashed away her tears. "Tell me who you are!"

The world around them crashed back as another explosion rocked the Shambles. The tenement block they stood on jerked. Plumes of smoke and dust enveloped them. An uneasy sensation washed over Rook, the same unsteadiness that came with sliding on ice. But it wasn't her feet sliding over a frozen surface. It was the surface underneath her giving way.

"Kes!"

The roar of the building going down swallowed her voice. Rook sucked in a deep breath as the roof disintegrated beneath her, and she fell. Her eyes stung and her lungs burned from the dust and smoke. Nothing made sense amid the screech and howl of the tenement collapsing. Everything was gray.

Her father was dead, drowned in the Allen River from his own grief, gone forever. Just as Drainer had said, you can't undo a death, no matter how Skilled you are. Rook's hand went to her breast pocket, feeling for the watch lingering in the patched-up silk lining. That was the last thing she had of her father. Rook placed her other hand on the first, lingering on the sting of Billy Drainer's touch. Her father's touch?

But had it been him? She hadn't seen his face. But who else could it be?

Rook pushed the thoughts away. In this moment, it didn't matter. All that mattered now was surviving. Giving everything she could, she pulled on her Skill and prepared for impact. Maybe, just maybe, she'd survive.

An ironclad grip clenched her upper arm. Rook's eyes flew open and for a moment she saw nothing but a dark figure in the swirl of brick dust and belching smoke. The figure drew her up with the impossible strength of Skill, and Rook grinned. It was Kestrel, covered from head to toe in soot and grime. Trails of blood wept from her hairline. Despite everything, she grinned.

"What would you do without me, eh?"

Even amid the chaos, Rook managed a laugh. "I've no idea, Kes. No idea."

She took stock of their surroundings. Kestrel had pulled her onto a steel beam that gnarled like an ancient tree branch, yet somehow remained upright. Gunfire sparked beneath them, bright flashes in the gloom, and grenades sent more explosions rocking through the mangled streets.

Rook's moment of joy disappeared like a snuffed candle. The Saosuíasei who resisted were on the receiving end of those shots. Those who didn't? Coldness crept along Rook's skin like tendrils. They'd be shackled and marched away, off to be drained in Purgatory.

"Where's the Shadow?" Her words came out in a desperate squeak. "The Jaguar and his Shadowmen should be here to protect us. That's what they set out to do, right?"

"Right," Kestrel said. Her voice was low and weary.

A new sound rose. It seemed to come from every winding street. It started as a dull hum, but as the source drew closer, it became more rhythmic. Rook tried to wipe the filth from her face as realisation came. It was drumming. Not the formal drumming of a military band, but the drumming of many pots and pans and lids and ladles.

The noise drew the soldiers' attention, and they stared in their blood- and grime-covered uniforms. The Shadow of Jaguars encroached upon them from every side, making their presence known only through sound. Rook frowned. From her vantage point, she couldn't see even one Shadowman. Below, the soldiers glanced at each other in confusion.

Then the Jaguar stepped into the breach. Out of *nothing*.

Rook blinked. He'd materialised in the middle of the soldiers, as if he'd stepped out of thin air. How?

Kestrel groped for her friend's hand, bringing it to her face. "Slap me, please," she said. "I'm seeing things. This head injury is worse than I thought. The Jaguar just appeared out of nowhere. Please knock the sense back into me."

"You have sense enough," Rook said. She reached for Kestrel, but instead of slapping her, she grabbed her hand. "I saw that too."

Kestrel shook her head. "We're both seeing things them. Perhaps we're dead. This can't be real."

The Jaguar raised a hand, and all around him his Shadowmen appeared from the ether. They stepped into the streets as if from nowhere, filling the Shambles with woolen coats and flat caps and determined eyes. At another signal from their leader, they lifted their pots, pans, lids and ladles, and once more began their drumming. It started slow, the tempo rising until the air filled with nothing but the hammering of metal on metal. The Stamchester Defense League stood still, bewildered to a man.

The Jaguar jerked a fist into the air, signalling for his men to cease. Silence fell. Rook's breathing was shallow as she waited for the Jaguar to open his mouth to speak noble words. Instead, he flicked his hand from a fist to a point, and anarchy erupted once again.

Kestrel and Rook shared a single nod, before steeling themselves and jumping into the fray. The soldiers were in retreat now, the Jaguar's amazing feat having stripped the will from within them. Rook and Kestrel fought side by side with the Shadowmen, their questions at bay—for now at least. As she swung her cane at a soldier, Rook's mind spun. Her eyes hadn't deceived her. Kestrel had seen it, too. The Jaguar, and every one of his men, had stepped out of nothing. That wasn't possible. It wasn't a Skill. Her amazement tinged with the sting of betrayal. It also wasn't something the Jaguar had seen to share with the Conventicle. Well, Rook corrected herself as she slammed the heel of her palm into an Avanish soldier's nose, it wasn't something he'd shared with her. Perhaps Mama Magpie had known. But, she thought with another twinge of indignation, if that was the case then Magpie had kept the secret from her too. Rook delivered another blow to the soldier, sending him toppling to the ground. She wasn't sure which outcome was worse.

It took only minutes for the Shadow to clear the streets of the Shambles of Avanish green. What remained behind was a maelstrom of destruction on a sea of collapsed buildings. They picked their way through the debris. Rook called out as the Jaguar's familiar figure rose to the crest of an uneven pile of concrete and bricks.

"You've got some explaining to do, Dru," she said.

The Jaguar, though breathless and sagging from exertion, flashed her a grin.

"I do at that," he said. "I do at that."

TWENTY-ONE

They stood for a moment, unsure of the next right move. They'd pushed the Avanish back, but the danger was still there. A muffled cry came from within the debris at their feet. It shot through Rook like a lightning bolt. Their battle had turned to a rescue mission.

"We have to get people out."

"Agreed." The Jaguar, his movements still languid from a lack of blood, placed his fingers between his lips and whistled. His men gathered, many bloodied and bruised from the fight and some swaying with fatigue. "Our job is far from over," the Jaguar said in a voice that echoed amid the cragged remains of the Shambles. "We still have a lot of work to do."

His deputies sent groups of men to find shovels, spades, or anything that would help them dig. Others started clawing at the debris with their bare hands. Rook pulled in a long breath, prepared to dig herself, when a voice called across the chaos.

"Rook!"

She turned, sending a pile of rubble scattering at her feet, and managed a smile. Crake crossed the devastation, with what looked like the entire surviving Conventicle of Magpies behind her, spread out in a wide line. With the buildings razed, the low sun shone bright behind them, casting long shadows before them. Rook raised a hand in greeting, unable to tame her smile.

"Glad to see you living and breathing," Crake said as they gathered at the bottom of the hill of destruction.

"Same to you, all of you."

Crake and the others remained in place, waiting as if for instructions. It wasn't until Kestrel jabbed her in the side with an elbow that she remembered. Magpie had made her the leader in her absence. They *were* waiting for instructions.

"All right," Rook said as she picked her way to the bottom of what had once been a building. "The Jaguar and his men are digging out survivors. Those of you who have enough blood left to Skill your strength need to help them. The Shadow has..." She stilled for a moment, wondering how best to explain the extraordinary events she had seen. "...Spent much in fighting the Avanish back. It's our turn to burn some blood."

"Some of us have done that too," Sparrow said. "I can't be the only one with not much left."

"Understood." Rook shot her a grin. "I'm the same. Those of you who don't have safe reserves need to tend to those we pull out. Find somewhere with a bit of space and set up a place for us to bring the injured. We'll need a shelter, some blankets, and a fire to keep them warm."

Pelican raised a hand. "I'll co-ordinate that."

Rook nodded. "Good." She caught the eye of each of the Conventicle one by one. "This might feel like an end, but it's just the beginning. We may have driven the Avanish out, but they'll be back. Don't doubt it. Now's our time to keep doing what we've always done: to protect the Saosuíasei. Questions?" None of the women spoke, only murmuring their agreement and conviction. "All right. Off you go." As the others left, Rook raised her voice once more. "Crake!"

The pale woman stopped and turned, casting her nonchalant gaze over her new leader. "Yes?"

"What about Magpie?" Rook asked. A tendril of dread pulled within her. "Is she safe?"

Crake pursed her lips. "I don't know. Last I saw, she was with the Jaguar's men."

"Grab Redshank and go find her. If she's trapped or injured, she doesn't have the strength to endure much more than she already has."

Her expression betraying no feeling, Crake nodded and took off in the direction Redshank had gone. Kestrel, now the only other woman with her, placed her hands on her hips. "That won't go down as the most rousing and inspiring speech in the history of leaders, but it wasn't bad for a first try."

Rook lifted a hand, showing her friend the back of it. "More of that disrespect and I'll give you something that'll rouse and inspire."

Kestrel's laugh echoed through the surrounding ruins. "Oh please, tell me another one. You won't hit me. You won't even raise a hand to Maird."

Rook's chuckle joined Kestrel's. "You're right." Their mirth dissipated as nearby, a Shadowman pulled a small girl from the mess of brick and wood that was once her home. "Come on," Rook said. "Let's get to work."

The recovery mission went on all day and into the night. The street lighting, along with the rest of the infrastructure, was destroyed, so the only illumination came from hand lamps and torches. Rook peered into the hole she and one of the Shadowmen were digging, trying to spy even the slightest of movement in the darkness. She'd lost count of how many people she'd extricated from the dirt so far. Some had been dead, others had been alive, and some were teetering on the edge of the next world. Exhaustion flowed through her where her blood had once been. It was only a matter of time before she would need to stop before she collapsed, yet a sickening force pushed her on. If it hadn't been for the Jaguar's carriage and wagon, finding her sisters would be her only focus, just like the mothers and fathers who'd escaped the destruction. Fatigue pulled on her like iron chains, but she kept going. Her family had been lucky, and she wasn't about to take that luck for granted.

"Do you see anything?" the Shadowman asked.

"No," Rook replied. She glanced up at the boy who held their lantern. "Bring it a little closer."

The boy, no older than Faibh, complied. The fear that shone in his eyes along with the sallow lantern light spurred Rook on all the more. How many boys and girls like him were wandering the streets in search of missing parents and siblings? She set her jaw and began digging anew. One was too many.

Dirt and shards of brick and rock tore under her nails, and her fingers were shredded. Beside her, the Shadowman was in a similar state, but they kept going. Rook's battered hands came upon something soft and stringy. Her heart quickened. That wasn't debris. She scrabbled at it.

"Lamp!"

As soon as the light hit it, she knew what it was. Hair.

"There's someone here. Quick!"

They dragged the mess of crumbling brick and mortar from the head, revealing a woman's face covered in bruising and blood. Together Rook and the Shadowman wrenched away as much as they could. The more detritus they discarded, the more dread rose in Rook's throat. When she touched her hand to the woman's skin, she sat back on her haunches and shook her head.

"She's gone."

The Shadowman swore and despite his exhaustion, grabbed a chunk of brick and launched it across the darkness. The young boy said nothing, but the light from the lamp trembled. Rook shook her head and returned to digging out the body. Her movements were reverent now, no longer frenzied, since the woman had long since passed. When they freed her enough to lift her, Rook and the Shadowman carried the body down to the street. It was a testament to the number of dead that at the sight of them pulling another body from the wreckage, a young girl came to them with a ragged sheet and smoothed it across the dirt.

They settled the body on the sheet and Rook knelt by the woman's side. The boy's lamplight flickered over her face, casting dancing shadows beneath her eyes. She was young, perhaps not much older than Rook. There were no tattoos on her, no sign of any affiliation. Whoever she was, she was no threat or enemy to the Avanish. Whoever she was, she hadn't deserved this end. No one did.

Rook arranged the woman's arms over her chest, straightened her legs, and pulled the edges of the sheet over her body. The girl who'd brought it set to twisting the ends and tied them off with charred offcuts of thin rope. As Rook stood, two men bent to bear the body away.

"It doesn't get easier, no matter how many times you see it," the Shadowman said. His voice was thin with weariness.

"No, it doesn't." Rook gave him a slight smile. "It's time to take a break. I think you need some rest."

"Only if you do, Rook," he said.

His use of her name caught her off guard. She tilted her head. "How do you know my name?"

The Shadowman shook his head. "Everyone in the Shadow knows your name. Now are you going to pack it in for the night or not?"

Reeling a little from his words, Rook managed a nod. The Shadowman pulled his cloth cap from the waist of his trousers, where he'd kept it tucked all day, and planted it back on his head, and gestured for her to walk first. "After you."

Though she'd intended her break to be temporary, just a brief close of her eyes to ward off fatigue, when Rook awoke it was light again. She shot up in a makeshift bed she hadn't fallen asleep on and whipped her head around, trying to find her bearings. She was still in the Shambles, still outside, although inside an improvised shelter with walls of faded cloth. The dry stench of concrete dust and smoke had dissipated, replaced with the familiar smell of flatbread cooking on a fire.

She slid her feet, still wearing her boots, onto the packed earth that had once been a road and hauled herself up. The world spun in dizzying circles and she stumbled, but righted herself. She'd made the right choice to stop along with the Shadowman. Had she pushed herself further, she mightn't have woken again.

Rook slipped out of her bedsheet and curtain tent, and utter strangeness greeted her. She had to blink several times, trying to force her mind to comprehend her surroundings. The cragged edges of what remained of buildings surrounded them, and where had once been a maze of streets and yards and alleys was now an undulating mass of debris. Amid the hills and valleys of destruction were similar makeshift shelters, and thin fingers of smoke rose from cooking fires.

"Rook!"

The shout drew her attention, and Rook turned to see another strange sight: the Conventicle sitting around a pit fire. Kestrel, who'd called out, waved her over. The gravel crunched under Rook's feet and she winced, hoping she wasn't walking over more buried bodies.

"You lot have made yourselves comfortable," she said, gesturing at the flatbreads cooking on a skillet. "Where did you get that?"

As Sparrow slid a knife under the bread to extricate it, Kestrel reached for the teakettle boiling beside it.

"The Undténsians sent some secret aid packages, despite the Avanish trying to stop them," she said. She poured tea in the hodgepodge of battered cups and mugs before her.

Rook sat down beside Crake and counted around the circle, ticking off names in her head. There was one missing. "Where's Redshank?"

Kestrel handed her a cup with so many chips in the rim, Rook wasn't sure which edge was safest to drink from. "She's with Greenshank. And Magpie."

Rook almost dropped the cup. "Magpie's alive?"

"Yes," Crake said as she accepted her own battered mug. "Both she and Greenshank are recovering in one of the Jaguar's safe houses."

The relief threatened to topple her. "Thank god." The mention of a safe house brought new anxiety. "Kes, do we know if Ma and the girls got out of the city?"

Kestrel paused, the teakettle hovering in anticipation over the next cup. "I wish I could tell you otherwise, but we've had no word. We've no confirmation that they got out, but none that they didn't, either."

Rook accepted the piece of flatbread Sparrow offered her and nodded. "That's better than knowing they didn't get out." She turned to Kestrel. "What about Pit?"

Her friend's face fell. "I don't know where he is. I doubt he was here during the attack, and even if he was, he would've been on the Avanish side." She shook her head. "Wherever he is, I hope he's safe."

"He will be," Rook said. "He has to be."

The Conventicle shared their bread and tea amid an alien landscape, beneath a slate grey sky. So much had happened in the past week. It made Rook's head spin anew. Dreidchain's extermination plans, the Nest's destruction, Magpie's arrest and their escape mission, the revelation her sister was likely alive, her mother and sisters fleeing the city, the massacre of the Shambles, the Shadow of Jaguars and their impossible feats, not to mention Billy Drainer's strange words and actions. Rook shuddered. Kestrel placed a hand on her shoulder, mistaking it for a shiver.

"I'll get you a blanket."

As Kestrel rose, Rook followed. "It's all right. I'm not cold." Every set of Conventicle eyes looked at her, and the weight of leadership hung heavy around her shoulders. If there was one thing she couldn't show, it was weakness. "Let's take a walk instead."

Kestrel gave her a side-eyed glance, but obliged. The two made their way to the top of one debris mound, and Rook folded her arms tight across her chest. "I don't recognise this place anymore."

"Neither do I," Kestrel said. "It's not just all this"—she waved her hands at the ruins surrounding them—"it's something more than that. There's a tangible hate in the air. We always knew the Avanish hated us, but now they've turned their hatred to active destruction. Everything's changed."

Their breath mingled in the frosty air. "It has." Rook shook her head. "I need to speak to the Jaguar. We need to know what's next, but more than that, I need to know how the hell they appeared out of thin air. It's impossible."

"Yet they did it," Kestrel said. "I think I know where to find him."

They picked their way through the jumble of odd tents and shelters. The Saosuíasei mothers were doing what they had always done, and making do with what they had. Thanks to the Undténsians, they would get by for now, but they needed a new normal to survive. A burst of warmth erupted within Rook as she thought of her own mother. No matter what life had thrown at them, Ma always made it work. *I hope you and the girls are all right*, Rook thought. *I know you'll make wherever you are and whatever you have work now, too.*

For every mother tending a fire and every father pulling what he could from the debris to shelter his family, Rook knew there was another family that wasn't as lucky. She'd pulled out too many dead bodies to think otherwise. She didn't doubt there were children with no parents, and parents who'd lost their children, and Rook knew these were all problems that needed attending to. With hope and a bit of luck, they would rebuild. But before the rebuilding could start, the war had to be over. From the Avanish's actions the night before, that possibility was far in the distance. It wouldn't be long before the militia, the army, the Stamchester Defense League or whatever they called themselves, would be back, with more firepower than before.

The cluster of Shadowmen around a long shelter made of draped sheets in many patterns gave away the Jaguar's position. Bruises and lacerations marred the men, but most kept their flat caps and expressions of steel. One face was friendlier, and Rook smiled as Cian doffed his cap.

"Miladies," he said. "Here to see the Jaguar?" At Rook's nod, he rapped on a plank of wood serving as an upright. He ducked his head between the faded floral curtains that served as the entrance, said something, then withdrew again. "Go on in."

They slipped through the slit between the curtains, and the Jaguar greeted them with a wide smile. "How do you like the new place?"

Rook pointed at the strange patchwork of old and filthy fabric around them. "You've got interesting taste in decoration."

The Jaguar gestured for them to come to the table he was leaning on. "If 'interesting' is code for 'none,' you're correct." Cian barked a laugh, and the Jaguar shook his head at his own humor. When Rook and Kestrel reached the table, he sobered. "I suppose you've come for answers."

"And plans," Rook said. "I want to know how you and your men managed what you did, but I also want to know where we go from here." She pointed at their fabric surroundings again. "We can't live like this, and I don't think the Avanish will give us much chance to live at all. They'll be back, with more force and more anger. We need a plan."

The Jaguar nodded and licked his lips. "That we do. But first," he said as he pulled up one sleeve, "an explanation."

From under the tattered fabric of his shirt sleeve, a contraption not unlike Rook's own bracer appeared. But it was larger, with multiple needles buried in the Jaguar's skin. Instead of one vial of blood, there were many.

"Dreidchain isn't the only one experimenting with blood burning and what more it can do," he said. "We're just going about it a different way."

Rook stopped herself from reaching for his bracer. "That's a lot of blood."

The Jaguar nodded. "It is. What we're learning to do needs a lot of fuel to burn." He slipped his sleeve down again. "For years, centuries even, everyone's been taught that you can only Skill something you already possess, like speed and strength, agility and tolerance of pain. And I still believe that to be true. But with the access to more stores of blood than we've ever had before, we're beginning to realise we have more potential." He placed a palm over his breastbone. "There's more Skill to discover. We just didn't know it was inside us."

Memories of Mónnuad Artur's bedtime stories flooded back. Her mother knew the Tuachiannad off by heart, and every night wove them tales of the heroine Líbhas, who cast herself into the sea to save her people, only to be saved by Tuachiad himself, who transformed her into a magpie. Rébh and all her sisters, even dour Maird, had lain transfixed by the adventures Mónnuad took them on, filled with tales of people who could disappear, who could manipulate objects and the elements, even people who could fly. But they'd been fables, tales told to children to keep them entertained when the nights were long and cold. Tales told by her mother on street corners to earn the extra money needed to feed their ever-growing family. They weren't real. They couldn't be.

The Jaguar gave a soft laugh. "I didn't believe it either, Rook. At least, not at first. It sounds like something from legend, right?"

"Right," Kestrel said, her eyes still fixed on the Jaguar's arm. "It's like something from the Tuachiannad."

"Maybe those stories from the homeland aren't just stories," the Jaguar said. "All this time we've thought they were myths, but they're not. With strong enough Skill and enough blood, we can do the impossible." He tapped the bracer under his sleeve. "This is our turning point. While Dreidchain works on trying to control others, we'll work on ourselves. We'll become those figures from legend and we'll fight back just like in the stories. Maybe Tuachiad himself will stand with us."

"And Líbhas too," Kestrel said.

The Jaguar's eyes turned to Rook and glinted with sharp determination. "We can show the Avanish we're not lesser than they are. We can show them we're *more*."

Rook clenched her fists on the tabletop. "And we can stop his plans to enslave us for our blood." Her voice grew thick. "We can save Isianná, and any other Zeroes he might have."

Kestrel slipped her hand atop Rook's, and Rook flattened her fist at the comforting touch. She glanced at Kestrel, then at the Jaguar as he placed his hand on top of Kestrel's.

"We can save everyone," he said. "We can be free."

Rook kept her eyes on their hands, that word reverberating in her mind.

Free.

She grinned.

I'm coming for you, Isianná. I'll bring you home.

The End

ABOUT THE AUTHOR

L.M.R. CLARKE IS A WRITER from Northern Ireland who writes Young Adult fiction, primarily in the Fantasy genre. She writes with inclusion in mind, especially LGBT+, and explores themes such as sectarianism, racism and other forms of discrimination in her books. She does not believe in shying away from difficult issues in YA. In fact, LMR thinks it's vitally important that young people are given access to difficult topics through fiction in order for them to see the consequences of actions as well as the ability for characters to conquer adversity.

BOOKS BY THE AUTHOR

Novels

ARC OF THE SKY (3 BOOK SERIES)
The Moon Rogue, book 1
The Sun Emperor, book 2
The World Breaker, book 3

BLOODSKILL DUOLOGY (2 BOOK SERIES)
A Conventicle of Magpies

Most books also available in ebook, paperback and audiobook. Visit www.castrumpress.com for more.

Printed in Great Britain
by Amazon